WHERE THE WIND BLOWS

SIMONE BEAUDELAIRE

ACKNOWLEDGMENTS

I want to thank Julie.
With all your many hats... friend, critique partner, editor, and
so much more.
I couldn't do it without you.

For Dr. V. Choir directors with heart make all the difference.
Best wishes on your retirement.

CHAPTER 1

"'The Priiiiiiiiince of Peeeeeeeeeeace,'" Brooke sang, eyes closed as the sound reverberated through the university's choir room. Music rolled over, under and through her, soothing away the stress of the day.

"That sounds great," Dr. Davis gushed, clapping his hands together. "In fact, all the *Messiah* sections are coming along beautifully. This concert is going to be amazing. Now, for the carols. Please take out the packets I gave you last time. Sopranos?"

Brooke lifted her head from her music and regarded the director intently.

"There's a descant on 'Hark! The Harold Angels Sing!' Only do it on verse five. The rest of the time, plan to carry the melody. We'll have the first altos only on the alto line, and second altos on the tenor line. Everyone understand?"

Heads nodded around the choir room.

"And there's a bass solo on 'Lo, How a Rose.' Kenneth, I know I didn't mention it when I asked you to do the bass solos on the *Messiah*, but do you mind?"

"No, that's fine," a low, mellow voice replied.

Despite promising herself she wouldn't look, the sound drew her gaze to the upper row, where a tall, bearded black man shuffled through his music.

"In German?" Kenneth asked.

"Yes," Dr. Davis agreed. "That's the only verse we'll do in German. After your verse, we'll invite the audience to join us, and end with low light, candles and 'Silent Night.'"

Murmurs broke out in the choir. "That will be lovely," the elderly woman beside Brooke breathed.

"I agree," Brooke whispered. A strand of medium brown hair slipped out of her messy ponytail and obscured her view of the stately bass. Impatiently, she smoothed it back. *Quit staring,* she ordered herself. *You're thirty, not thirteen. Just because someone is talented... and handsome doesn't mean you should drool. Sing, Brooke. Eyes on the music.* Her gaze remained fixed, drinking in the details of the oh-so-handsome Kenneth Tyrone Hill.

"All right, everyone," Dr. Davis said, calling the attention of the room back to him. His voice never rose above a whisper, but the way he ran his hand over his shiny, bald head and ruffled the wisps of silver hair above his ears showed he was ready to move along. He turned to the tenor section. "Gentlemen, please note that on page twelve the arranger has changed your harmonic line. It's an interesting line, but one you might not be expecting, so please note the changes."

Paper rustled. Pencils scratched. Brooke continued to gaze at Kenneth. *Just one moment more,* she promised herself, *and then I'll go back to concentrating.*

At that moment, Kenneth turned in her direction. His warm brown eyes lit up and crinkled in the corners as he gifted her with a friendly smile.

Brook's cheeks heated. Swallowing hard, she willed herself

again to look away, but it was impossible. Kenneth Hill had the most compelling gaze.

"Ken, would you please?" Dr. Davis said.

Kenneth broke eye contact with Brooke, and his cheeks darkened. "Certainly. Accompanied?"

"No," the director replied. "Here's your note. I'll get you a pitch pipe next time. Miss Schoeppner?"

The accompanist cleared her throat and played a single note on the piano with the gravity of a performance for a king or emperor.

Kenneth lifted his music, inhaled deeply. A moment later, his robust basso rolled through the rehearsal room. "'Es ist ein rose entsprungen,'" he sang.

The low, sweet tone of his voice crept up Brooke's spine, and agreeable shivers rolled down her arms, setting her fingertips tingling. *I haven't been this attracted to anyone in so long. Even better that he's safely unavailable.*

Smiling to herself, she returned her attention to the director, waiting for the cue.

"'Lo, how a rose e'er blooming,'" she sang, enjoying the old, familiar tune. Through and around the many voices of the symphony chorale, she could pick out Kenneth's appealing tone. It gave her a thrill. *What would it be like to sing a duet with him? I think I would enjoy that.*

A smile tugged at her lips as the familiar carols wove a magic spell on her senses. *One thing that's nice about singing is that we can start Christmas in October and no one worries about it. Of course we have to practice.*

The rehearsal ended happily, with chatter and snippets of music from various singers.

Brooke indulged in another lingering look at her favorite bass, as he made his way slowly through the rehearsal room and out the door. Then, with nothing left to capture her interest, she meandered to the coatrack and retrieved her jacket.

"Wow, Brooke," Mrs. Schumacher said gently, "you should take a picture. It would last longer."

Brooke's cheeks heated. "He's just so talented. I hope it wasn't too obvious."

"It was," her colleague assured her, "and so you should talk to him."

"Oh, I couldn't," Brooke replied. "I'll just have to be more discreet."

"Why couldn't you? He was looking at you too when you weren't paying attention. You know, both minutes."

Brooke laughed nervously. Setting her music on top of the water dispenser, she shrugged into her coat. "Don't make fun of me, Mrs. Schumacher."

"You should call me Nancy. We're not at school in front of hordes of teenagers here."

"Nancy, then," Brooke agreed. "He's way out of my league; a professional opera singer about to embark on a European tour. I'm the assistant director of a high school choir."

"A very prestigious magnet school for the arts," Nancy corrected.

Brooke pushed open the heavy metal doors of the rehearsal room. She stepped out into a courtyard with a fountain in the center, her friend in tow. The water sprays threw colored lights into the night sky, catching the woman's eye and making her smile.

"And," Nancy continued, "you're not just my assistant. You're also the director of an award-winning girls' choir and freshman choir."

"I know," Brooke said, "but that still doesn't seem equal. Watch your step!" She shoved an abandoned broom handle out of the walkway with her toe.

"Thank you, Brooke," Nancy said, patting her arm. "Oh, and you should know, I submitted my retirement to the human resources department and the principal last Friday, effective the last day of school." She cackled with glee. "Arizona, here I come, and may this be the last winter I ever shovel snow again, as long as I live."

"That's great, Nancy." Brooke paused squeezing her friend's hand gently.

"Yes, I'm so ready, but that changes things too, you see. I mean, think about it. Once I retire, we'll need a new *head* director, which is an even more prestigious position. Sounds like exactly his league. Besides, I've always heard he's very nice."

"So have I," Brooke mumbled. Then, not wanting to say anything more, she yawned a big, fake yawn. "Listen, I'm beat, and I have class bright and early tomorrow morning, plus sectionals. I'd better get home while I can."

The fountain lights changed colors, illuminating Nancy's dubious expression in a soft, pink glow. "All right, then. See you in the morning."

Brooke hot-footed it into the parking lot, dodging around various cars and motorcycles as she made her way to her aging Freestar. Quickly turning the key in the ignition, she skirted the line of exiting singers and made her way to the rear exit of the parking lot, preferring the long drive on city streets to the freeway. Even late in the evening, she didn't care for the speed or density of the traffic.

Twenty minutes of twisting, turning and waiting at red lights led her to the base of a four-story building. Once, it had been a stately home, but now, the interior had been carved into apartments, including the attic walk-up efficiency she shared. Thankful for a designated angled space along the curb, she parked her vehicle, locked it up, and headed inside.

5

The formerly-grand staircase only contained vestiges of its former beauty. Time had rendered the luxurious scarlet carpet thin and flat. The ornate handrails sported scratches and fingerprints. The owners had long since enclosed the stairs with drywall in order to create apartments on either side.

Up and up Brooke climbed toward the attic, passing cheap doors decorated with plastic zombies and paper ghosts in preparation for Halloween. Her own unadorned door awaited her, its white paint peeling. She knocked twice and waited. No one answered, so she pulled her key from her purse and let herself in.

The dark interior had the empty silence of an unoccupied room. Another minute of quiet listening did not reveal her roommate's quiet breathing from behind her privacy curtain in the east-side alcove, so Brooke turned on the overhead light, revealing a threadbare sofa facing a small, wall-mounted television, a table with two chairs in the center, a kitchenette along the rear wall, and a pocket door that lent a hint of privacy to the diminutive bathroom.

Brooke quickly rounded her own privacy curtain and hung her purse from the footboard of her bed. Yawning, she ducked back out again and made her way to the kitchenette, where she retrieved a gallon of milk from the 3/4 -sized refrigerator and poured some into a mug, adding a sprinkle of cinnamon and nutmeg and popping it into the microwave.

Good thing Jackie isn't here. She always fusses about my hot spiced milk, even though I don't bother her to drink it. I wonder if she's spending the night with her boyfriend... or if she had to stay late at the hospital.

The microwave beeped. Brooke took her steaming mug to the sofa, sprawling across the fading green cushions. She felt no compulsion to turn on the television. Instead, Brooke sipped her hot milk, eyes unfocused as her busy mind played through the rest of the workweek.

Women's choir. Sectionals. Planning period. After-school rehearsals Tuesday and Thursday, and then on Friday, the opera. I wonder what the MJAMA Vocal Society will think. They're pretty hardcore musicians, but they're also high school students.

Brooke drained her drink, but cradled the cup in her hands another minute, enjoying what remained of the warmth. The building's heat struggled to compensate for the thin insulation in her attic, leaving a drafty chill in the room.

Her eyes slid closed. *Girl, don't pass out on the sofa again. Go to bed.*

Moving quickly, before fatigue could claim her, Brooke rinsed her cup and ducked into the tiny bathroom to brush her teeth. By that time, the last vestiges of her strength had drained away. She shuffled through the apartment to the entryway and switched off the light, then made her way by feel to her bed. She tossed her jeans and sweater into a tall laundry basket she'd tucked between her dresser and the wall, tugged on the nightgown she'd tucked under her pillow, and collapsed. Sleep claimed her in moments.

CHAPTER 2

"*T*hat sounds wonderful, ladies," Brooke cheered, making a closing motion with her hands. "This is going to be the best part of the whole concert."

Big smiles, some complete with braces, broke out on the faces before her.

"Don't get complacent. It's a long time until our concert, and we have much, much harder pieces to learn. Now, go home, and don't forget; those of you who are coming on the field trip need to be back in an hour and not a minute more."

A blonde girl raised her hand.

"No, you didn't turn in your paperwork on time. I told you I needed permission slips and payments no later than yesterday or you won't be on the list. You'll have to come with a parent."

The girl sulked as only a disappointed rich girl can while the rest of her class meandered down the risers, their sneakers stomping on the metal planks. The heavy door of the choir room groaned open as the girls dispersed in a chattering herd.

"Brooke?" Nancy called from her office, which was set off

to the rear of the choir room, with a glass wall so she could oversee rehearsals she wasn't leading.

Brooke crossed the room. "Yes, Nancy?"

"Are you sure you don't mind staying so late? I swear you work until seven every night."

"As opposed to what?" Brooke teased. "I share an efficiency with a near-stranger. There's nothing there to hold my attention. I'd rather be here. This is my true home."

"You might try a date," Nancy suggested.

"What's that?" Brooke cupped her hand around her ear. "I can't hear you." She giggled and changed the subject. "Anyway, I won't be here until seven tonight. The school bus is leaving for the opera hall at six. And on that note, I have a couple of things to finish up before I head out."

Nancy gave her a purse-lipped frown. "Before you run off, I heard a rumor that they're planning to post the head director position. I'm sure it's a formality. Rules, you know? But you have to go through the motions. Just wanted to let you know. Be on the lookout."

"Thank you," Brooke told her colleague sincerely. "I will certainly do that."

Waving to Nancy, she made her way into her office, tucked between Nancy's and the corner. Unlike her boss's, hers had a solid wall and a non-soundproofed door. Still, it was a nice place to escape to.

Brooke plunked into her comfortable office chair and rolled her mouse to activate the computer. One click started her classical music soundtrack. Another brought up the internet, where she quickly updated her participation grades before taking a final check of her plans for the rest of the evening. *Permission slips. Tickets. Paperwork for the bus. Roster checklist.* The ritual comforted her ever-present anxiety to a certain degree. The minutes passed quickly as she busied herself with mundane tasks until the time arrived to meet the students in front of the school in the bus lane.

Darkness had long since fallen, ratcheting mid-fall chill down to wintery iciness. *Winter. Ugh. It's going to be so cold. No matter how many years I spend in this city, I can't adjust.* Zipping her coat, she stepped out beside the bus. The driver operated the arm to open the door.

Various cars waited in the student parking lot. Some belched exhaust from their tailpipes as shivering parents waited to ensure their child's safe delivery to the bus. Others sat empty, the students having gathered inside the school's vestibule to pass the time chatting.

At Brooke's arrival, students surged around her like a wave from the ocean. *Or maybe from Lake Superior,* she thought wryly. *The ocean's a long way from here.*

Though the actual number of students attending the opera was small, a pack of high school students always sounds like a flock of tropical birds; a chirping, chattering cacophony of hormones and conversation. Brooke loved their energy.

"Miss Daniels," one young woman shouted, not because she was angry, but because her normal speaking voice was incredibly loud. "Miss Daniels, my dad sent the money after all. Can I go?"

"Melissa, you and your dad should drive along behind us, in case I can't get last-minute tickets."

"You didn't buy them?" the girl demanded, incredulous. "I told you I was going."

"And I told you," she reminded her student gently, "that you had to pay by yesterday. I'm not saying no. I'm only saying you don't want to be stuck in the lobby. Have your dad drive you to the opera hall. If we can get tickets, fine, but I can't guarantee it at this late time."

Melissa sighed and stomped back to her dad's Mercedes.

Someday, I hope she learns that deadlines apply to her, just like they do to everyone else, regardless of her dad's income.

"Now then," she pitched her voice higher, so all the chattering teens could hear her. They continued unabated, so she lowered her volume. "I'm going to stand over here by the door to the bus. You all listen for your name. You may board the bus when I call you. Janet Anzaldua."

Janet obediently stepped forward, and Brooke smiled. The quiet senior always set a good example for her younger, more rambunctious classmates.

"Janet, I have your letter of recommendation ready to go. I'll drop it in the mail tomorrow."

"Thank you, Miss Daniels," Janet said earnestly. She tugged her letterman jacket tighter around her body, adjusted her gloves and climbed up the noisy steps onto the bus.

"Aimée Borden. Sophia Cardini. Damien Fernandez. Jorge Gutierrez." One by one, she ticked off the students and ushered them onto the bus. Then she boarded behind them.

The stinking beast lurched away from the curb, pulling cautiously into the stream of traffic that continuously flowed past Mahalia Jackson Art and Music Academy. It headed downtown toward the opera hall and the students' first experience with live musical theater.

It always surprised Brooke how many people attended opera performances here in this city. The crowd surrounding the opera hall hindered the bus's forward movement. Three busses ahead of them also crept toward the front doors inch by painful inch.

The huge white structure with its three mismatched towers loomed over them.

"Wow," Sophia breathed. "It's so pretty."

"The angles and roof lines are appalling," Aimée snapped.

11

Brooke grinned at her impatience. *She's going to be one hell of an architect someday.*

The bus finally inched its way to a stop in front of the building. The door hissed open, and Brooke descended, blocking the exit with her body. The students crowded up.

"Okay, guys. Stay with me, all the time now. I don't want to lose any of you. I'll be calling roll when we leave the will-call desk and when we get to our seats, so do not wander. Bathroom only with a buddy. Everyone understand?"

Nods and affirmative responses greeted her.

"Okay, let's go." She stepped aside, and her twelve young music-lovers filed off the bus and gathered on the sidewalk, shivering and blowing frosty breath in the air. *Wow, it's cold for October.*

After a quick count of heads, Brooke pointed at the doors. In a knot, they climbed up to massive double doors, now flung wide and flanked with ushers. Entering an opulent, crowded lobby, she herded her young charges toward the will-call desk beneath a ceiling of crossing beams and gleaming pink panels in diamond shapes.

From behind a heavily-carved desk, a uniformed man with long sideburns asked, "Can I help you?"

She smiled at him. "Thirteen tickets under the Mahalia Jackson Art and Music Academy account."

He raised one eyebrow, but dutifully punched keys on his computer. A moment later, he passed a thick stack of small rectangles printed with the opera's logo.

"Thank you," she said, collecting the tickets.

From the corner of her eye, Brooke saw Melissa and her father, matching scowls on their faces, stomping out of the opera house. They headed away from a ticket window from which a sign bearing the words SOLD OUT hung.

Brooke grinned. Then she sailed through the lobby, leading

a trail of teenaged ducklings into the concert hall. With a bit of help from a female usher, she found their seats, along the aisle in three partial rows. Brooke claimed the rear corner seat, where she could keep tabs on all her students.

"So, guys," she said, luring heads in her direction, "take a look at your program. This opera, as we've discussed, is called *Faust*. Many composers have set it, but this particular one is by Charles Gounod." She enunciated the name carefully in French. "It tells the story of a doctor who sells his soul to the devil. The devil is called Méphistophélès, and you should pay close attention to his famous aria, where he laughs. It's a famous and surprisingly tricky role..." She cut off, realizing she was rambling.

The lights flashed.

"Okay, kiddos. We're about to start. Last potty call until intermission."

Three girls scrambled up the aisle together. The rest of the kids settled in, some reading the libretto, others idly chatting, until the lights went out again. Then, the music rose. First, a strong cord. Then, the low strings began a pulsing beat, which the violins transformed into a mournful yet passionate melody, rendered strange by unexpected accidentals. Another, higher cord rang through the concert hall. The low strings again built into a sad, tender melody as the stage lights illuminated a scholar at a table, wrapped in a red blanket.

The music and story immediately swept Brooke away. In the long minutes that followed, she had no idea whether her students chatted, slept or pulled out their phones to distract themselves. The stage, the music and drama thereon, captivated her.

At last, the moment she'd been waiting for. Méphistophélès appeared.

Even from this distance, Brooke could make out the soft

fullness of his form. The gleam of his dark skin. The coarse crinkles of his thick beard. He enunciated the French lyrics flawlessly, with a sincerity that surpassed mere acting. His serenade began, teasing her senses with a roguish charm and a wicked chuckle that had been written into the music. The whites of his eyes flashed as he rolled them in fiendish delight.

I'm being seduced by the devil, she thought, not sure whether that amused or alarmed her. *How long has it been since I was seduced? Too long, my sister would say, and yet, it doesn't seem to have been nearly long enough. Not after...*

Her mind veered away from painful memories. *The opera, Brooke. Watch the opera. There's no harm in crushing on a handsome bass. He's unavailable and way out of your league, just like a celebrity. A safe crush. It's perfect.*

So, she allowed herself to wallow in his gorgeous, low tone, his handsome face, his delightfully charming evil persona. Time passed. Faust faced his eternal reckoning, choosing damnation to save his beloved. The devil took his due.

As the final notes faded away, Brooke sank back in her chair, saturated in music and infatuation. She closed her eyes, letting the moment seep into her soul.

Light flared behind her closed lids.

"Miss Daniels," an adolescent female voice cut into her awareness. She opened her eyes to see Sophia peering at her curiously. "Miss Daniels, did you fall asleep?"

She shook her head. "No, of course, not. I was just taking it in. Well, ladies and gentlemen, what did you think?"

Blank, bewildered faces met her gaze.

"Need some time to process it?"

Nods.

"Okay, let's make our way back to the doors. Again, stick together. I don't want to lose anyone."

They rose and made their way toward the rear of the hall.

"Miss? Miss Daniels?" A hand tugged at her sleeve.

"What is it, Lupita?"

"I need to use the bathroom."

Brooke suppressed the urge to roll her eyes. "Okay, Lupita. Better now than halfway back to school, I guess, but there may be a long line." *Actually, waiting a few minutes in line here in the warm building might be preferable to waiting on the cold, stinky bus.*

"Change of plans, everyone. We're making a potty stop. Take the opportunity, because it's a bit of a drive, as you might recall, and the traffic downtown is heavy, even late at night."

The boys groaned in annoyance, but relief blossomed on several female faces. *Bingo. I had a feeling.*

After stepping from the concert hall into the expansive lobby, they picked through a massive, roaring crowd, executed a sharp left turn, and headed toward a discreet sign nearly hidden in the dark wood paneling. As expected, a long line of women, many wearing fur wraps and glittering gowns, waited for their turn. Outside the men's room, two gentlemen in suits chatted, not clearly in line, but not clearly out of it either.

Typical, Brooke thought. *Venues should make twice as many ladies' rooms as men's rooms. That would help.*

To their credit, her girls stood sedately in the line, chatting at a quiet volume and not dancing in place as they waited. Their school-issued performance gowns, while not as fancy as the blue-sequined sheath on the woman in front of them, didn't look out of place.

The boys approached their restroom, quietly questioning the waiting gentlemen, and upon hearing that they were, in fact, in line, took their places behind.

Keeping part of her attention focused on her students, Brooke allowed herself a moment to people watch, wondering if she'd see anyone she knew. *Even in a big city, the music*

15

teacher community is not so big we can't occasionally meet up. She scanned the faces but didn't recognize anyone.

As her students inched toward the restroom, a bit of conversation, pitched at a different volume than the rest of the crowd, cut through to her.

"Sir, are you aware that your role, Méphistophélès, represents the devil?"

"Well, of course," A richly-dark tone replied.

Brooke's head turned involuntarily, snapping to the side as she gawked, stunned, at the familiar dark face and full beard of her favorite bass.

"Gentlemen, I've spent the best part of a year preparing this role. Aside from the fact that we're singing, not speaking, this is an acting job. I had to consider the character; his motivations, drives and weaknesses so I could bring it to life. I knew before I began that I was playing the devil. I knew before I began rehearsing what *Faust* was about."

It's an interview, Brooke realized, eyeing the two pale young adults. *They're covering the concert for something, possibly a school project or student newspaper.*

They glanced at each other with the oddest expression on their faces. The taller of the two, a slender young blond who looked like a runner, cleared his throat. "Don't you think their casting is a bit inappropriate?"

Kenneth's dark eyebrows drew together. "What do you mean?"

Oh, God. I know where this is headed. Kenneth doesn't deserve this. Not when he's on a post-performance high. That alone could be enough to make his answer less than thought out and measured, which will only fuel their nonsense. She waited, curious how these dweeby social-justice warriors would handle their extremely rude and ignorant questions.

"I mean, as a person of color, it's typical to be cast in the antagonist role, while the Caucasian gets the lead. It makes me question the motivations of the opera's leadership."

Kenneth's face twisted. "Um, I don't think that's right, I..." He stuttered, brow furrowed, seeking words to explain the situation. "It has nothing to do with that."

"But how can you be sure? This sort of racism is often covert."

"That's not what this is about. I, uh..." he struggled again, the words refusing to form.

I know what that feels like. It's such a shock to the system, trying to think moments after a heady performance. They're going to make him sound like an idiot because their questions are so far from where his mind is at.

Brooke had heard enough. Stepping away from her students, who had nearly reached the front of the line anyway, she barged up to the group.

"You guys knock that shit off," she snapped.

They turned to stare at her. Her cheeks heated at her own unexpected boldness, but if there was one thing her father had always taught her, it was that you should never back down. *Especially since I'm righting a wrong, not that Dad would care about that.*

"Look," she explained, trying to rein in her temper, "you've just taken in a gorgeous musical performance, one that represents years of planning, months of rehearsal, and all you can talk about is your own white guilt? You'll need to find better ways to assuage that than harassing an artistic genius moments after he leaves the stage. But let me make one thing perfectly clear. You are so far off base with this line of questioning, you might as well just stop. Rewrite your questions so they're not stupid and try again later."

"Ma'am, I know you think you're helping," the tall one said, condescension dripping from his tone, but..."

"But nothing," Brooke interrupted. "Your questions are ignorant. *Faust* calls for a tenor as the lead, a bass as the antagonist. Mr. Hill is not a tenor. That role would have been out of his vocal range. He would never have been cast that way, not because of his race but because his voice won't go that high. It's as simple as that."

"Then perhaps," the shorter blond boy gently suggested, "they might have chosen a different show..."

"Why?" Brooke demanded. "If the opera company's tenor were black, or if the whole cast were white, we wouldn't be having this conversation, would we? There's nothing wrong with the opera. In reality, the company has selected singers without consideration of race, caring only for their musical talents and the skills they've developed."

She drew in a quick breath and ranted on "They cast those musicians in the roles to which their voices are best suited. Isn't that the goal? For each person, no matter their skin color, to be selected for the position for which they are best suited?"

The two young men stared at her. A hint of understanding dawned in the eyes of the shorter one again, but the bigger one still looked confused.

"Instead of prodding into an accidental alignment, why not comment on the beauty of the performance, the incredible way in which all the singers—including Mr. Hill—executed their roles. I mean, it's actually rude of you two to assume that he somehow didn't know what he was taking on. He's a professional musician and actor. He knows what his role represents. If it had bothered him, he wouldn't have agreed to it, and for you to imply that he didn't understand what he was doing is actually far more insulting than him taking on a challenging, famous operatic role and executing it convincingly."

"Well," the taller student snapped, his challenged ego puffing up, "I think you're..."

"Stop, Brett." The shorter one laid a hand on his arm. "She's right about at least one thing. Our assumption about Mr. Hill's awareness was way off base. I think we should rethink some of our questions. We don't want to write an ignorant piece, do we?" He closed his hand on his friend's arm and all but dragged him away.

In the wake of the tense confrontation, Brooke sagged.

"Thank you," the deep voice said softly.

She inhaled, and the scent of cologne and perfect male filled her in every cell of her body.

"I know you," he added. "Where have I seen you before?"

"Symphony chorale," she pointed out.

Awareness dawned. "Yes, that's right."

"Miss Daniels?" Sophie asked.

Brooke glanced behind her to see her gaggle of students gathered around her, finished with their pit stop.

"Ready to go?" she asked. They nodded. She turned her attention back to Kenneth. "I have to get my students back to school now. It was nice to meet you, Mr. Hill. The performance was glorious. Guys, did you like the show?"

"I like how you laughed in your solo," Damien said. "I'm a bass too. I think I'm going to learn that one for my college auditions."

Kenneth beamed at the youth. "You do that. It's tough, but if you can handle it, you'll really set yourself apart. Swing for the fences, young man."

Damien beamed.

See, that's what I'm talking about. Artists encouraging each other.

"Thank you again, Miss... Daniels was it?"

"Yes. Brooke Daniels." She extended one hand. "It's an honor to meet you, Mr. Hill."

His hand, warm and slightly damp after so much time under stage lights, engulfed hers and sent a tingle all the way up her arm. "Call me Kenneth. It's great to meet you." He turned to her students, shaking each one's hand and thanking them for coming.

At last, Brooke led her group out to the bus. She took roll with only the slightest attention to the names on her roster.

Still in a daze, she delivered the students to their waiting parents, floated to her office to retrieve her satchel, and drove home without noticing the road. She barely remembered the rule she and her roommate had put in place and didn't turn on the lights, lest Jackie be sleeping.

She wasn't.

Soft groans and squeaking springs greeted Brooke as she crept in the door.

Not wanting to interrupt, she slipped into the bathroom, brushed her teeth, and made her way to bed in near silence.

The sounds of her roommate's ongoing encounter blended with images of a handsome, bearded face, the sound of a rich, low voice, the scent that still lingered in her nose, and the sensation of his hand on hers. Wrapped in overpowering sensations, she slipped into a long and passionate dream.

CHAPTER 3

*B*rooke took a bite of her sandwich, searching YouTube for recordings of Kenneth singing. She found a student recital and clicked on it, relaxing to the sound of his gorgeous voice.

Inside her desk, her cell phone began to chime.

Brooke sighed, paused the music and went digging for it, catching it just after the ringing stopped. Glancing at the screen, she realized it was her sister, so she quickly pressed the button to return the call. Autumn answered on the first ring.

"Hi, Sis," Brooke said. "Sorry about the delay. My phone was in my desk."

"I figured," her sister replied, and Brooke could practically see her tossing her long mane of thick blond hair over her shoulder. "That's why I didn't go anywhere. I know your schedule pretty well by now."

"I'm sure that's true," Brooke agreed. "So, what's up, Sis?"

"Nothing much with me. Work. Spending time with Dad and River, dating a bit here and there but nothing serious. However, I had a feeling I needed to call you because something important had changed, so mainly I called to ask what's up with you?"

"Huh." Brooke took another bite of her sandwich, savoring the flavor of ham, cheddar and tomatoes. *Psychic sister strikes again. Nothing has changed though.* She swallowed. "I went to the opera last night."

"On a date?" Autumn asked hopefully.

"With my students," Brooke replied. "They really enjoyed it, or so they said. I know I did. I'm lucky to live in a city where so much incredible music is happening."

"There's music in Texas too," Autumn pointed out, sounding deflated. You know you can do something other than work once in a while, right?"

"I do," Brooke replied. "Going to the opera wasn't work. I enjoyed it. I also sing in the symphony chorale. That's just for me."

"Why do you?" Autumn asked, and Brooke could hear that probing note in her voice that meant she was about to do something spooky.

"Why do I sing? Sis, you know I love to sing."

"Yes, I know." Autumn sounded even farther away, like she was inside a tunnel. "You love to sing with... him. Him who, Brooke?"

"Stop being spooky, Autumn," Brooke exclaimed, rather louder than she should have given that Nancy was sitting in the next office with her door open. "There is no him." She could hear the lie in her own voice.

"Ha, now I know there's someone. Why, Brooke, are you in love?"

Brooke rolled her eyes. "In love is a bit much. I don't even know the guy. We only introduced ourselves yesterday. It's just that he's really handsome and a fabulous singer. I guess you could say I have a little crush. But listen, he's a rising star in the local opera scene. I've heard rumors he's taking off for a European tour with them starting after Christmas. He's like a celebrity. Celebrity crushes are no reason to break out the champagne."

"Wow, you sure said all that fast. Are you trying to convince me or yourself?" Autumn asked, a hint of a chuckle lingering in her voice. "Anyway, I wouldn't assume you're as safe as you think you are. You sing in an ensemble with him. You say you introduced yourself last night? You may see him as a celebrity, but I'd be willing to bet he sees you much more as an equal. Don't rule anything out."

"I introduced myself because I chased away a couple of social justice warriors who were killing his concert buzz. I also wanted my students to get a chance to meet him. He was really encouraging to them."

"You? Quiet Brooke? Chasing away people due to an overheard conversation? That's not like you."

"It is too," she replied. "I chased bullies away from you all the time."

"Yes, from me. Your family. I think you have to admit you see him as more than a handsome, musical stranger, at least in your heart."

Brooke opened her mouth to protest but found herself unable.

"There, you see?" Autumn told her gently. "It's easier if you don't fight yourself. What's this music god's name?"

"Kenneth," Brooke replied. "Kenneth Tyrone Hill. He has a whole page to himself on the opera website if you want to take a look. Great headshot."

She could hear some clicking sounds on the other end and knew Autumn had taken the bait.

"Oh, wow," her sister breathed a moment later.

"Handsome, right?"

"I had no idea you liked his type."

"What type? Do you mean because he's black? You know I don't restrict my attraction by race. Jordan's Asian, and remember Juan back in high school?"

"I mean the teddy bear type," Autumn replied idly. "He looks nice to hug. Also, there's gentleness around his eyes and humbleness to his expression that tells me he's not nearly the big star in his own mind. If you decide to go after him, I bet he'd be receptive."

"Come on, Autumn. I can't do that. What would Dad say if I got together with another musician?"

"Brooke, you have to stop making decisions based on what Dad would say. He doesn't mean any of it. He just likes to give you a hard time. If you stand by your convictions, you'll realize that he may bluster, but he actually respects it."

"That's hard for me," Brooke told her sister. "Besides, I have no idea whether Kenneth is even interested."

"He is," Autumn said. "I can feel it. I'll run a tarot spread later on if you'd like."

"No cards," Brooke replied. "You know I don't believe in that."

"It's real whether you believe or not," Autumn reminded her, "but I respect your decision. Take care, Sis, and don't sell yourself short. You have a lot to offer, and Mr. Kenneth Tyrone Hill would be lucky to have you, not just the other way around."

"Maybe, but that's not what I'm looking for," Brooke replied.

Autumn paused for a long moment. At length, she sighed. "I don't believe that either, but it's clear, for the moment, that you do. I won't push. Only, if your feelings change, don't fight them. Let life happen to you once in a while."

"I'll think about it," Brooke replied noncommittally.

"All right. I'll go now. Have a good day, Sis."

"You too."

Brooke ended the call quickly, but the feelings elicited by her sister's words lingered with her.

Throughout the day, a sense of something she couldn't name teased the back of her mind. It left her unsettled, but not in a bad way.

The next day, and the next, images of Kenneth popped up frequently in Brooke's mind. The memory of his face, of his voice, the scent of his cologne, the electric sizzle of his touch, all lingered with her.

The following Monday, when she arrived at symphony chorale practice, she struggled to concentrate on the music she loved so well. Strained to hear the bass line, she found Kenneth's velvet tone. It caressed her like a touch to the back of the neck, which made her feel like a petted kitten. She wanted to wrap herself up in his voice and purr.

Then, the director cut off the singing with a closing motion of his hands. "Excellent, everyone. The music is coming along beautifully. Tonight, I have a special treat for you. Our own Kenneth Hill, who will be the bass soloist for our performance, has agreed to let us hear his 'For Behold, Darkness Shall Cover the Earth,' as a special preview. The other soloists do not participate in the chorale, so we will have to wait to hear them until the week before the concert. To make this authentic, when he's finished, prepare to come in with 'And He Shall Purify.'"

Brooke dutifully opened her *Messiah* score and waited. To practice the transition this early—the second week in October—was almost unheard of, but she had no complaints.

The piano played the opening line, a strange series of notes rocked back and forth until they finally tripped downward in a minor key, signaling Kenneth's entrance.

Until then, Brooke had forced herself not to look at him; to keep her eyes on her music, but she couldn't sustain it. The moment the first long, sustained note broke on her ears, she lifted her head, gazing at him with unbridled admiration.

He'd gotten his hair cut, and it sat close to his scalp, a dark cap on his dark skin. His beard remained full, drawing attention to his warm, brown eyes, which twinkled with mischief and joy and framed his mouth as his plump lips formed the words. In the middle, a broad, square nose completed the face she'd been obsessed with for the last month. Maybe longer.

I noticed him last year, she recalled. *How handsome he is, how beautifully he sings, but my obsession started more recently.*

It struck her, in a moment of amused irony, that the last time she'd heard him sing, he'd been playing the devil, and now he was singing a hymn in praise of Christ. *Music can lead to the most surprising juxtapositions,* she thought with a grin.

Her smile coincided with a pause in the recitative, and in that moment, Kenneth glanced her direction and returned her smile with one of his own.

For a moment, Brooke forgot to breathe. Even her heart paused in its beating. Then, he resumed singing, trading the slow, measured exhortation "Who shall stand when He appeareth? for the fast, driving melismas of "For He is like a refiner's fire."

Brooke's heart slammed in her chest, pulsing painfully into her throat. Her breath resumed in a noisy whoosh that drew the attention of several of her fellow singers. She ignored them all, focused as she was on the sound of his voice. *If Malachi had sounded like this, the children of Israel would have repented on the spot.*

The solo ended, and the choir came in rapidly, leaving Brooke spluttering. The singer behind her elbowed her in the ribs. She coughed, cleared her throat and found her spot, but her singing lacked its usual attentive execution. She couldn't help it. Kenneth Tyrone Hill had sunk deep into her awareness, and nothing could extract him.

The rehearsal ended in confused frustration and many grumpy looks from her fellow sopranos.

Annoyed with her own distraction, Brooke stepped down from the risers and tucked her folder into its cubby. Then she turned toward the coatrack in the hallway at the entrance of the choir room but found it crowded with departing singers. She lingered on the fringes.

"Hello, Brooke," a low-pitched voice breathed in her ear as a warm hand closed on her elbow.

She whirled around. "Oh, um, Mr. Hill—Kenneth, that is— hello," she spluttered. She cleared her throat. "How are you?"

"I'm well. You, on the other hand, sound like I did the other night."

Brooke's face flushed. *Who was I to think he needed my help?* she realized for the first time. *I jumped in, unasked for, assuming he needed my help. I'm no better than those twerpy students.* Aware of how badly she overstepped, she lowered her lashes, breaking contact with his velvety dark eyes. "I'm sorry," she said.

"Sorry for what?"

"For jumping in. I'm sure you can handle yourself. I didn't mean to presume. It's just, they were going to twist anything you said. Elevate their own wokeness by implying you didn't understand what you were doing. I couldn't stand it."

"I..." he scrutinized her. "I can handle myself, but still

appreciate your intervention. I'm not offended." The softly slurred way he formed his words suggested he had come from a more southern place.

"I had a feeling you might be on a concert high. It's hard to think after a performance," she blurted, not sure what else to say.

"That's for sure." He grinned.

His smile drew an unexpected one from Brooke. She bit her lip, feeling shy.

"So, anyway," he continued, "I wanted to thank you for sticking up for me. I appreciate it."

"It's no credit to me," she murmured. "I had no idea you even wanted my help."

"Well, I did," he replied. "I'd like to do something for you."

"Oh, that's not necessary," she said, her stomach jumping as unwarranted possibilities crowded her mind.

"I want to. Besides, those students of yours intrigued me. I remember being that age, loving music but not knowing what to do about it. I'd like to show them the possibilities."

Right. An opportunity for the students. That's a good thing, actually. "Maybe coach them a little?" Brooke suggested. "Like a masterclass?"

Kenneth's eyes lit up. "Yes, exactly like that."

"I'll have to talk to the principal, and you'll have to fill out a background check form, but I think it would a lovely thing for you to do." This time, her smile felt wide and genuine. *What a great guy. Even nicer than I thought.*

"I'll do that. Oh, and one other thing..."

She regarded him expectantly.

"Are you busy this evening? I'd like to take you out for a cup of coffee or a glass of wine or something."

Whoa. That's not work-related, it's personal—a date! Kenneth is asking me on a date? Mercy me. Do I dare say yes?

Practicality warred with temptation. *Work. Early morning. It'll already be ten by the time you get home.*

But this is Kenneth, her heart reminded her. *Don't miss an opportunity like this.*

"It's okay if you don't want to," he added, clearly able to read her conflicted expression.

"Kenneth," she said seriously, "there's nothing I'd like more than to accept your invitation. However, it's pretty late and I have to be at work by 7:30 for my freshman girls' choir rehearsal. If you know anything about high school freshmen... Well, I have to be 100% on, which means skipping out on rest is not advised. Is a raincheck possible?"

Kenneth glanced at his wrist, at a chunky, masculine watch in a dark silvery finish.

Brooke found it appealing that he chose a watch rather than digging for the cell phone she could see outlined in his shirt pocket.

"You're right about the hour. I forgot. Since I've been in grad school, everything happens late. The classes I took before I began my opus used to begin at 6:30 at night. The classes and lessons I teach are in the afternoon. All right then, hardworking lady. If we're going to take a raincheck, that'll be fine. Better, actually, because then I can ask you to dinner. Friday?"

Dinner on Friday? Hot damn, that sounds like a date. A date with Kenneth? Wow. "Of course. That sounds great."

"Where shall I pick you up?"

"Um, let's meet at the restaurant, okay? Here." She pulled out her phone. "Tell me your number. I'll text you. We can work out the details."

This time, he did fish his phone out of his pocket. He read off the numbers as she typed them in before sending her name. His phone chirped. "Brooke with an e, eh? I was wondering that. I figured I'd have to check the concert program."

Brooke giggled. "You could have just asked."

"What a funny conversation starter that would be," he replied. "Hi, how do you spell your name?"

They laughed, and in the midst of laughing, their eyes locked.

A sensation of being caressed with something warm and soft crept down the back of Brooke's neck and along her spine. *He's so compelling he's dangerous to my peace of mind. I can hardly concentrate on anything but his presence,* she thought, not caring.

The crowd around the coatrack had thinned, so they stepped forward and retrieved their outerwear. In companionable silence, they made their way out of the choir room and along the university's sidewalk to the parking lot. Brooke made her way toward her car, and Kenneth walked beside her.

"Cold, isn't it?" she murmured. "It's only October. Five years up here and I'm still not used to the weather."

"Same here. Where are you from?"

"Texas," she admitted. "I moved for work. You?"

"Georgia. I moved for school." She could see his grin flash in the light of the streetlamp. He then grasped her hand. "Sharing warmth is a good way for two southerners to weather a northern fall, but what will we do in the winter?"

"Snuggle?" The suggestion slipped out without her full consent, and she gasped when she realized what she'd said.

"Deal," he agreed amiably as they reached Brooke's car. Slowly, he drew her toward him.

She stared in fascination as his handsome face moved toward hers. His lips gently touched her cheek. The warmth and scent of him rendered her into a puddle of molten Brooke-goo, and the scratch of his beard on her skin set her tender places ablaze.

"Is this you?" he asked.

She nodded, uncertain of her ability to form coherent words.

"Then, good night, my dear. I won't wait three days to contact you, I promise." He strode away, and a lilting whistle split the night in a cheerful tune.

Brooke fumbled her keys out of her purse and struggled to click the unlock button on the fob. In her state of distracted disbelief, it took three tries. Suddenly her safe crush on a local celebrity had all the earmarks of an early relationship.

At last, she slid into the driver's seat and cranked the ignition. "Oh, dang," she breathed. "Now what am I going to do?"

CHAPTER 4

"*He* asked you OUT?!" Autumn squealed into the phone.

Brooke moved the device away from her ear.

"Please, tell me you said yes."

"I said yes," Brooke replied, "but I'm having second thoughts..."

"Oh, no you don't!" Autumn shouted.

Brooke edged the phone farther away. "Please, lower your voice. You're going to blow out my speaker."

"Tough noogies," Autumn replied, thankfully at a more normal volume.

Brooke considered for a moment, and then pressed the speaker button.

Autumn, as expected, continued her tirade without a pause. "Don't reconsider. In fact, don't think about it at all. Just go. Go on your date. Eat. Drink. Kiss. Get busy. Anything. Just don't sit in your room and let another good man hang out to dry."

"How do you know he's a good man?" Brooke challenged,

interrupting her sister. "You've never met him. Hell, I've barely met him. I've talked to him exactly twice. That isn't much of a basis for anything."

"Every relationship has a first conversation," Autumn pointed out, "and I know he's a good man because of the way you talk about him, because of a feeling I get, and because I looked up his profile on the opera company's website. Charity work with urban youth. He even credits his mama. All signs point to a keeper."

"I don't want a keeper," Brooke pointed out for what felt like the hundredth time.

"Bullshit," Autumn replied. "If that was the case, you wouldn't have said yes. You're not asexual, you're just afraid. Not everyone is as cruel as Jordan. Not everyone wants to take advantage. If Kenneth the Opera God asks you out, chances are, he's interested in dating you. You don't need more than that. Not yet. It's time for you to open yourself to it."

That irritated Brooke. "Don't you think it's my decision?"

"Yes," Autumn replied promptly, "if it was a decision based on your higher good, but I know you, Sis. You're making decisions based on fear, and on protecting your ever-so-limited comfort zone. It's not good for you. You create arguments so fast, even you can't keep up with them. They become contradictory and stilted. You need to move past your... well... your past to discover your destiny."

Though she wanted to protest, honesty compelled Brooke to consider her sister's words. Leaning back in her office chair, she scanned the wall in front of her desk; the corkboard plastered with family photos and outdated fliers, one poster of the Three Tenors and another of Chanticleer. Behind the clustered images, the pasty-white wall behind soothed her eyes. "He hurt me so bad," she admitted softly.

"I know, honey," Autumn told her gently. "It was totally

uncalled for and wrong. Kenneth, however, had nothing to do with that."

"I can't believe you're advocating this hard for a total stranger," Brooke said, a hint of a sulk in her voice.

"Oh honey, no," Autumn assured her. "I'm advocating for you. You deserve to be happy, but that can't happen if you're making your decisions based on fear rather than trust."

"Trust in what?" Brooke demanded. "Trust in a handsome stranger? Yeah, because *nothing* ever goes wrong with that."

"Trusting the universe to bring what's best for you."

Brooke sighed but could find no retort. "Goodbye, Autumn."

"Go on the date," Autumn insisted. "Even if it's nothing, at least you will know."

Brook touched the screen to disconnect the call and laid her head on her desk. *Ten minutes until class. How on earth will I concentrate on my work?*

Her cell chirped again, and she lifted her head, expecting to find one last message from her sister. Instead, the message she saw made her heart pound.

Got plans tonight?

Gasping, Brooke stared at the message. *Oh, shit. He didn't wait three days at all.* She gulped. **No, I'm actually off early… well on time.**

What's on time? The response appeared instantly, signaling that Kenneth hadn't dropped his message and run off.

Concentrating on her shattered breathing, Brooke typed **4-ish. The kids leave at 3, and I have a bit of paperwork.**

The reply came in seconds. **Cool! The class I'm teaching ends at 4:45. If you're still on for that dinner, can we meet at 6pm?**

Where? She responded, her pulse hammering in her ears.

Believe it or not, there's a decent BBQ place near the university. Thoughts?

She considered his suggestion, and the watering of her mouth told her what she needed to know. **Sounds good. Text me the address. Meet you there at 6.**

Great! Can't wait to see you, Brooke.

Brooke didn't respond to the text. She closed her eyes. Mixed emotions warred in her, but one thing had been determined. She *would* be going on the date, just as Autumn had urged. Accepting had not required a thought process. She'd just gone along with it, and all the mental gymnastics she'd been performing for the last few days melted at the very memory of Kenneth's velvet voice and winning smile.

Autumn would say my higher self made it happen. That it's tired of me making decisions based on what I don't want rather than what I do want. She rejected the thought of fear, though in her deepest heart she recognized its truth.

"This is not going to help me pay attention," she told herself with a sigh.

Though her predicted distraction did prevent her from pushing her students as hard as she normally did, she managed to take them through decent rehearsals. They practiced dynamics—an easy objective to observe—and introduced a new song for the Christmas concert with her freshman choir so they could work on the notes.

All I hope, she thought as she ran the tenor line on the piano with clumsy fingers, *is that once I've had this date and gotten Kenneth out of my system, I'll be able to go back to normal.*

After work, she scurried through the clogged city streets

back to her apartment and crept through the door. She found Jackie sitting on the sofa, watching a reality show.

"Hi, Jackie," Brooke greeted her roommate. In reality, despite the year they'd shared the tiny space, they had never really gotten to know each other, apart from setting some ground rules to preserve their privacy.

"Hi, Brooke," Jackie said, though without her usual enthusiasm. She didn't look herself at all. Her long red hair, normally perfectly styled, hung in a lank clump. Her black turtleneck and trousers were crumpled and had a noticeable stain. A sallow tinge yellowed her complexion.

She looks ill. I hope she's okay. Of course, Jackie is a nurse, so if she was sick, she'd probably know it.

Despite her desire to rifle through her closet in search of the perfect date outfit—which she did not possess—Brooke couldn't help but plunk down on the sofa next to Jackie. *Just for a minute. It's not like new clothes will appear if I get there fast enough.* "Is everything okay?"

Jackie clicked the remote. The overly made-up woman blabbering in a whiny, east coast accent disappeared. "Not really," she said, turning to Brooke and frowning.

"Can I help with anything?"

Jackie shrugged. She considered Brooke for a long moment, as though weighing some heavy options in her mind. "I don't know. It may be that you need to find a new roommate, though I'm not sure yet. Maybe you should make up an ad? I'll let you know if you need to run it as soon as I decide."

Brooke raised one eyebrow. "That sounds heavy." A thousand questions zoomed through her mind, but her roommate's expression didn't invite her to ask them. *Heavy for sure. I hate hunting for roommates. Jackie and I might not exactly be friends, but we've had a cordial, respectful existence here. She's quiet and doesn't bring weirdos into our space like that last one did.*

"Too heavy to bear." Jackie's voice broke. She swallowed convulsively and covered her face with both hands. Her normally well-manicured hands looked rough and red, the tips ragged with hangnails.

"Can I do anything?" Brooke asked again. "Get you a drink or something to eat? Call someone? Give me your boyfriend's number if you want. I'll let him know you need him."

"I'm not ready to talk to him," Jackie said. "If I had a bottle of vodka, I'd drink the whole thing... no I wouldn't. I don't know. Can you get me a glass of water?"

Uh oh. I know what that sounds like, Brooke realized. "Of course I will."

As she filled the cup with crushed ice from the dispenser on the door and added water, her runaway thoughts kept churning. *If I'm right, it would explain everything. Why she doesn't want to call her boyfriend, or drink, or make a decision whether to move out. She doesn't know what she wants to do yet, but she's leaning toward... toward...* she hesitated to complete the thought, realizing that despite all evidence, without Jackie's confirmation, it was just speculation.

"Here's your water," Brooke told Jackie, handing her the cup.

The young woman looked up at her with wild, frightened eyes.

"You know, it's going to be okay."

"How can you say that?" Jackie hissed.

Brooke furrowed her brows. "You know, I'm not sure. It's just a thing to say, but you're absolutely right. I have no idea what's going on with you, so predicting the outcome is pretentious. I'm sorry."

Jackie's expression softened. "I know, Brooke. I know you had good intentions, but the fact is, I have no idea what to do with myself, so until I make that decision, there's nothing anyone can do to help."

"Well, let me know if there's anything I *can* do, other than putting my foot in my mouth. Meanwhile, I'm going out tonight. I'm not sure how late I'll be, but I'll come in quietly, so I don't disturb you."

Jackie blinked, seeming to reset her thinking. "Going where?"

"Oh," Brooke said off-handedly. "I have a date."

"You?" Jackie's eyebrows shot up so high, they nearly touched her hairline. "You haven't been on a single date since I've lived with you. Who is it?"

"Just some guy from choir," she replied. *Jackie's not the only one who doesn't feel like our relationship is right for full disclosure.*

"Great!" Jackie's face lit up, and Brooke could see that she looked more green than sallow. "Common interests are the best. What are you all going to do?"

"Go out to dinner. He suggested barbecue, which sounds great. I haven't had any since I left Texas five years ago."

"You know," Jackie said, "you say you're from Texas, but you don't have the accent."

"Not all Texans have an accent," Brooke pointed out. "Country folks do more than city folks. I'm from Dallas, which is really cosmopolitan. I guess I just never picked it up. Kenneth is from Georgia, he says, and *he* has an accent. It sounds so nice."

"Woohoo!" Jackie hooted loud enough to make Brooke worry about the thin structure of their apartment. Sure enough, the downstairs neighbor thumped the floor.

Jackie shot the finger to the unseen person and returned her attention to Brooke, lowering her voice. "Southern with a sexy accent *and* a singer? You may have met your match, Brooke."

"It's a bit early for that," Brooke said, and again the implication irritated more than it should have.

"Nah." Jackie waved away the protest with a casual hand gesture. "Every true love has a first date, and the people in question rarely see it as soon as us bystanders. Oh, one suggestion though..."

Brooke looked at her and waited.

"Use protection. You won't know for sure if he's the one for a while. It would be a shame to get... into trouble."

"I have no intention of having sex with this man. Not for a long, long time... if we make it that long. It's just dinner."

"Take this anyway," Jackie urged, grabbing her purse from where it sat by her feet and digging out a ribbon of plastic packages filled with concave rings. "Goodness knows I won't need them for a while."

Bingo. I knew it. Projection much, Jacqueline Castellani? Brooke accepted the six condoms with a wry pursing of her lips.

"You never know if the mood might take you," Jackie pointed out. "It's better to be prepared."

Brooke didn't argue. Instead, she laid a hand on her roommate's shoulder. Giving her a gentle, caring look, she said, "I was right before. It is going to be okay. I know that now."

Jackie narrowed her eyes. "You know something, Brooke? You're spooky."

I am? she wondered to herself. *I thought that was my sister's thing.* "I guess it runs in my family. Okay, I need to change."

"Why?" Jackie demanded. "You only have work clothes, unless there's a little black dress in there that I've never seen. Trading in that outfit for another won't make it date wear."

"Nah, no dresses. Too cold for that here. I guess Kenneth will have to take me as I am," she replied, "but I'd still like to put on something that doesn't smell like a high school."

"Good point," Jackie pointed out, wrinkling her nose. Then, her eyes went wild, and she abruptly jumped to her feet and ran for the bathroom at the back of the apartment.

Shaking her head, Brooke made her way to the curtain that hid her sleeping alcove and tugged the chain on the naked bulb above the bed. Scanning her garments, she realized Jackie was correct. All her clothes had a schoolteacher vibe. The only festive note was the ugly sweater she wore around the holidays.

I knew I'd just be trading in one bland, boring outfit for another, she thought. *I don't have anything sexy to choose from... Wait, sexy? Where did that come from? I just told Jackie I wasn't having sex, so what difference does it make? I wonder if Kenneth wants to have sex.*

The thought sent a foreign thrill to the apex of her thighs. Her long-neglected womanly parts reacted with an uncontrolled clench. *Get your mind out of the gutter,* she warned herself sternly. *You are not a sex-on-the-first-date kind of woman, and if that's what Kenneth intends, he's going to have to wait.*

As she rifled through her sweaters, she failed to notice that once again, she was thinking in affirmatives and certainties, as though their final union were just a matter of time.

Eventually, she settled on a blue cable knit sweater and a pair of faded and comfortable blue jeans. *I hope this will work. From what I've seen, all the restaurants near the university are pretty casual. Plus, who ever heard of fancy barbecue? A casual dining option makes sense with a graduate school budget. Technically, I could afford more, but with my savings plan, I prefer not to.*

She made her way out of her alcove to find Jackie slumped on the sofa, clutching the glass of water in her trembling hands. Brooke regarded her with sympathy. *There's a lesson for you, miss. Keep your wits about you.*

"Have a good time," Jackie said weakly, burped, and took several slow, deep breaths.

"I will," Brooke promised. *After all, I'm eating barbecue with Kenneth. What could go wrong?*

"Famous last words," some unknown voice whispered in the back of her mind.

She pushed the threat away, but it left an unsettled feeling behind. Shaking her head, she made her way down the staircase. No other tenants appeared to greet her.

Her car waited in its usual spot along the curb, but the driver in the next spot had parked poorly and was much too close to her front bumper.

She looked at the car beside her, and the traffic streaming past and sighed. "Forget it," she said aloud. "I'm taking public transit."

Twenty minutes later, she walked through growing twilight down a chilly street crowded with undergraduates. Tall boys in football and basketball jackets hollered at young women, trying to score a touchdown. Girls rolled their eyes and ignored them, hands thrust deep into jacket pockets.

One boy, a towering young man of indeterminate race, with a gelled mess of black hair, whistled as he passed Brooke.

She rolled her eyes. Then, the scent of tomato, spices and slow-cooked meat wafted out to meet her. Turning, she saw the neon sign with the name Kenneth had texted her.

Shaking her head at the shenanigans in the street, she ducked through the heavy glass door into a room that had a comforting familiarity. Small round tables covered in plastic sat under hanging lights in colored shades. Booths lined two of the walls. The smell of barbecue, so appealing in the street, punched her with nostalgia that brought tears to her eyes.

"Brooke," that so-compelling voice she'd come to adore broke through her homesick moment. She turned to see Kenneth seated in a booth in the center of the west wall. "Is this all right?"

"Booths are great," she replied, smiling. "Good to see you, Kenneth." She slid into the bench across from him.

He reached across the table and clasped her hand.

She allowed it. Her fingers tingled at his touch, and a lovely heat spread up her arm, warming her neck and face. *God bless America, I'm blushing like a Victorian lady.* She broke contact with his hypnotic brown eyes and looked demurely down, completing the effect. *Holy cow.*

"So, how was your week?" he asked.

She shrugged. "The same as always. Rehearsals galore. You?"

"Just the usual. Mid-semester voice lessons."

A server turned up with glasses of water. "Can I get you two something to drink?" she asked, pen poised over a small notepad.

"What have you got on tap?" Kenneth asked.

"We feature local small breweries," she replied. "There's Wild Horse IPA, Northern Lights Lager and Coalminer Stout."

"I'll try the lager, please," he requested.

She nodded and turned toward Brooke.

"Just water please," Brooke requested.

The waitress wandered away.

Brooke and Kenneth looked at one another.

"Uh, what do we talk about now?" Brooke asked.

Kenneth shrugged. "Not sure. I'd like to know you better—I want to—but where should we start?"

"At the beginning, I guess," Brooke suggested. "I know you sing bass. I know you're in the opera, and I know you like to encourage students. Beyond that, you're a bit of a mystery. So... um... I know the musician, but not the man. Who are you, Kenneth Tyrone Hill?"

"Asking me to define myself, but not by my career? How revolutionary." He laughed, and his pleasant chuckle sent an answering shiver up her spine. Clearly, Kenneth noticed her reaction because his expression turned to concern and he asked, "Cold?"

She shook her head. "Not particularly. You just have a nice voice."

He grinned. "Thank you. Okay... basic facts then?" He looked to her for confirmation, and at her nod, explained, "I come from a pretty big family. My parents, Walker and Shayla Hill, are both teachers. Mom teaches in the special ed resource room at an elementary outside of Atlanta. My dad is a football coach and administrator at the local community college. I have three brothers and a sister."

"Wow," Brooke commented. "Does she ever get to date with all those brothers?"

"Not much," Kenneth admitted with another shiver-inducing chuckle. "We'll ease up on her when she's grown. She's only fifteen now. No rush."

Brooke grinned. "And you're the oldest, right? With you being in grad school and your sister only a teenager, I'm assuming."

"Yup, oldest," he replied. "I was kind of a surprise. I mean, my parents graduated high school about a month

43

before I was born. My next oldest brother is ten years younger than me."

"Oops," Brooke commented. "Something similar happened to my sister. She had to drop out of college the second semester of her freshman year so she wouldn't miss too many credits when she delivered her son. It worked out in the end anyway."

"Exactly," Kenneth agreed. "My grandfather passed away shortly before I was born. He had a nice life insurance policy, enough for my parents to live at home and go to college while my grandmother watched over me."

Brooke chewed her fingernail, not sure what to make of that. "Does your grandmother still live with your folks?"

"Sure does," he replied. "The household wouldn't run properly without her."

"Interesting," Brooke said because she didn't know what else to say. She filed the information away. "Before I respond in kind, maybe we should choose something to eat?"

Kenneth looked askance at her, so she indicated the server, who was bearing down on them with his glass of beer and a little notepad.

He nodded.

Brooke glanced at the menu with its dizzying array of options. "Kenneth..." she began and then trailed off.

He raised his eyebrows at her.

"They have beef ribs on the menu. That's way too much food for one person. I haven't had a rack of beef ribs since I left Texas. How would you feel about sharing?"

The waitress arrived at their side and handed Kenneth his drink.

"Well," Kenneth sipped his beer, "in Georgia, like in most of the South, pork is the tradition. Tell you what; Let's get the beef ribs today and next time we get barbecue, we can get pork ribs. Deal?"

Next time? Wow. He's planning another date? She swallowed hard. "Deal."

"So, the beef ribs then?" the waitress asked, pencil poised.

"Yes, ma'am," Kenneth said easily.

"Sides? It comes with two."

"Salad," Brooke replied. "If I eat a few veggies first, I can pretend the meal is healthy."

"Mac and cheese," Kenneth added. "If it's down-home night, might as well go the whole way."

"Coming right up," the waitress told them. She sailed away again.

"Okay, Brooke. Time's up. Spill," Kenneth quipped.

Brooke swallowed again and took a sip of water.

"Uh oh. Complicated family?"

She shook her head. "Not so much complicated as... troubled, I guess. My mom died when I was five. I don't even remember her."

He lowered his eyebrows. "That's sad. What happened?"

Brooke shook her head. "Childbirth complication when she was delivering my younger sister. She had a hemorrhage."

"Ouch."

Brooke nodded. "That's for sure. My dad raised us, with a string of nannies and housekeepers helping out. He's a finance banker. A high roller." She shook her head. "He's a hard man to know."

"High standards?"

"Impossibly. He wanted me to major in finance, like him. I tried..."

"Couldn't do it? I don't blame you."

"I could," she replied. "I was actually doing rather well, at least in terms of grades. The problem was, I hated it, so I switched to music. I don't think he'll ever forgive me for that." She laughed but knew it sounded tense. Not wanting

45

to delve too deeply into the topic on their first date, she hurried on. "I mentioned I also have a younger sister, Autumn. She's great. A free spirit. She majored in business at the community college and opened a palmistry and tarot shop in Dallas. She does what she wants, and she's always successful at it."

"You mentioned she has a son?"

Brooke nodded. "River. He's seven. Great kid."

"You all are really into nature names, aren't you?"

She nodded. "Seems to be a theme."

Further conversation was cut off by the arrival of a rack of ribs big enough to have come from a dinosaur.

"I was wrong," Brooke said, eyeing the monstrous slab.

"How's that?" Kenneth asked, awe in his voice.

"It's not too much for one. It's much, much more than that."

Kenneth laughed. "Well, we'll do our best and take home the rest, I suppose."

Brooke nodded. "Sounds good."

"Wait, where are our sides?"

Brooke shook her head. "At this point, who cares?"

They laughed and turned their attention to carving up their portion of beast in sauce.

Kenneth escorted Brooke out into the cold darkness of an October evening. "Are you ever going to let me pay?" he asked.

"I haven't decided yet," Brooke quipped. "I guess it depends."

"On what?"

"I'll let you know." They exited the restaurant and the slap of cold air momentarily cut off Brooke's breath. "Oof."

"I agree," Kenneth said. "It's quite a night. One has to

46

wonder why anyone thought this cold, snowy place would be a good location for a major metropolitan area."

"And yet, there are several," she pointed out. "It would seem some people enjoy the cold."

"Those same people would probably complain so bitterly about the heat down south."

"Right. We don't have to let them know that EVERYONE complains about the heat down south, even the natives."

Kenneth laughed. "That's one way to look at it. Well, Brooke, I hate for the evening to come to an end, but..."

"I know what you mean. It's too cold to stay outside... too cold and only October. What a sorry state we're in. What on earth could we do next? Best to call it a night." *Which is a shame,* she added silently *It's been a lovely night. I doubt we'll have another opportunity. He's going to be busy with teaching and classes and preparing for the next opera... and his big European tour. I have concerts and contests coming up...*

"Are you sure? You can't think of anywhere to go in this whole big city?"

Brooke shook her head. "It's important to know when something is ending and not wreck it by pushing. It's like a television series. Know how when they go on too long, they get pointless? Let's not let tonight get pointless."

"I suppose that's wise. There's always next time."

She didn't respond, not sure a next time was wise... or likely.

"So, where's your car?"

"Oh!" Brooke suddenly remembered how she'd arrived. "I took the 'L'. My neighbor wedged my car in, and I couldn't get it out."

"How nice of them," Kenneth said dryly. "It's awfully late for public transit. The creeps have probably emerged from their holes by now. I know you're trying to be very safe and cautious, but it would be hard to let you go into that environment. I'd worry about you too much. Would you please permit me to give you a ride home?"

Brooke bit her lip, considering. All evening, she'd gotten nothing but positive vibes from him, not to mention all the good feelings she'd gotten from him over the months and years since she'd first noticed him across the choir. *Autumn suggested taking risks. This is actually a pretty small one, isn't it? To get into a car with someone I like a lot.* "Okay."

Kenneth's huge smile shone in the darkness.

Brooke bit her lip against the irresistible tingles of pleasure triggered by his expression.

"This way." He laid his hand in the center of her back, and she could have sworn she could feel the warmth through her sweater and her jacket.

Acting on impulse, Brooke stepped away from his touch. Grasping his hand in hers, she laced their fingers together.

Kenneth paused for a heartbeat. Then he gently squeezed her hand and led her forward. Silence closed in around them as words gave way to a more primal form of communication—no, communion—with one another. Brooke could feel Kenneth's presence seeping into the far corners of her being and taking up residence there.

It felt so perfectly right, and at the same time, absolutely terrifying. She longed to curl up in his arms and let him permeate every fiber of her being exactly as much as she wanted to shove him out, to push him away and run. Unable to decide, she did nothing, passively letting Kenneth guide her toward his car, which turned out to be a small gray SUV that had seen better days.

He opened the passenger door. "I hope you don't mind. My southern gentleman won't allow for anything else."

"You're fine," Brooke said. "I'm from Texas, remember."

"Of course."

She sank into the seat and he shut the door behind her. It creaked on its hinges but agreed to latch properly. A moment later, Kenneth jumped into the seat beside her. The car groaned under his weight.

"Oops," he joked. "Too many ribs."

She reached across the center console and took his hand again. Again, that sense of oneness swept over her, and from the way Kenneth's self-deprecating smile eased into comfortable calmness, Brooke could see he felt it too. It scared her.

Frozen between fear and comfort, Brooke endured the ride in silence. The contradictory impulses left her uncertain and more than a little unsettled. At war with herself, Brooke chewed her lip, and then she moved on to the nails on her free hand.

"Is everything all right?" Kenneth asked as he pulled along the curb half a block from her building. "You seem... upset."

"I'm fine," she said quickly. "Just tired. It's been a busy week."

"That's for sure." She glanced at him and saw that his expression didn't buy her simple excuse, but he would take it for now.

I have to watch it with this guy. He's entirely too intuitive. Taking her inane comments to a new level of pointlessness, she said, "Lucky to find a spot so close."

"It certainly is," he agreed. "Let me walk you to the door."

She gulped, and her throat felt so tight, her spit almost choked her. Her heart gave an almighty thump that made her ribs ache. "Okay," she croaked. Not waiting for him to circle the vehicle, she vaulted out of the seat and made her way through the cold to her front door. She could hear his footsteps as he crunched fallen leaves underfoot.

Brooke fumbled her key out of her purse, fitted it into the front door and then paused. She felt more than saw Kenneth lean against the wall beside her.

"I had a great time tonight, Brooke."

She nodded, unable to speak past the lump in her throat.

Kenneth leaned in. He moved slowly, allowing Brooke time to react, but she was frozen. Until his lips touched hers. Then the most comforting warmth she'd ever experienced sparked in her lips and spread. Her scalp tingled. Her pounding heart slowed to a pleasant, steady throb. Her hands shook as she lifted them to his shoulders. Her knees weakened, and she leaned into him for support.

Kenneth engulfed her with one arm, pulling her tight to the softness of his chest and belly. His arm felt strong, but his body molded to hers.

Brooke sighed. The embrace felt like a warm blanket on a snowy day. Like a cup of coffee on a cold morning. Like a hot shower after being caught out in the rain. She melted in his arms, at peace and completely whole.

And then he lifted his head.

Cold air stung her moist lips like a slap... or a punch. Reality shattered the moment. Brooke stepped back with a gasp. "I have to go."

Without another word, she fumbled the key in the lock until the door swung open, and then she ducked through, shutting and locking it behind her.

Her phone chimed, but she didn't look. Instead, she began the long climb up to her attic apartment. She burst through the door and flicked on the lights, completely forgetting the rules. Luckily, Jackie had gone out.

She tossed her purse on the sofa and ran for the bathroom, turning on the faucet and letting the water run hot. Over the whoosh of water, she could hear the chime of her phone a second and then a third time.

"You're acting like a weirdo," she told herself as she pumped facewash into her hands and began rubbing it over her skin to remove the makeup. "You had a great date, a great kiss, and you ran like a rabbit."

She splashed water over her face to rinse off the soap and then patted the water away with the hanging hand towel. A quick smear of nighttime moisturizer and she emerged, heart pounding, ready to see what her text messages had to say. *Probably go away. Too weird. Too mixed up,* she thought bitterly, *as if I didn't know that. Kenneth deserves a woman whose heart is as open as his own. That can never be me. I have so many hang-ups.*

Again, the tight sensation of fear rose up in her throat, and again she tried to swallow it down, but it lingered, choking her with meaningless suppositions and the sensation that something vague was threatening her. *But it's not Kenneth,* she reminded herself. *Whatever you're feeling comes from you, not him.*

Her heart and intuition agreed. Not one thing he'd said or done in all the time she'd known him had given her a minute's pause. "Nope, it's me. And because it's me, it would be unfair to subject him to my fearful self."

She lifted the phone, and her heart tried to stop. **I had a great time tonight.**

Brooke closed her eyes. *So did I,* she admitted to herself. *I just overthink everything.*

She forced herself to look at the second message. **I'm good with taking things slow, but I'd really like to see you again. Let me know if...** The message cut off abruptly, as though he'd hit send in the midst of rewriting it.

Then, a final message waited. **I can see you have some concerns. I'm still interested if you are. If you want to go out again, let me know. —Kenneth.**

Again, Brooke's eyelids slid shut. The eager way her heart had leaped when she saw his messages told her something. *Told me I'm stupidly infatuated and desperate to accept what he's offering,* she admitted to herself. But no sooner did she consider another date, then the fear rose up in her throat, choking her. *I need therapy.*

"Home already?"

Jackie's arrival startled Brooke so badly, she dropped her phone. Luckily onto the sofa.

"Sorry. I guess if you're back at..." she glanced at her own device "9:37 p.m., you didn't have a great time?"

"I did have a great time," Brooke replied. "We embraced our southern heritage by eating barbecue and our music nerd status by talking about work. It was fun."

"Then why..."

"It was time to call it a night, that's all," Brooke snapped.

Jackie's face scrunched inward in surprise.

"Sorry. I don't mean to be rude to you. I just have a lot of things on my mind, and all of them contradict each other."

"Well, I can certainly relate to that," Jackie said. "Shall we leave it for now?"

Brooke nodded eagerly. "Best idea I've heard so far."

Though she didn't feel particularly sleepy, chit-chatting with the roommate she wasn't particularly close to didn't sound like fun either. She retrieved her laptop from on top of her dresser and carried it back to the sofa.

Jackie had done the same thing, sprawling on the love seat that lined the wall below the apartment's east-side window. The way she constantly clicked the touchpad showed Brooke she was likely researching.

No surprise there. Brooke, however, had other plans. Opening the school's website, she made her way to the employment page and began filling out the application for the head choir director position. *It may be a formality, but I have to do my best anyway.*

CHAPTER 5

*H*eart pounding up into her throat, Brooke slowly typed one letter at a time into her phone. **I had a great time. You're an amazing man. I wish you all the best, but another date is not a good—**

An incoming message interrupted her. Of course, it was from Kenneth. **A friend gifted me tickets to Les Miz. This Saturday. 7pm. Interested?**

Brooke's half-typed message disappeared when Kenneth's text arrived.

"Stupid phone," she muttered under her breath, even as her fingers, of their own accord, typed **Sounds like fun. See you there.** She hit send and then stared at what she'd done. *Damn it. This is getting away from me.*

The phone chimed again. **What if we meet downtown? Get a bite to eat, and then take the 'L' to the theater. Save on driving in the traffic.**

He'd presented the perfect solution, of course. Trapped by

her own overeager heart, she typed **OK** and sent it. Then, the bell rang, so she added, **Class starting. Gotta go.**

Ducking out of her office, Brooke took her place at the music stand in front of the risers. She waited to direct her students, as always, to stop loitering and chatting, and get into place.

"So, guys, you've been doing great so far," she informed them, starting rehearsal on a positive note. "I'm really pleased with your progress on the fall concert music. But we're not going to repeat last year's successes if we stick with easy stuff. I want to give you one more piece, a really difficult one, that will challenge you and prepare you for the more advanced music to come. Are you ready?"

Nods and a few excited expressions.

She pulled out a manila envelope she'd left on her music stand and withdrew a stack of sheet music, handing them to her students to pass down the rows. "This is by a composer named Anton Bruckner. He lived in the 1800s. This piece is called 'Os Justi.' It will involve all four parts splitting, so I'd like Kelly S., Lupita and Julie to sing first soprano, Jasmine, LaKeisha and Kimberly on mezzo, Susana, Kelly P., and Eliza on first alto, Mel, Jenny and Carly on second alto, and Tonya, if you can join the first tenors, that would be a big help. Joey and Kyle also on first tenor. Alfonso and Traevon on second tenor, Arnoldo, Jack and Peter on baritone and Darion and Martin on bass. Sound good?"

Nodding again, the students moved into their groups.

"Now, I'm not guaranteeing we'll have this ready for the fall concert. We'll perform it if we're able, but I wouldn't be surprised if it's not ready until Christmas. Since the UIL Concert and Sight-Reading Contest is in the spring, we'll be okay for that, I'm sure."

A few faces showed relief.

"Oh, you wound me," Brooke cried dramatically, laying her hand on her heart. "Do you think I would allow y'all to perform a work that isn't ready? I didn't get where I am by doing that. Now, the flip side is, you all have to work hard and do your best. You have some big shoes to step into, but I have no doubt you'll live up to it."

A hand shot up.

"Yes, LaKeisha?"

"What does it mean?" the curvaceous, dark-skinned girl demanded, smoothing straightened, dyed-blonde out of her eyes. "You said it's important to *believe* what we're singing, to give our music authenticity. What's the song about?" She flipped through the pages. "I can't read Latin."

"Of course," Brooke replied. "I had planned to explain that shortly. This is a song about justice. Follow along with me as we go over the pronunciation and meaning of each line. Pencils ready!"

The students dug their pencils out of their folders while Brooke focused on her notes, determined to dispel images of Kenneth from her mind... and heart... and body. *Surely Latin will help. Surely it must.*

It didn't.

Saturday at 5:30 p.m., Brooke stepped out of a downtown parking lot near the 'L' station and approached a small assembly of food trucks. For once, the temperature had risen into the sixties, a tolerable temperature even for her thin Texas blood. Her light jacket sufficed, though her gloves remained tucked into the pockets, as it would be fully dark and cold by the time the show ended.

A huge crowd of hungry tourists and locals crowded

around the trucks, but somehow, Kenneth's tall frame and bright smile drew her eyes like a magnet. He stood in the center, a foil-wrapped packet in each hand.

She approached cautiously, drawing near, but not near enough to touch. Even from that distance, she could *feel* him, as though the warmth of his body had hands and could reach out to her.

"Hi," he said. "I hope you like tacos. I was concerned, with this crowd, that if I waited for you to get here, we wouldn't have enough time to choose anything before we had to get moving again."

"I love tacos," Brooke replied. "That was pretty smart." Still, she didn't approach. Kenneth's appealing, wistful smile threatened to drown common sense altogether. She wasn't ready to lose her willpower, not yet.

"Beef or chicken?"

"Um, beef," she replied, and he extended a warm, foil-wrapped packet. Inside, she found four obviously fresh, handmade corn tortillas, filled with tiny cubes of meat, and a little plastic cup filled with diced onions and cilantro. A second tiny cup contained salsa.

Brooke popped open the salsa and tasted it with the tip of her finger, smiling at the burn of chilis and the sharpness of tomatoes. "This is good. Most authentic I've had outside of Texas. Thanks, Kenneth." She poured the salsa over the tacos, added the onion and herb mixture and took a bite. "Beautiful evening, isn't it?"

"Yes, I'm enjoying the warmth quite a bit." He doctored his own tacos, leaving out the salsa, and began to eat.

"Anything new happening on the college front?"

He swallowed and considered. "I defended my master opus today."

"That sounds heavy. What does it mean?" she asked. "Is that like a dissertation?"

He nodded. "I composed a piece of music—a short, comic opera for children. I had some students perform it while I directed. I showed them the video and explained my choices for the plot, the music, and so on."

Brooke's eyebrows shot toward her hairline. "You *wrote* an opera? Wow, Kenneth. That's amazing! How did the defense go?"

He shrugged. "Hard to say. They had some compliments, but they also wanted me to make some changes to the score. They suggested I fix up some awkward chord progressions, and they questioned the necessity of one of the minor characters. A few things like that. If I make the changes they recommend, I pass."

"Nice. What else will you need to do in order to graduate?" Brooke wanted to know. "I mean, I have a master's, but the process of getting a doctorate seems so... scary and mysterious to me."

"Not much. Just make sure my students—both in lessons and in class—have every opportunity to pass and don't drop the ball on my grading, but that doesn't matter. The process is *still* mysterious and scary," he admitted. Taking another bite of a taco, he chewed and swallowed while pondering his answer. "It's... I feel like... like a fraud sometimes. I'm studying a couple of small things, and people will think, because I have a doctorate, that I'm some general expert on music."

"I can relate to that," Brooke replied. "It's not getting your education that teaches you what you know. It's using it. Don't worry. You'll get over that feeling after you've been out of school for a while. What do you have in mind for a career? You're graduating in December, right? That's an odd time to get a teaching job..."

"Well, I'm going on that European tour this spring," he reminded her. "That will keep me busy from January to April. The pay is decent, so if I'm careful, I should be okay until fall. After that, I'll hopefully have a better idea what's next. The fall job postings should open early in the new year, so when I'm not performing, I'll be plastering the world with applications."

"Sounds wise. I remember doing that," Brooke replied. "It's scary but led to some really interesting opportunities. Do you have any regions or even countries you're interested in?"

He shrugged. "It depends." A hint of intensity in his voice teased her, and again her heart pulled toward him while her sense pulled away.

It's too soon to talk about things like that. Wait, what? Too soon? You haven't even decided this is a relationship. It's just a date.

"How did you decide on Chicago?" he asked her, drawing her runaway mind back to the present. "Weren't there any jobs in Texas?"

"Not really," she replied. "I looked, but jobs in Texas are hard to come by. It's a high-pay area compared to the cost of living, and in magnet and charter schools, the opportunities are less. I got an offer from a regular high school along the border, but I thought I could handle cold better than that kind of heat. After weathering a couple of winters up here, I'm not as sure, but now..."

"Now?" he took a bite of his food and regarded her with his eyebrows raised.

"Now I have a chance at a big promotion, and I'm crossing all my fingers and toes, even though there's every likelihood I'll get it."

He grinned. "That's great. I hope you do."

"Thank you." The sight of his warm, open-hearted approval caused a bit of the wall around her heart to crumble.

They finished their tacos in silence. The sun sank lower in the sky, and the pleasant afternoon began to cool. The tempting warmth of Kenneth's body drew Brooke closer. Every shifting half-step she took in his direction seemed to wrap her in more bands of comfort. At last, they stood shoulder to shoulder.

He reached out but paused, as if uncertain whether he ought to touch.

By now, Brooke had fallen completely under Kenneth's spell. The scent of his cologne, his warmth, his smile and some other, less tangible force had taken her over. She reached out and grasped his hand, lacing their fingers together. "Is it time to go?"

He checked his watch. "I think so. Shall we?"

They headed toward the 'L' station, dropping their wrappers into a convenient trash can. Already, a crowd had gathered at the station They waded, hand in hand, through the milling mass of fellow commuters onto the train, and managed to find two blue seats, which they sank into.

Kenneth dropped Brooke's hand and casually laid his arm along the back of her seat.

She snuggled back, willing him to embrace her.

He did.

She closed her eyes, drinking in the sensation. *Peace. Safety. Oneness. Acceptance.*

Across from them, a snort sounded, breaking into their quiet union.

Her peace shattered, Brooke looked at an old woman with a triangle of plastic tied over her hair. The woman shook her head, her mouth turned down in disapproval.

Brooke glared, refusing to back down as the judgmental stare carried on. Awkwardness rose. Brooke made no move to look away.

At last, the woman broke eye contact, turning to the side.

Brooke smirked to herself. *Nosy old busybody. Welcome to the 21st century. I'll date a black man if I want to, so suck it.*

Feeling pleased with herself, she let her eyes close, sinking again into Kenneth's compelling aura.

Going from one downtown location to another didn't take long. However, while they'd been inside the train, the sun had set further. A cool breeze ruffled Brooke's hair as she stepped away from the platform, her hand again firmly laced through Kenneth's.

They approached a grayish-tan brick building with a red marquee above the entrance. Ducking through the front doors beneath the marquee, they quickly navigated the check-in process and found their seats. They sat off to one side of the stage, but not too far back.

"Would you care for a glass of wine?" Kenneth asked.

Brooke shook her head. Instead, she grasped Kenneth's hand and laced her fingers through his.

A broad smile broke across his face. He tugged gently on their joined hands and laid them both on his knee.

Within a short space of silent time, the lights dimmed, and the music began. While very different from the opera, the compelling tune wove a spell of pathos that sucked Brooke in. She drew closer to Kenneth until her head rested on his shoulder, and his tempting warmth and scent added their magic, until she released conscious thought altogether and let her feelings take over.

Kenneth leaned over toward her, and she obediently lifted her chin, allowing him to claim her lips.

"Ahem." A voice behind them urged them apart, but Brooke couldn't keep a smile, or maybe a smirk, from spreading across her face.

~

Brooke's back compressed against the side of her car, and still, she squeezed tighter, wanting to engulf herself completely in Kenneth's warmth. His lips parted, and she allowed him to deepen the kiss. His tongue slid along hers.

Heat flared in her belly, welling outward in a bubble of desire that spread to the far extremities of her body. Her fingertips trembled. Her toes curled inside her shoes.

"Get a room," someone shouted, voice echoing through the parking garage.

Kenneth lifted his head. Brooke rested her forehead against his chest, panting.

"Come home with me," he breathed.

It sounded amazing. Tempting. *Perfect.* "I can't."

"Too soon? I understand. But, Brooke..." he trailed off.

Cold reality seeped between them, shattering the evening's magic spell. "Kenneth..."

He cupped her cheek in one big hand. "Don't run," he urged. "Tell me what you're feeling. I want us to be on the same page, but how can I if you shut me out?"

Brooke lowered her eyebrows. "Shut you out? We're not married, Kenneth. We've had two dates and a few conversations. We're not even a couple. Don't push it."

He met her look of consternation with one of his own. "But you can feel it. I know you can. You can feel this... thing that wants to grow between us. When you get out of your head, when you let yourself feel, you're as caught up in this as I am."

His words teased a hidden part of her heart, one she rarely consulted, or even acknowledged. Beyond reason, beyond sense, her innermost being responded to Kenneth in a way she couldn't explain. However... "Attraction and even infatuation can be a good start, but neither one is a reason to abandon sense. What did you say you were doing in the spring?"

"Touring Europe," he replied. "But that's only for a short time—"

"And then what?" Brooke interrupted. "You'll be applying for jobs all over the country, and maybe even all over the world, right?"

"Well, yes," he agreed.

"Then is it really wise for us to throw caution to the wind and succumb to this mad attraction, knowing that it is almost certainly going to be measured in weeks? How old are you, Kenneth?"

He pursed his full lips. "Thirty-two."

"I'm thirty. Aren't we past the age of wild flings?"

"But, that's not what this is," Kenneth protested. "There are options..."

"And you're going to limit your options for someone you just met? That's crazy."

"What are you saying, Brooke?" he demanded. "You might say that after two dates, we're not at a level of deep intimacy. I even agree to a certain extent, but I feel like there's something you've been trying to tell me since our first date, and then changing your mind. Is that true?"

Brooke bit her lip. A hot, painful feeling raced through her. It made her eyes burn. She cleared her throat. "Yeah, it's what I just said. The more attraction we feel, the less appropriate it is for us to act on it because there's every likelihood that our chance to be together is so short. Why invest ourselves in something with no future, and why promise a future when we've just met? See what I mean?" She blurted it all out in a rush, and it hurt. Hurt so much more than it should have.

"Why are we here then?" he asked, his handsome, open face shutting down into angry lines that slashed deeper at her pain.

Damn it. "I'm trying *not* to hurt you, Kenneth. I wish I

could make that make sense. When you asked me out, I couldn't say no. I just couldn't. You're... God, you're amazing, but—"

"But you don't see a future in it."

She squeezed her burning eyes shut tight. "What do you want, Kenneth?" she demanded. "Do you want a fling? A two-month quickie before you take off for Europe? And even if you come back, how long will it be until you leave for new adventures? What are the odds I'll even see you again?"

"I don't know," he replied, his voice flat and his face set in lines of deep disappointment. "I don't always need to know the answers. Sometimes what could be is enough. How did you ever get through a music degree, knowing that musicians barely make a living?"

She shook her head. "I planned to teach. Always. I never invest in risks beyond my comfort level."

"Child of a banker, eh?" the bitter irony in his voice seemed at odds with the situation, much like the agony tearing at her heart. "Never invest more than you can afford to lose?"

She nodded.

"Hearts don't work that way, Brooke. If you're not willing to risk, you may never find your soulmate... or rather, you may not be willing to 'invest' in him."

Oh, God, he's talking about me. About us. Her throat closed, but she still managed to choke out. "You don't understand."

He shook his head. "You're right. I don't."

"I mean, suppose you're right," she blurted. "What do you want me to do? You go off into the wide world out there, following your star, as you should. You will probably have to move several times before you find your destination, and what about me? Am I just supposed to follow you where the wind blows on the basis of a nice attraction and a couple of dates? Come on."

"I would never ask you to give up what you're building," he said.

"Nor would I ask it of you," she cried, perhaps more loudly than she needed to. "Our paths are diverging, Kenneth. You need to accept that. It's not my fault. Fate can be cruel, but there's nothing we can do about it."

Kenneth lifted his hand to his face and toyed with the hairs of his beard. "I see. Well then, I guess it's good we didn't let this get away from us. Thanks for the company. Best wishes." He turned and stalked away.

Brooke longed to call out to him, but she didn't quite dare. *It's what you asked for—no. It's what you demanded. It's also the right thing to do. Let him go. He's a true keeper. Let him find his perfect match when he's more settled. You have everything you need here.*

Sucking in a shaky breath, Brooke fumbled at the door of her car. Finally opening it, she slid into the driver's seat. Locking the door behind her, she leaned against the steering wheel, panting with distress. Her swollen heart felt like it had suddenly constricted.

Clearly, trying to turn a crush into a relationship is a bad idea. The logical thought did nothing to calm her, and it took her over half an hour before she felt calm enough to fire the ignition. Then, she inched onto the crowded streets toward her home.

Home, she thought bitterly, *is an efficiency apartment I can only manage and still follow my savings plan because I share it with a roommate. That's insane. In Texas, I could buy a house already.* Suddenly soured on everything, she made her slow way back to her building.

Her overactive mind had already shut down. She eased into her spot, barely fitting between her more conscientious neighbor's car on one side and the usual jerk who parked over the line on the other. Muttering to herself, she jumped out of the car, clicked the lock button and made her way along the sidewalk. It took far too long for her to get the front door key into the lock, but she managed in the end.

A crowd hovered around the front door, chatting in a worried undertone.

"Oh, hey," a delicate man of about forty with gelled, sandy hair and big dimples said, "it's the girl from the attic. Have you heard the news, Brooke?"

"News, Stanley?" Brooke asked, forcing her wildly firing brain to focus on the conversation. "What news?"

"They've put the building on the market. At the price, it'll take a while, but there's no telling what will happen if it does finally sell. Someone might want to restore it, make a B&B, or fix it up and raise the rent, which is likely due to all the gentrification going on around us."

Brooke scowled. "Well, it's good to have warning. Still, finding a new apartment is a pain. Hope I don't have to."

"We're all saying about the same," a lady whose apartment was on the ground floor cut in. "This building has its issues, but the rent is decent and it's not too bad."

Brooke nodded.

"Are you all right?" another woman Brooke had seen in passing asked. "Your eyes are red."

Brooke swallowed hard against a sudden burn in her throat. "I'm just tired," she said. "Long hours at the high school, you know?"

"Teachers work harder than anyone gives them credit for," Stanley said, gaining Brooke's eternal gratitude.

"Have a good night, everyone. I'm going to go lie down. Lots to think about."

Some of the assembled crowd waved, others ignored her. She made a decisive move to the stairwell and began the long climb to her space. Again, a state of agitated lethargy descended upon her, so that with each step, her feet felt heavier and heavier until she could hardly lift them. Still, two flights remained.

Brooke paused, leaning her forehead against the cheap drywall, breathing slowly in hopes of regaining some strength. *Your bed is up there,* she reminded herself.

At last, she forced herself to make one slow, painful step, and then another, until at last, her door lay before her. She gently worked the lock and eased the door open, only to curse in frustration. It appeared Jackie was entertaining again.

I wonder what, if anything, that means for her predicament, Brooke thought. She crept through the dark apartment, trying to give her roommate as much privacy as possible while she set aside her purse, brushed her teeth, and got into bed.

Only then did the full frustration of life's unfairness break over her. She buried her face in the pillow, feeling miserable and alone. *I could have spent the night with Kenneth. It might have been wrong, but the temptation... He's such a good guy.*

"But he's not *your* guy," she reminded herself in an undertone. "That doesn't make sense. Now go to bed."

Ordering herself to sleep had no effect. The long, lonely hours stretched out.

Long after Jackie and her companion subsided into silence, Brooke lay awake staring at a dark wall and wishing life didn't have to be so filled with impossible decisions.

CHAPTER 6

"**E**xcellent, girls," Brooke exclaimed, making the 'cut-off' motion with both hands. The sound rang through the room, much louder than anyone would have expected of sixteen teenagers, even if they were the best at a school specially designated for people with exceptional artistic talents. "The fall concert is going to be spectacular."

"Miss Daniels," Salome Jaramillo asked, raising her hand, "have you selected our contest music for this year?"

"I've got most of it," Brooke replied. "We'll be ready to start next week."

"Good," Salome replied. "Are we still going on that tour in January?"

"That's the plan," Brooke told her. "Tour in January, camp in March, and then UIL in April. State in the summer, I have no doubt."

Grins broke out.

"But it's not going to be easy. Reputation alone is not enough to guarantee success, and only about half of you have experience with this. The rest of you will have to get with the program. Get on board. Work hard. Starting with rehearsal tonight."

Murmurs broke out.

Brooke lowered her voice, barely whispering to force them to listen. "Yes, tonight's rehearsal is for our concert on Thursday rather than a competition, but winners go above and beyond, without complaining, making excuses or putting it off. Winners make commitments. You all are the best of the best. There are seven girls who auditioned and didn't make it. They'd be beyond happy to get another chance, even if it means extra rehearsals."

The murmuring fell silent and matching expressions of determination hardened the girls' jaws and narrowed their eyes.

"Okay then," Brooke said at her normal volume. "I'll see you all tonight at five. I'll have you know I'm missing my own choir rehearsal—the only time I get to sing instead of directing —so I'm sacrificing for this too."

The bell rang.

The girls scattered.

Brooke sagged. The ends of rehearsals always left her exhausted. Introversion closed in on her, sending her stumbling into her office, where she flopped listlessly on her chair. Her head fell back in extreme fatigue, and when her phone chirped, she contemplated not answering it.

The sound stopped, and she closed her eyes. *How am I going to get through the entire afternoon and an evening rehearsal too? Thank goodness I have an excuse to skip chorale tonight. I'm not ready to see...* Her mind veered away from Kenneth's name, but an image of him floated up in her mind.

"Stop it," she hissed under her breath. "It was nothing but a celebrity crush and a couple of casual dates. No need to obsess like you lost your one true love."

The thought of true love triggered a welcoming surge in her innermost being. Tears stung her eyes, so she kept them shut tight. "Stop being stupid."

The phone rang again. Suddenly desperate for a distraction, she opened her desk drawer and dug out her purse, fumbling for the phone just as the ringing stopped again. A quick swipe and press showed her sister's number, and she called back immediately.

"Brooke, what the hell is going on?" Autumn demanded without preamble.

"What do you mean?" Brooke asked, rubbing her eyes and faking a cheerful tone.

"Don't pretend with me," Autumn snapped. "I didn't even need the cards to tell me you're in a bad way. What happened? Did something go wrong with Kenneth? I could have sworn he was your soulmate..."

"Nothing happened, Autumn," Brooke insisted. "We went on a couple of dates. That's it."

"Then why is your pain reaching me all the way in Texas?"

"I've never been able to explain your spookiness," Brooke quipped. Her foul mood turned her playful comment snarky, and she instantly regretted it.

"I'm not asking you to explain what I can do." Autumn snapped back, "I'm asking you to stop shutting me out. You're my sister and I love you, so since you're hurting and anxious, and it's messing with me, I want to know what's going on."

Brooke opened her mouth, another snarky reply lingering on her tongue, but then she stopped herself. *It's not Autumn's fault. She's only trying to help.* "I'm not sure. I heard our apartment building is being sold. I don't like the idea of having to find a new place. I'd have to dip into my savings for first and last month's rent, security deposit and all. That's about five months' worth of savings gone and sets me back on buying a house."

"Hmmmm. That's a pain, but you don't sound *that* upset about it. More irritated. That's not what I'm feeling, though I'm sorry to hear you're troubled."

"And my roommate might be moving out. I think... Well, I don't want to gossip about her, but I suspect she will not be coming with me, so along with finding a new place, I have to find a new roommate."

"All that sounds pretty far off," Autumn pointed out. "Months away. Maybe by then, you'll be ready to move in with Kenneth."

"No," Brooke said sharply. "It will never happen."

"Whoa." She could almost see her sister pulling back in surprise. "That's a bit extreme. Why on earth not? You said nothing was wrong and you've been on two dates. Why would moving in never be an option?"

"Because he's leaving," Brooke explained, unable to keep the harsh bitterness from her voice. "He's graduating in December—that's only two months away, remember— and in January, he's going to Europe for four months, and then..." She trailed off.

"And then?" Autumn pressed.

"And then he's off to the ends of the earth," Brooke burst out. "Off to find his place somewhere out there in the world, while I stay here. If I'll never see him again, why would I invest in this now?"

Autumn sighed, a sigh that seemed to encompass the entire world of frustration and disappointment. "You're overthinking it."

"No, I'm not," Brooke protested. "I'm being *sensible*. I'm protecting my heart and his from being broken. Since there's no future, and since we like each other so much, there's no benefit in starting something that simply cannot continue."

"Brooke," Autumn said gently, "that's not how it works. You don't know there's no future. You can't see all the outcomes. Listen to your heart. If something is meant to be, the universe will handle the details. Nothing truly fated will fall apart."

"How?" Brooke demanded. "How will the *universe* make this fated relationship between people who are moving in opposite directions?"

"You don't *know* you're moving in opposite directions," Autumn pointed out. "What if he's planning to stay in your area?"

"He didn't say that. He's going to apply everywhere. And he's good, Autumn. Amazing. People all over will want him. I can't limit his future that way."

"A future is more than a job, Brooke. A job is only the way to fund your life. Yes, work is good for us, and if we like our jobs, that's even better. Best of all is a calling, a vocation. But all those things are still only part of the picture. Maybe Kenneth understands that, even if you struggle with it."

Brooke opened her mouth and then shut it again. The voice of reason rebelled against such a worldview. Again, she tried to speak, but the words refused to come out. At last, she admitted, "I really, really like him. That's why I have to let him go. I can't allow us to get closer when there's no likely future."

Autumn sighed loudly, making the phone crackle. "Maybe you're right."

Brooke blinked. "In all these years, you've never agreed with me. Why now?"

"Because you're settled on this idea. If Kenneth is a really great guy, he doesn't deserve to be jerked around by a woman who doesn't know how to adapt or compromise. Let him go so he can find someone who loves him back."

The words stabbed deep into Brooke's heart. "Autumn!"

"What?" her sister demanded. "Either you're willing to adapt or you're not, and everything you've just told me says you're not. If that's truly how you feel, then you did the right thing. Go with it. Stop feeling sorry for yourself because this is one hundred percent your choice."

"Autumn..."

But Autumn had hung up the phone, leaving Brooke alone with her sister's all-too-logical conclusions. They rang in her head like a clanging gong, making her ears hum. *She's right. I hate it, but she's right.*

Tears welled up in Brooke's eyes. When the bell rang, she wiped them away angrily with the back of her hand and firmed her jaw. *Time to learn new, really hard music. No time for all this lovey-dovey nonsense.*

Brooke would have liked nothing better than for Monday night to take a year to come, or maybe a decade, but skipping out on the high-intensity, auditioned group in which she was privileged to participate didn't sit right with her. *The Christmas concert is right around the corner. Only six rehearsals left. I can't skip any. I'll just focus on my music and ignore... the bass section. Surely, I'm professional enough to handle that, right?*

Wrong.

The second she walked in the room, Kenneth's compelling presence reached out, potent as hands, to touch and caress her soul. It hurt. *And why not? The potential is compelling even if the timing is wrong. We weren't drawn to each other because of our mutual incompatibility. He's a high-level, talented musician* who also turned out to be friendly, kind, attractive...and a damned good kisser.

The memory of his lips lingering on hers made a tingle run up her spine. *He invited you to come home with him, and you wanted to go. That's what made you run. Not him. Not the situation. You can't control yourself when you're with him.*

The truth of the realization hit her like a bucket of cold water. She actually gasped as it raised goosebumps along her arms. *I had to break things off because I wanted this too much. Because I was already on the verge of falling madly in love with a near-total stranger. I knew Jordan for a year before we started dating, dated a year before we moved in together. Now, I'm here with Kenneth for a handful of choir rehearsals and a couple of dates and I never want to leave his side.*

The low rumble of his voice reached her eardrums, and she looked up, unable to resist. He stood chatting idly with the man next to him as they rifled through their music.

Rehearsal, Brooke. Wake up. Checking the board, she realized that the concert order had been sketched out in yellow chalk. Forcing her mind onto the task, she began to place her music in the correct sequence, but all the while her ears strained to hear even a hint of conversation from Kenneth. She heard plenty, and every time she did, she shivered. *His voice is so beautiful.*

Dr. Davis bustled out of his office, a notepad in his hand. "Good evening, everyone," he said softly.

The murmuring of conversations and the rustling of pages instantly died as everyone strained to hear the director's instructions.

"The symphony board is going to begin creating the program soon, and they need everyone's name and the part you sing. I know a couple of people retired or moved after last season, and I think someone got married, so if you would, please, find your part, write your name in your *most legible* handwriting." He leveled an accusing glance at a local physician who sang in the baritone section. "Then, pass it on. Hopefully, we can get through that quickly during the announcements and be ready to start rehearsal shortly."

He handed the notepad to the woman in the back row of the soprano section and moved to the front of the room, taking his place on a small riser behind a black music stand. "As you can see, the board has decided on the order for the concert, and I've written it for you. We will sing in the second half of the concert, after intermission. The first half will be instrumental only, as usual. We will reserve our section of the balcony so that you all may enjoy it."

Brooke's attention wandered. She'd heard the speech before and knew what was coming. The notebook came to her, and she dug her pencil out of her folder and wrote her name beneath the underlined word Mezzo-Soprano in a careless but readable scrawl. Without paying much attention, she passed it to the right.

A compulsion overtook her to look up, not at Dr. Davis's earnest and wrinkled face, but at the bass section... *at Kenneth. At his warm brown eyes. At his irresistible smile. How on earth am I going to go to rehearsal from now until the Christmas concert, look at this man, and do nothing?*

Her reason didn't respond. It seemed to have fled in the force of his presence.

Gee, thanks. Leave me miserable and alone, and then ditch me with no backup. This isn't going to end well. I should just quit.

The thought produced a ripple of unhappiness, but she didn't delve into its sources. Thankfully, Dr. Davis retrieved the notepad from the far end of the bass section. *Good. We'll start singing soon.*

His movement drew her attention across the choir, and sure enough, her gaze went straight to the one person in the room she didn't want to look at, the one person she couldn't resist.

He was looking at her.

Kenneth's intense, brown-eyed stare captured Brooke in unbreakable bonds. Anger, sadness and confusion twisted his expression to one she'd never seen before. One that accused her of much more than just cutting off a pleasing potentiality.

Brooke swallowed hard, not with her usual fear of intense feelings, but with something else. Something *more*. Kenneth's compelling presence seemed to reach across the room, skipping over every other person until it wrapped her up. Then, the piano crashed out a chord, breaking her concentration and leaving her scrambling for her music, lest she miss her entrance.

Despite her best efforts, concentration remained a struggle throughout rehearsal. Every time she looked up from her music in an effort to keep pace with Dr. Davis's conducting, Kenneth drew her gaze. Every time the basses sang, his voice stroked her.

By the time they closed the final cadence and began packing up their gear, she felt like weeping. Every molecule in her body cried out for Kenneth, as though they'd starved her whole life for some vital nutrient, and now, after only the tiniest taste, had been cut off again forever.

Potent grief, much too strong for the shortness of their association, tore at her. Reason, logic and common sense offered a weak protest, but their shrill voices, which sounded altogether too much like fear, did nothing to comfort her. *I let go of the best thing that's ever happened to me.*

Finally, Brooke waded through the crowd to her cubby and dropped off her folder. In the last two weeks, the temperature had noticeably dropped, especially at night, so heavier coats had become a must. She had to navigate another mob of people around the coat rack.

People brushed against her. Loud voices shouted to be heard over one another. They jarred her badly as they warred with her pained contemplation. Behind her, she could hear Kenneth's luscious voice matching pitch with the piano as he practiced his solo for the carol section of the concert.

It was one blow too many.

Ignoring manners, Brooke pushed her way to the front of the group, grabbed her coat and fled without putting it on. Outside, the chilly night cooled her burning face, but nothing could touch the aching agony in her heart. *Life is unfair. This whole situation is unfair. Why would I meet someone so wonderful, someone who wants me as badly as I want him, at exactly the wrong moment?*

Brooke caught her lip between her teeth. *I think Autumn might be right. Fate exists, and it has a nasty sense of humor. I've been the butt of more than one cosmic joke in my life, but this really takes the cake.*

Ducking around the corner away from the parking lot and the crowd of singers who chattered like magpies as they exited the choir room, she sank to a seat on an abandoned bench. Burying her face in her hands, she trembled. *It's too much,* she told herself fiercely. *Too much emotion for someone you barely know. Too much reaction.*

Her heart, it seemed, did not care.

The darkness had already long since fallen, and bitter night chewed at her skin, but she didn't mind it. It matched how she felt on the inside. *Cold and bitter. I'm already well on my way to misery, all for trying to be sensible and fair and not limit the options of a person I care about.*

"You sure did take on a lot that wasn't yours to decide, didn't you?" a voice in her head that sounded like Autumn commented. "You decided for Kenneth that he wasn't allowed to limit his job search. You might have had good intentions, but you treated him like you knew better than he did what was best for his life. You have no idea whether this relationship would have been worth that kind of sacrifice in the end because you never let it develop. In fact, you never even found out if it would have been a sacrifice for him at all. There are dozens of universities and just as many community colleges, if not more—not to mention high schools and private music lessons—within a reasonable commute. He's already a core member of the opera society. Does that really sound like a sacrifice?"

Brooke opened her eyes, and the cold air stung the tears shimmering in her eyelashes. "It's too late," she told herself, her resolve firm but her voice wavering. "You told him you were done, and he agreed. Go home. Look at your bank account. Remind yourself of your life goals. Your chances with Kenneth are over and no amount of regret will undo what you did so live with it."

Shivering, she rose to her feet and finally wrapped her jacket around her frozen torso.

The noises from the parking lot had faded to the roar of tires on nearby roads. This suited Brooke just fine, as not dealing with people and traffic seemed like the best plan of action. Exhausted, she trudged toward her car, digging her keys out of her pocket as she went. "Go home," she told herself. "Drink some hot spiced milk and get some sleep. Tomorrow is a big day... like all the days."

A car alarm beeped, indicating that someone remained in the parking lot, and Brooke turned to look, out of idle curiosity.

It was Kenneth.

He half-turned his body as he pulled open the driver's door of his SUV, and the movement brought him face to face with Brooke. Their eyes locked, and they both froze.

Brooke's heart stopped beating for a second as Kenneth's potent aura seemed, as always, to reach out and caress her. This time, though, her resolve shattered. She took a hesitant step in his direction. Then another. Then, time seemed to bend or warp.

One second, she stood a dozen paces away, and the next, her body crashed into his. She threw her arms around his neck and rose up on tiptoes, capturing his lips with hers. Desperate, she clung to him, trying to express her volatile, contradictory emotions in a kiss that surpassed mere verbal expression.

Kenneth remained frozen against the onslaught for a long moment, and then, as though against his will, began to respond. His full lips pursed against hers. Parted. Allowed access for her tongue to slip past and tease him.

A guttural growl started in his chest. A moment later, Kenneth reversed the kiss, driving his tongue into Brooke's mouth and staking a primal claim on her.

She melted in his arms. This time, though her heart pounded with fear, she surrendered herself fully to the inevitable.

It is inevitable, she realized. *Come what may, I cannot face a future without at least having tried.*

Kenneth cupped her bottom in two big hands, tugging her forward until he had her fully plastered against his body. A growing fullness in the front of his jeans told her that maybe, just maybe she hadn't blown her shot after all.

"Oh, Kenneth," she breathed against his lips.

He lifted his head. As she watched, the wild passion in his eyes faded to confusion. "Brooke, what are you doing?" he asked.

I don't know," she said honestly. "I don't know how we make this work, or what the future holds, but I realized one thing. If you're not in it..." she shook her head. "I don't want to know what that's like anymore. Please tell me I'm not too late. Do you have it in your heart to give me another chance?"

Tension melted from his shoulders. "Do you mean it?"

She nodded.

"Come home with me," he said, closely watching her reaction.

It's a test, she realized. *He wants a commitment. He wants me to take a risk for him. After what I put us both through, it's no surprise.* Her already-pounding heart increased in tempo, but the sensation of moisture in her panties told her what she needed to know. "Yes."

His eyes widened.

She wriggled out of his grip and scurried around the SUV, letting herself into the passenger seat.

Kenneth stepped through the open door and flopped hard onto his own. "Yes? Are you sure?"

"Drive," she ordered.

Kenneth's lips twisted wryly to one side. Then he obeyed, cranking the key in the ignition, shifting the vehicle into reverse and backing out of the parking space. They sat in silence as he drove through the streets.

Brooke's tension ratcheted up higher and higher as it slowly sank in what she was doing, what she had agreed to. *I'm going to Kenneth's apartment for sex. I agreed to it, and I'm going to go through with it. That kiss told me everything I needed to know. It sure has been a long time, though, since I went to bed with anyone, let alone someone new. Holy cats.*

Her heart pounded so hard, her chest hurt. Her head, too. Tension pushed at her eyes and tightened her jaw.

Within a few short minutes, they pulled up to a rather ugly, glass-fronted high rise. In the dark, the balconies looked like scraps of paper clinging to the façade. The dead flowers in the window boxes and the laundry hanging from a few of the balconies only added to the effect of a huge pile of trash towering above the trees.

The way we live. She shook her head as Kenneth drove down a ramp into an underground parking ramp. *Money just doesn't go as far up north. In Texas, I could easily buy a home with what I've already saved, and the alignment between the cost of living and salaries is so much better, but it's so hard to get a job.*

"Shut up," she whispered to her chattering brain.

"Is everything okay?" Kenneth asked. "If you're worried or not ready, it's fine."

"No, I'm ready for this," she argued. "I want it. I need to do *something* to tell my overactive mind to shut up and let me *live* for once."

"Oooookaaaaay," he replied, drawing out the word to show his confusion. "Is there something I need to know, Brooke?"

"Lots of things," she replied obliquely. "I'm a bit of a mess, to be honest. But if you're willing, let's make this relationship into something I can't argue with."

He shifted the car into park and turned to face her, one eyebrow raised.

"I don't do casual," Brooke explained. "It's against my personal code. So, if we go to bed together, it must be a relationship, and relationships are worth fighting for, so..."

"Do you always overthink everything?" Kenneth asked, pushing his lips forward at her.

"Oh, yes," she replied eagerly. "Always."

"Good to know. Sooooo, you want to go up?"

"I do," she agreed. "At any rate, I don't want to spend another week like the last two for a long, long time."

"Now that I heartily agree with. Shall we?"

Brooke popped the button on her seatbelt and let herself out of the car. Kenneth emerged on the other side and gestured to her. She reached out as she moved forward, laying her hand in his. He rushed forward, his long legs eating up the distance. Brooke had to trot to keep up.

To stave off panic over her impulsive behavior, she kept her mind completely blank. Instead of her usual, busy thoughts, she focused on the tempting way in which Kenneth's presence touched her. It felt more intimate than fingers on flesh, and she had no defense against it.

I don't plan to defend myself against it, she reminded herself. *I'm going to wallow in it until my resistance melts away. I wonder if he's a good lover.*

They crossed the chilly interior of the parking garage to the elevator and rode up to the lobby. There, other residents called out greetings, but Kenneth didn't respond to any of them. Instead, he hurried Brooke through a linoleum-floored space to a second elevator and pushed the button several times in rapid succession. As he waited for the car to arrive, he dragged Brooke back into his arms.

Only a single, deep kiss later, the bell dinged, and the door in front of them slid open. When it did, he guided her inside and pushed the button labeled 'seven'.

The door slid closed, and Brooke ran the fingers of her free hand up Kenneth's arm. She cupped her hand around the back of his neck and tugged him down, pursing her lips slightly.

He acquiesced to her urging with a brilliant grin, letting her claim his mouth in a kiss of eager passion. Their tongues tangled.

Brook's skin warmed in Kenneth's embrace. Her breasts tingled, and the tingle spread through her belly. Long-forgotten sensations awakened her intimate flesh, moistening it as her body prepared itself for sex. A shiver ran up her spine.

Before they could get into too much mischief, the elevator stopped its slow climb, and the door opened on a floor that resembled a clean and newly-updated but far from inspiring cardboard box. Tan tile. Tan paint and tan doors. Boring.

"It's not much," Kenneth said, suddenly looking worried as he stepped back from Brooke and led her out of the elevator into the hallway.

"I share an efficiency apartment with a roommate. It's in the attic of an old mansion, emphasis on the *old*. Besides, you're still in grad school and housing in this city is expensive. I'm not worried." She said it all in a rush, hurrying to erase the thought that she might care about something so silly.

He paused and turned to look at her. "Thank you, Brooke."

"Which one is you?" she asked, indicating the hallway.

"Down to the end," he replied.

"Show me."

He grinned again, taking her hand and leading her forward. "I must admit, I'm stunned by the sudden about-face."

"Me too," she admitted. "I usually avoid doing impulsive things."

"So then?" He dug in his pocket and drew out a key, inserting it into a doorknob on the right side of the hallway.

"I don't know," she replied. "I've been fighting myself for two weeks. It was all I could do to make myself believe that I was doing the right thing. And then I saw you. I heard your voice. I was lost. It doesn't matter what it takes, I can't deny this connection."

"There's always a way to make it work, Brooke," he pointed out.

"You'll have to show me," she replied. "I don't know how to do this."

"I will," he promised, "as long as you don't overthink this into oblivion again."

She nodded.

He opened the door and ushered her into a tan efficiency whose tile and paint matched the hallway.

The space consisted of two matching loveseats set at right angles to form a seating area in front of a wall-mounted television. Behind, a bed thrust into the center of the room. Across from the sitting and sleeping areas, a small table and three chairs created an eating space. The kitchen dominated the rear wall.

Everything was new but deeply bland and boring. Everything, except for a gorgeous framed painting of a jazz club that hung beside the dining table. Done in shades of deep blue and black, it featured a dark-skinned man at a piano while a woman with marcelled brown hair leaned against the instrument's curve, a microphone clutched in her hand. Her head thrown back, she seemed to be singing a long, loud note.

"I love that," Brooke said softly.

"It's my grandparents," he replied. "When I moved up north, my mom insisted I bring it. She said it would keep me grounded."

"It's beautiful," she breathed.

Brooke's nerves rose up again. Too many minutes had passed since she'd drugged herself with Kenneth's touch. Rational thought—including the realization that she had agreed to and was about to have sex with a man she'd known for less than a month—bubbled up in butterflies that made her stomach clench.

The door shut loudly, and the lock clicked.

Kenneth must have seen her jump because he asked, "Brooke, are you all right?"

She didn't know how to answer the question, so she remained silent.

"You know we don't have to do this right now, right?" he reiterated. "I won't write you off for good if we wait to make love until we've had a few more dates. It was only a request, not an ultimatum."

"I know," she replied. "If I thought you were pressuring me, I wouldn't be here. My intuition—which I have despite being really bad at listening to it—feels you're worth it. I mean, I want to. That's why I'm here. I'm wildly attracted to you. I just get cold feet a lot. Even when I do plan things out and take my time, committing to a particular action always has me second-guessing myself."

"What do you need, then, to feel comfortable?" he asked. "How can I help you relax?"

"Kiss me again?" she pleaded.

Kenneth's expressive face lit up. "That's easy." He reached for her.

She stepped into his arms.

The moment his lips touched hers in a kiss of aching tenderness, Brooke's nerves melted away. Rightness that surpassed sense and even thought welled up within her. She relaxed into the embrace.

I can't get over how powerful this feels. She parted her lips, deepening the kiss, but that sense of warmth and caring never faded, even as passion grew. Her body tingled and heated. Her heart felt safe. Nurtured. *Loved... but it's too soon for love.*

"Stop overthinking it," she ordered herself silently. "Just let the moment take you." She released Kenneth's lips and drew her sweater, along with the long-sleeved tee shirt underneath it, over her head.

Kenneth looked down at her tenderly, taking in her plump breasts, cradled in a lacy bra, the soft convexity of her belly, her rounded arms, and the swell of her hips where her jeans hugged them. He grinned, drawing his own sweater and turtleneck up and off, revealing soft skin dotted with sparse, coarse hairs. No six-pack of unnatural muscles marred the smooth line of his chest or belly, but his biceps did possess a manly bulge.

Just two regular folks with natural bodies, she realized, finally dismissing the idea that Kenneth was some kind of classical music version of a rock star. *He's all about the substance. The package is... cute, but not really the point.*

She leaned forward, hugging him this time. He engulfed her, opening the hooks at the back of her bra. The garment slipped to the floor. She expected him to reach right for her breasts, knowing that many men would find their generous size appealing, but he didn't. He let her adjust to being topless with him by fully aligning their bodies and soothing her with a brush of his fingertips up and down her back.

Her nipples hardened as they came into contact with the soft skin on his chest. A few hairs tickled the sensitive peaks.

"Hmmmm," she hummed, the sound borne more of relaxation than arousal, though the warmth between her thighs let her know her engine was still firing. *Soon,* she thought. *When I'm ready. When he is. There's no rush. There's just us and we fit together. We feel good together. We belong together.*

As one, they reached out for another kiss. Lips parted. Tongues tangled, but always that sense of calm rightness overlaid the interaction. *There is no decision to be made.* Fear had fled the moment she stepped into Kenneth's arms.

Here, she could release her busy mind's overwhelming urge to pick everything to pieces. Here, she could just be, feel, live. Her heart thumped, moving blood to her intimate places. Her breathing deepened and slowed, drawing his essence into her.

Again, she broke the kiss, stepping back so she could reach the buckle of his belt, where it dug into his skin. She manipulated the leather through the metal that clasped it. The button of his jeans surrendered easily to her questing fingers.

Kenneth's pants sagged to the floor, and he stepped free.

Brooke led him toward the bed.

He acquiesced without hesitation. Tossing the comforter aside, he stretched out on the sheet in his underwear, his arm up under his head. Then, he waited, watching what she was going to do.

Brooke released the button on her own jeans and shimmied them over her round bottom and down her thighs. Her shoes got in the way, and she used her toe to pry one off the opposite heel. *How elegant,* she thought, rolling her eyes at herself. *I hope he can appreciate eagerness. I'm not up for sultry tonight.*

At last, she wrestled off her pants and shoes, then approached the bed in her panties. Biting her lip, she took in the long, dark stretch of Kenneth's skin. He looked relaxed yet ready; his expression as eager as the thick swelling that tented his dark blue boxers.

"Ready?" he asked.

Words failed, but Brooke stepped forward with a nod.

Kenneth reached out one hand. When Brooke laid her palm against his, he drew her forward, gently coaxing her onto the bed so she could straddle him.

As the fullness in his groin came into contact with her panties, her core clenched hard. *God bless America, it's been a long time.* Grasping both of Kenneth's hands, she drew them forward and laid them on her breasts, eager to be caressed.

He chuckled as he cupped the plump mounds and teased her nipples with a playful pinch that left her gasping. Then he grasped her hips and rolled her to the side. Laying her on her back beside him, he leaned up over her.

Kenneth claimed Brooke's lips in a tenderly passionate kiss that made her feel as though a cocoon of perfect trust and safety had enveloped her. *Nothing can harm me here, in Kenneth's arms. Our lovemaking is protected and safe. We're free to touch each other without fear of the outside world intruding.*

Conscious thought fled as he released her mouth and kissed his way down the side of her throat and across her upper chest while his hands made free with her breasts. Tingling arousal spread out to Brooke's core, her limbs, her fingertips. Her toes clenched and her belly jumped as he kissed his way to one breast and awakened her nipple with a wet lick.

Brooke clutched the back of Kenneth's head, her fingers sinking into the thick, coarse hair. Her hips bucked a bit. She traced her hand down to his shoulders, where she caressed him. His skin felt unbelievably soft.

He moved to her other breast, nibbling and sending shocks of pleasure straight to her intimate flesh.

"Kenneth," she moaned.

"Ready for more?" At her affirming whine, he rose up to his knees and slipped his fingers into the sides of her panties, drawing them down her thighs and over her feet, tossing them aside. "Open, honey. Let's see what you've got."

Feeling no awkwardness—she couldn't when it was Kenneth ready to plunder her—she spread her thighs wide. As he gently cupped her mound, Brooke arched into his touch.

"Easy," he said with a laugh.

Brooke had no ability to take it easy. Her body ached to be touched. Years of touch deprivation left her weak and needy. "Please," she whimpered.

"Okay," he agreed easily, sliding his fingers along her seam before applying just enough pressure to part the lips and discover the folds within. "Damn, you're wet, girl," he informed her.

More moisture surged to meet his words.

Kenneth caressed each fold, spreading the lubrication evenly. "This is gonna be good."

"Oh, yes," she agreed in a moan. "So good."

His thumb homed in on her clitoris, which had risen up full and proud, and hestroked the tender flesh.

Brooke cried out loud, arching her hips.

He gently worked her, drawing her pleasure higher and higher.

It won't be long, she thought, and sure enough, her pleasure peaked in a wild orgasm. She bit her lip against a scream of pleasure.

"That's it," he encouraged. "Come, baby."

"Kenneth, please. I need you," she gasped.

Obediently, he reached out one long arm and opened the drawer in his bedside table. Tugging his boxers down his thighs, he used his teeth to rip open the condom packet. Her orgasm began to wane as Kenneth rolled the condom over his straining erection. Then, he eased down over her.

She wrapped her legs around his waist, urging him closer. Trailing her fingers down his chest, she wrapped her hand around his erection and led it right to the opening of her body.

He arched his hips, and her body yielded easily to his penetration. The glide of his thick sex into her drew a small squeal from her.

"Aww, yeah," he groaned. Leaning down to kiss her, he surged deep, pulled back, and surged again. Kenneth took Brooke in a fast, hard rhythm born of wild attraction, and she met him thrust for thrust, just as undone as he. They pounded each other, each as desperate as the other to bring maximum arousal, maximum closeness.

A second orgasm lingered on the edges of Brooke's awareness. She tried to delay it, tried to focus on Kenneth's pleasure, but her body took over. With a surge of release, her sex clamped down on its welcome invader.

Kenneth groaned as her passage fluttered on him. Groaned, and then growled as his own peak locked him deep inside her.

They clung to each other as pleasure peaked, plateaued, and finally waned into a deep and relaxing sleep.

Brooke awoke with the disconcerting sensation that she didn't know where she was. Even stranger, though mildly irritating, the feeling didn't make her panic the way it normally would have. She felt warm, safe and comfortable... as well as lost.

Opening her eyes, she stared up into a dark room with a low ceiling of soft tiles, barely visible by the thin sliver of moonlight shining in a window she didn't recognize. *My apartment is always darker at night, both because the building next to us blocks out direct light, and because the window is on the other side of my privacy curtain.*

A soft rumble drew her attention to the warm, soft bulk cuddling against her back. Shifting, she rolled over. Kenneth snorted and shifted back in her direction, urging her against his chest.

Oh, that's right. I'm with Kenneth. A gentle tingle reminded her of their evening's activities. Grinning, she settled in and closed her eyes. *Maybe I'll have better concentration for my teaching, now that I'm not suffering from unrequited passion.* Her eyes shot open. *Teaching? Oh, God.*

Wriggling out of Kenneth's grasp, she fumbled for the lamp and switched it on, hunting for her clothing across the floor.

"Brooke?" The sexy voice, pitched lower than ever with sleep, chased up her spine with a pleasurable shiver.

"I have to go," she blurted, tugging her sweater over her head. Her underwear still eluded her, but her socks sat in a pile on the floor. She planted her bottom on the edge of the bed and stuffed her foot into one.

He sighed. "Again?"

Brooke paused. *Oh, crap. He thinks I'm freaking out about us.* "I mean, I need to go home. I'm teaching tomorrow..." she glanced at the clock. "...later today. It's Tuesday. No jeans allowed until Friday. My car is still at the university. This doesn't work. I don't regret... what we did. I don't regret that we're together, but I have to get home now so I can get ready for work."

Kenneth sagged back against the pillows. "Oh."

"Um, we are *together* now, right?"

One corner of his mouth turned up. "We're as together as you want us to be. I'm not the one who's struggling with doubts about this."

Brooke pursed her lips. "Sorry for being cautious," she said, a touch of sarcasm rising in her voice. "I was trying *not* to hurt you. I still don't know how exactly all this can work out, but I'm willing to let go of that, even though not having a path mapped out makes me anxious. I want you more than I want to know the plan. That's a good thing, right?"

She found her panties tangled in the bedsheets and retrieved them. Quickly, she finished pulling on her clothing and stepped into her shoes. *Now what? I'm here, my car is there, and my apartment is not that close to either.*

The bed shifted as Kenneth rose, stepped into his boxers, and circled around to her. He reached out both hands, and she allowed him to grasp hers. He drew her up to stand against his body, wrapping her in a warm embrace. "I'm sorry. That wasn't called for."

"Perhaps, but it's also not surprising," she replied, trying to be fair. "I didn't handle things as well as I could have."

"I was afraid you were going to disappear..."

Oh, no! Not that. Never again! "It didn't even cross my mind," she hurried to assure him. "I just don't want to turn up to work tomorrow in jeans and dirty underwear."

"I understand."

"Can you take me to my car, please?" Brooke requested. "Next time we spend the night, let's plan it out. I'll bring clean clothes and my toothbrush. That will work a lot better. But I don't have any regrets. It was lovely."

"Now that I heartily agree with." Kenneth's voice seemed to be grinning.

She looked up and saw a broad smile light up his handsome face. Laying one hand against his cheek, she drew him down for a kiss.

CHAPTER 7

*a*n hour later, just as the clock on her dashboard showed 3:24am, Brooke eased into her parking space. She frowned again at the poor parking of her neighbor. Shaking her head, she hurried through the cold into her apartment building. Making her way quickly up the stairs, though perhaps not as quietly as she should have, she wrestled the door open, hoping to slip into bed without disturbing her roommate.

Inside, the room was brightly lit. Jackie sat on the couch, staring at the door. Her long red hair hung down around her shoulders, and she twirled it around her finger as she gnawed on her lip. "Where have you been?" she demanded.

"Out," Brooke replied, confused. "Why do you ask?"

"You're *always* here," Jackie insisted. "You never stay out late, especially not *this* late. I was worried something had happened to you."

"I lost track of the time," Brooke said.

Jackie raised an eyebrow. "There's nothing open late enough for you to lose track of the time, and it's not like it's summer where you might go hang out in the park or something. Brooke, it's after three. Where were you?"

"Kenneth's place," she mumbled.

Jackie's other eyebrow joined the first as they made a quick ascent toward her hairline. "What was that?"

"I spent the night with Kenneth, okay?" she hissed.

Jackie looked confused.

Brooke sighed. "The choir guy I mentioned earlier, remember? We were, you know, together. We fell asleep."

"Oh, wow." Jackie giggled. "I thought you were a virgin."

Brooke pursed her lips. "I went to college, you know. I'm not opposed to sex. I just haven't had the opportunity until... now."

"Okay, okay." Jackie raised both hands and surrendered her teasing.

"So anyway, I had to get home because I work tomorrow."

"I get it. So, walk of shame it was."

Brooke shook her head. "I don't want to fight with you, Jackie. It's the middle of the night, and I'm tired, but that's a dumb expression. What should I be ashamed of? Do *you* feel ashamed after sex?"

"Of course, not. Sorry. I know I'm being insensitive." Jackie bit her lip, and her shoulders drooped. "I've had a lot on my mind lately."

Brooke sighed. "Have you made any headway on that? Should I start advertising for a new roommate?"

"I'm not sure yet," Jackie said.

"Then let's go to bed," Brooke suggested.

Jackie nodded and trudged over to her curtain.

Brooke quickly brushed her teeth before retreating behind her own, tugging off her clothing and dropping a nightgown over her head. Though the bed looked inviting, sleep eluded her. The peace she'd felt in Kenneth's arms had melted in her rush to get home, and her rational mind refused to stop questioning the wisdom of committing.

"Shut up," she told herself sternly, but it was no use. By the time the alarm buzzed, she'd scarcely managed to do more than drowse a couple of times. She felt like a zombie as she dragged herself out of bed, showered and drank coffee.

Time seemed to jump after that, and her next flash of awareness came when the tardy bell rang for her first class. She had no recollection of driving to work or the hour she'd spent in her office. She did realize, as she approached the podium, that her shoes did not match. *Wonderful.*

Fuzzy sleepiness overtook her again, and the rehearsal, like her morning commute, passed on autopilot. *I definitely need to plan out any future late-night activities more carefully.* A tired tingle affirmed the desirability of this action.

By lunch, Brooke had passed sleepiness and fallen into a sick sort of exhaustion. Her belly churned and her head ached. When her phone, again tucked in her purse inside the desk drawer, began to ring, she considered not answering. As she pondered, the ringing stopped. Only then did it occur to her that it might be Kenneth. She dug the phone out and activated the screen.

Two text alerts popped up on the screen. **Last night was great.** Then a second message right below it, asked, **Can I see you this evening?**

Not sure how to respond to that, she checked the call log. Autumn. *Of course. She usually calls at lunchtime, and she can get a bit testy if she thinks I'm ignoring her.*

Sighing, Brooke returned the call.

Autumn answered before the first ring ended. "Brooke, I'm so glad you called me back. I needed to talk to you. Please don't be mad at me. I know you have doubts about dating Kenneth, but I think you need to reconsider. There's something there. I can feel how broken up you are about it. My intuition is screaming at me and—"

"Autumn," Brooke said, trying to cut through the mad gush. "Autumn, hey."

"What?" Her sister stopped chattering and waited.

"I had sex with him last night."

Silence.

Then... "You did? You?"

Brooke rolled her eyes. "Well, yeah."

"But... but..." Autumn spluttered to a halt, clearly speechless.

"I know it's a rapid change in my attitude. Frankly, I'm a bit surprised at myself, but when I saw him at rehearsal, I knew I couldn't hold out any longer. Kenneth is too special to pass up, so I stopped fighting it."

"Oh." Autumn paused again, long enough to make the silence awkward. Then she blurted, "What are you going to do now? How are you going to handle the separation and his career?"

"I don't know," Brooke replied. "Didn't you tell me not to worry about that? I'm trying not to."

"Right. I have to say, Brooke, this is unusual for you. Did you make a spreadsheet?"

"Of course not," she replied. "There's no spreadsheet for something like this."

"'The heart wants what it wants,'" Autumn replied, quoting Emily Dickinson.

"I've never given mine so much leeway to make decisions, and I'm far from comfortable with it, but fighting it was futile. It was wearing me down and hurting him, so that's all bad. I can only hope that giving in won't end up in some kind of worse problem down the road."

"Now that's the Brooke I know," Autumn said, amusement

in her voice. "Try to have faith, Sis. The universe won't give you a perfect love without also providing the means to keep it, and before you argue, just because love is in its infancy doesn't mean it's not real."

"Perfect love? How can you even say that? We still barely know each other." The thrill in the region of her heart named the thought a lie even as it formed.

Autumn just waited.

"Okay, okay." Brooke yawned. "It's a big deal. My plan at this point is to go with the flow and see what happens."

"My timid sister having a hot love affair? A hot *interracial* love affair? That's definitely a big deal. You're right about that. Care to overshare?"

"No. Even if I weren't trying to get through a workday on not enough sleep, that's not your business."

"You're mean," Autumn grumped, a pout in her voice. "Okay, okay. You have to at least tell me if it was good."

"Yes, Autumn, of course it was. We're not teenagers, you know? We both know what we're doing." Another thought occurred to her. "The sex felt good. Really nice, but there was something more."

"Good? Nice? That's tepid," Autumn pointed out.

"Don't think like that," Brooke urged. "Listen, all orgasms feel pretty much the same, right?"

"Well, right," Autumn agreed.

"So, yeah. Good. I had a couple. They were great, but the physical sensation isn't what I can't shake. There was... there was something else I haven't been able to define. I just felt... warm. Emotionally warm. And safe. It was like, in Kenneth's arms, nothing could ever hurt me. I've felt it every time we touched, even if it was just a handshake. I felt it in every kiss. Last night, it was insanely intense. He's like a blanket of peace."

Autumn didn't say anything.

"Sis?"

"I think you'll figure out what it means in time," Autumn said at last, "as long as you don't chase him away. Some things transcend reason, and that's okay because that's what they're meant to do."

Unable to understand her sister's existentialist ramblings, Brooke replied, "I'm not chasing anyone away anymore, but I do need to finish my lunch and get ready for afternoon classes. Talk to you soon, okay?"

"Okay, laters," Autumn agreed cheerfully. A moment later, the line went dead.

Brooke lowered the phone from her ear. Kenneth's two messages still lit up the indicator at the top of her screen. Opening them again, she pondered and at last typed,

I don't know. I'm really tired.

A second later, the reply bounced back.

Does that mean no, or are you letting me know you're not up to anything too energetic?

Brooke pondered. **If you want, you can hang out at my place. I'm just planning on watching TV and eating takeout, but you're welcome to join me.**

It's a date.

Despite her fatigue, by the time she arrived back at the apartment, Brooke began feeling a few bubbles of excitement. *And why not?* she thought as she pulled into her parking space. Today, the parking spot neighbor with the poor skills hadn't arrived home yet, and she was able to position her car more comfortably. Yawning, she locked the door with an absentminded click of the key fob and made her way inside.

Again, a cluster of gossiping roommates hovered around the mailboxes.

"What's the word?" Brooke asked as she collected a pile of bills, notices, advertising and other assorted junk, most of which she dropped straight into a recycling bin near the front door.

"They've shown the building twice," a middle-aged matron called over her shoulder as she herded two teenage boys up the stars. "No information yet on offers."

"I heard one was a restoration fanatic who's spending his retirement refurbishing old houses like this one to their former glory before flipping them as big family homes and B&Bs," said a young man Brooke happened to know was sharing one of the ground floor apartments with a pile of roommates. Probably more than the fire code allowed.

"Hmmm, interesting," Brooke replied. "Well, we'll have to see how it all goes." Waving to her neighbors, she made her way up to her own room.

Immediately upon unlocking the door, she realized Jackie was not home. The apartment felt empty. Trudging in on weary, aching feet, Brooke kicked off her sensible work shoes and tucked them onto the shoe rack. Then she pulled back the curtain on her alcove.

Her black work pants felt sweaty and tight after her workday, so she shimmied them off and tossed them into the laundry. Her sweater had a dribble of salsa on the sleeve, so she dropped it in the laundry as well. The turtleneck was okay by itself, so she added a pair of ragged and comfortable jeans from her bottom drawer.

A glance at the clock told her Kenneth wasn't due to arrive for another hour. She plunked down onto the bed. *Just want to rest for a moment.*

A buzz woke Brooke with a start, and she jumped from the

bed in surprise. The building's intercom, which had summoned her from sleep, fell silent as she hurried toward the panel. Instead, her purse, which she'd dropped on the sofa, began to chime.

"Damn it," she cussed, swiping the bag into her hands and fumbling inside. She did not succeed in dragging out the phone before it stopped.

At last, she managed to extract it, just as a text message lit up the screen.

Brooke, are you there?

Sorry, sorry. She sent the message quickly, not wanting Kenneth to think she'd forgotten. **Are you still at the door? I'll let you in. Come up all the stairs to the attic. Room 400.**

She hurried to the panel. A small video screen showed a gray and grainy image of Kenneth, fidgeting on the porch. She pushed the button to release the door and activated the communication panel. "Come in," she called.

His head shot up, and she saw him try the door. This time, it opened, and he disappeared from view.

Heart pounding after being so startled, Brooke scanned the room, tossed a pair of dirty socks around the curtain onto her roommate's bed and put two coffee cups and two cereal bowls into the cabinet. *No time to vacuum, but the carpet doesn't look too bad.*

A moment later, a heavy knock sounded. Brooke scampered over, her socks swishing on the carpet, and unlocked the deadbolt. The second the opening door revealed the cuddly figure and smiling face of her favorite opera singer, she surged forward, drawing him into a long, warm hug.

He leaned down for a kiss and then slung a black backpack onto the floor.

Kenneth scanned the room, took in the crowded, threadbare furniture, the two privacy curtains over the sleeping alcoves—really the eaves—the clean, builder-grade kitchen. "Efficiencies, eh?"

She nodded. "This city is killer expensive. It's hard as hell to save money. Do you want me to make some coffee or something?"

"No thanks," he replied. "If I have coffee in the afternoon, I'll be up all night. I'd be glad for some water though."

She meandered into the kitchen area while he followed after her. She busied herself with gathering up two cups and filling them with water from a filtering pitcher she retrieved from the refrigerator.

"On the subject of finance," he added, making conversation, "I aim to break even, nothing more. I work as a teacher assistant, which takes care of my tuition, and between my stipend and the salary from the opera, I have just enough to cover my expenses. I haven't saved a penny in years."

She shrugged, turning to hand him his cup and taking a sip from her own. "You're not in the saving stage of life. That's understandable. I've been in the workforce five years. I'd never forgive myself if I wasn't in the process of trying to build my wealth, though I'm not sure I'll ever achieve objective wealth. Music teachers aren't known for that."

"I suppose not," he agreed.

Brooke's cheeks heated slightly. "Sorry. I'll just get off that soapbox now, shall I?"

"It's okay," Kenneth replied. He drained his glass and handed it back to her. She set it in the sink. "I don't think it's necessary to apologize for feeling how you feel or for talking about it. Didn't you say your dad was in finance?"

Brooke nodded. Drinking her own water down, she added her cup to his and turned to face him.

"Then saving and building wealth were probably your earliest lessons, well before music or anything else."

"Right," she agreed. "Financial security was so drilled into me that I feel intense guilt even for something as silly as getting fast food I didn't budget for. Moderate, planned indulgences are fine, but even then..."

"You have to use self-discipline to obey the budget rather than using the budgeted money for indulgences?" Kenneth guessed.

"Exactly. *Not* using the budget planned for indulgences is more expected than not."

"Always trying to beat rather than meant the goal?" he guessed. At her nod, he continued, "Is there any place in this worldview where money is the tool you use to enrich your life rather than the final goal in itself?"

Brooke shook her head.

"I mean, what are you building wealth for?" he asked. "Retirement?"

"I don't know that I plan to retire," she replied. "Provided my health holds into old age, teaching music doesn't strain the body much. I should be able to continue long past retirement age."

"Then?" he asked.

"You know," she replied, "I don't know exactly. I'd like to buy a house someday. Apartment living isn't much to my taste. I'd like a yard to sit in with friends on a summer night. A fireplace. A proper bedroom with a door. I mean, with my salary, I could have an apartment to myself, but it would slow down my plans. Having a roommate means saving faster. I've mapped out how to purchase a home in commuting distance to my work by the time I'm 35, and I'm on track so far."

"Nice," Kenneth commented. "Does it bother you that I

don't have such settled plans? I know that was a sticking point early on."

She shook her head. "I understand where you're at. You can't plan until you have the position, know it's where you want to stay, and know the prices and opportunities in the area. For instance, Chicago itself wouldn't have been my goal. It's too cold for my Texas blood. Too expensive. Too crowded. I'm willing to endure it all in order to keep this job because I love it so much. Given that, I made plans after I'd been here for two years."

She paused to take a sip of water. "You haven't found your final placement yet. If you use my techniques—which you might not decide to do at all as your background is really different from mine— you would graduate in December, travel through the spring while applying for many positions, interview when you get back, choose an opportunity and work there for a few years. If what I know about university teaching is true, you'd have to go on a tenure track. Once you achieved tenure, it would be time for long-term financial planning."

"Wow," Kenneth said softly. "That's... intense. I'm not sure I could even think that far ahead. Today's goal is enough for me." He regarded her solemnly before taking her hand and leading her to the sofa, where they sat, half-turned to face each other, knees touching, fingers laced together. "All this planning. Does it give you joy?"

She lowered her eyebrows. "What do you mean? Teaching and singing give me joy. Financial planning is like washing dishes. It has to be done, but it's not particularly pleasant."

"I see." Kenneth regarded her closely for another minute. Then he blinked a couple of times. "So, um, how have you been doing? You didn't have any trouble after our... impromptu night together, did you?"

"Apart from being so sleepy I sort of passed out waiting for you to get here?" she asked, smiling. "I won't lie that it was a long day after such an interrupted night, but I don't have any regrets. I haven't had sex in ages, and it was great." They sank wearily onto the cushions, side by side, fingers clinging.

He smiled. "We have a nice fit physically, that's for sure, and the emotional draw is undeniable. As for the intellectual..."

"That takes time," she agreed. "There's a vast amount of knowledge about each other we haven't discovered yet. We can only keep talking and planning and examining and figuring out how this puzzle that is *us* actually works."

He nodded.

A yawn fought its way out of Brooke's throat, and she covered her mouth with one hand. "We'll have to do that exploring another time, though. I'm so tired I can hardly think straight, and I'm more likely to ramble than converse at this point."

"Likewise," he concurred. "It's a good thing that the class I'm teaching is tomorrow and not tonight. I'd have struggled to pay attention in my current state.

"Oh, yes," Brooke agreed. "I predict an early bedtime tonight." She eyed Kenneth. "You're welcome to stay if you want, but the bed is narrow."

"I'd love to, and I'm sure we'll find a way to make ourselves fit."

She smiled. "Are you hungry?"

"I could eat."

Brooke pulled out her cell phone and swiped the screen. "Chinese? There's one nearby."

"Sure," he agreed easily. "I like sweet and sour chicken."

"Yum. I like lo mein. Maybe we can share?"

"Of course," he replied. "That's part of the fun."

Brooke brought up the website and pushed a few buttons.

"They predict 30 minutes or so. Um, what would you like to do now?"

"Not sit so far away," he told her.

Brooke scooted closer and Kenneth wrapped his arm around her. She leaned her head on his shoulder. As before, the luscious warmth of his body seemed to sink into her, bringing a sense of peace and safety. More than his physical warmth, some essential Kenneth-ness also wrapped around her.

Here, in his arms, all her frantic planning and saving seemed unnecessary. Here, everything worked out. It would have to. Nothing could go wrong while he held her.

She relaxed further, her body half-melting against his. His arm lowered to her waist, resting against her hipbone. Brooke grasped his hand and laced their fingers together.

"I could fall asleep right here," he commented. "You're so nice to hold."

"So are you," she informed him. "This feels good. Thanks for not giving up on me."

"I'm not sure I would have been able to, so I'm glad you changed your mind."

"Me too." Brooke stretched back, twisting slightly and reaching up to Kenneth. Laying one hand on his cheek, she drew him down so she could claim his full, tempting lips. The kiss lingered, long and tender, without urgency. Subtle shifts settled them more comfortably against each other.

It feels so good. So perfect. I could kiss this man forever.

The door flew open, slamming against the opposite wall with a bang.

Brooke jumped, accidentally jabbing an elbow into Kenneth's ribs.

"Oof." He grunted.

"Sorry." Looking up, she saw Jackie storm in. "What's up?"

"Oh!" Jackie froze, staring at them in consternation. "I didn't think you'd be home yet."

"Well, I am," Brooke replied dryly. "Jackie, this is my boyfriend, Kenneth Hill. Kenneth, this is Jackie, my roommate."

"Pleased to meet you," he said politely.

Jackie looked him up and down with a smile that almost looked like a smirk. "Likewise." She turned to Brooke. "I understand now what kept you."

Brooke's cheeks flamed, but she met her roommate's gaze with an unblinking stare. "Yes." Then she snuggled back into Kenneth's embrace. "So, what's your plan, Jackie? You staying in this evening?"

Jackie considered them for a long moment. "Nah, I have a dinner date. I'll be back later. What about you?" she asked Kenneth. "Will you be sleeping here?"

"I had thought I might," he replied mildly.

"We won't be up late, though," Brooke added. "We're both pretty tired."

Jackie poked her tongue into her cheek, making a sassy bulge. "I bet. Well, kids, I'm going to take a quick shower and be off again. Behave."

Brooke rolled her eyes but didn't answer as Jackie sailed out of the room.

"Is she always so charming?" Kenneth asked, a note of irony in his voice.

"Usually." Brooke snickered. "At any rate, she likes to tease me on the rare occasions we're home at the same time. Normally we just aim not to get in each other's way. Roommates have a way of making things... lively, don't they?"

"That they do," Kenneth agreed.

"Um, do you actually want to watch anything on television?" she asked, "at least until Jackie goes out?"

"I suppose," he said. "Do you like true crime shows?"

"They're not bad," Brooke conceded, "and there's usually one on." Reaching past Kenneth, she grabbed the remote and clicked it, quickly finding a gruesome crime scene investigation. "This work for you?"

"Sure," he agreed.

She settled back against his chest. He rested his other arm on her torso, fully embracing her. They let their tired minds go blank as their spirits tangled together, forming tighter and even tighter bonds between them.

Fatigue, chased away by Jackie's noisy arrival, crept back up Brooke's spine, making her scalp tingle. Her fingers and her eyelids grew heavy, and she closed her eyes... *just for a minute.*

A sense of movement drew Brooke up out of a deep sleep. "What's happening?" she mumbled.

"You passed out," Kenneth explained. His voice sounded strained and she realized, dimly, that he was carrying her. "It's ten fifteen. I was moving you to the bed. Is that okay? You never ate."

"Not hungry," she breathed, fatigue dragging her back down again.

"Okay, then. Let's sleep."

"Hmmmm," she agreed. The mattress compressed beneath her back. Comfortable at last, she let sleep drag her back under.

Kenneth stretched out on the sofa, staring up at the darkened ceiling. Fatigue welled up in him, making his eyelids feel like hand weights hung from his eyelashes. They crept downward.

Don't sleep, buddy, he reminded himself. *Your girlfriend is in her bed, the bed she's invited you to share. Do you want to sprawl on this sofa while your lady sleeps alone? Go brush your teeth.*

He heaved himself upright, gathered the uneaten Chinese food Brooke hadn't realized had arrived and tucked it into the refrigerator. Then he grabbed his duffle and made his way into the bathroom. As he spat toothpaste into the sink, a chirp sounded from the living room.

He could hear Brooke groan through the open bathroom door.

Oops. She's so tired. I want her to sleep. He hustled out, wondering who might be calling at such a late hour.

Two cell phones lay on the coffee table in front of the sofa. His own, with no case and its smear of fingerprints across the screen, lay silent. Brooke's, in its purple case with music notes, lit up bright.

Kenneth frowned at the screen and reached down with one hand, intending to reject the call. The moment he touched the screen, the call picked up. *Crap.*

He grabbed the phone and hot-footed it to the door of the apartment, stepping outside and shutting the door partway.

"Hello?" a female voice asked. "Hello? Brooke?"

"This is Brooke's phone," Kenneth replied awkwardly.

"Who is this?" the woman asked.

"Um, this is Kenneth. Kenneth Hill."

"No way. Wow, I totally get it now."

"I beg your pardon?"

"Sorry. Um, this Autumn, Brooke's sister. She told me you had a great voice, which I figured since you sing opera."

"Uh, thanks."

"Listen, is Brooke there?"

"She's sleeping," he replied. "She had a rough day. I was trying to send your call to voicemail so the phone wouldn't disturb her, but clumsy fingers, you know?"

"I do," Autumn replied. "Happens all the time. In fact, I was going to ask her to put you on the phone one day soon."

"Oh?"

"Yes," she insisted. "Brooke is my sister. I care about her. I've had a feeling from the beginning that there was something about you, about your relationship, that was important for her. I didn't know what it was, but I knew she absolutely needed to date you. Now that she's decided to take that step, I need to shift focus from what Brooke needs to do to fulfill her destiny, to sister mode."

"So, you're checking up on me?" Kenneth guessed.

"Yep," Autumn agreed. "What kind of sister would I be if I didn't?"

"True enough," Kenneth agreed. "I would do the same for my sister. My brothers would never put up with it, but she still lets me play the game now and again."

"You have siblings? That's good! I mean, I have nothing against only children. Everyone has the story they were meant to have, but having a sibling teaches a different skill set. With what Brooke's told me, I'd guess that's where you get your patience from."

"There may be something to that," he agreed. Then he lowered his eyebrows. *This is quite a strange conversation.*

"You only have strange conversations when you talk to me," Autumn informed him cheerfully. "I'm psychic, so the shallow pleasantries mean nothing to me."

"I see," Kenneth replied. *Now, what do I say in response to that?*

"Do you believe in psychic phenomena?" she asked.

"I don't know," Kenneth said honestly. "I'm not totally closed to the idea, but..."

"Skeptical?"

"Yeah." *Hope that doesn't piss her off.*

"Fair enough," she replied mildly. "Even if you did believe, it's never wise to accept someone's claim without evidence. No worries. I think you and Brooke have a long future together, so we'll have opportunities to get to know each other sooner or later. In fact, I would love to see you all. Let Brooke know that I've invited you for Christmas."

"I'll tell her," he promised. The surprise of the unexpected phone call faded, leaving him exhausted. A huge yawn, complete with creaking jaws, forced its way out of his chest.

"I'll let you go, then," Autumn said. "Get my contact information from Brooke's phone. I have a sense you're going to need it sometime soon. It was nice to finally talk to you."

"Likewise."

"Bye."

The phone went dead.

Shaking his head, Kenneth stepped back into the apartment, locking the door behind him but remembering not to set the chain in case the roommate returned later. He set Brooke's phone on the table and grabbed his own. *Autumn seems like a weird girl, but sure I'll get her information.* He transferred the number into his contacts, saved it, and made his way to the bed.

That's a small bed, he thought, *not even a queen. Will this big ol' body fit? Brooke's no heavyweight, but she's not a twig. Will we be able to get comfortable?*

Easing back the blanket, Kenneth climbed in. His butt hung over the edge. *Well, that's not going to work.* Reaching one long arm past her to feel the distance to the wall, he gently shifted Brooke's hips in that direction.

She murmured in her sleep and rolled onto her side, her back to him. Strands of warm, brown hair—black in the darkness—fell across his arm. His skin tingled.

Down, boy, he warned his impatient penis, which had

reacted to her nearness. *Second night together and no sex. Oh well. If Brooke's psychic sister is right, we'll have another chance. Besides, I'm tired too.* So tired that the blood drained quickly away from his hopeful erection, leaving him sleepier than ever.

Finally able to get his entire body onto the bed, he closed his eyes.

CHAPTER 8

"Well, I've decided," Jackie announced.

Brooke looked up from Kenneth's beautiful dark eyes to see Jackie standing inside the door, chewing her nail. "I didn't hear you come in," Brooke commented. "Are you okay? You look a little pale."

"Morning sickness," Jackie admitted bluntly. "It's a misery, but it will hopefully pass in time." She gave a dismissive wave of her hand. "Anyway, I've decided, and Joe agrees. We're keeping the baby and eloping."

"Oh," Brooke said mildly. "That's a good idea."

"Congratulations," Kenneth added kindly.

"When?" Brooke asked.

"We've got a Unitarian pastor reserved for Christmas Eve," Jackie said, "but we'd like to move in sooner. Now that we have all these plans, I want to get underway. Besides, I'm already waking up about twelve times a night to pee. If I'm going to disturb anyone, it should be Joe, not you. I know the lease is up in May, but do you think there's a way I can get out sooner?"

Brooke raised her eyebrow.

"I'll pay for December," of course," Jackie added, twining one strand of staticky red hair around her finger, "but I'd really like to save up starting in the new year."

"I'll have to think about it," Brooke replied coolly. "I get where you're coming from but finding new tenants in winter isn't easy."

"You could easily afford this place on your own," Jackie pointed out.

Well, bless your heart, Brooke thought, raising one eyebrow. "Nice try deflecting, but that's not the issue. You knew moving out early would be a problem. My ability to pay for the apartment has nothing to do with it."

"Well, keep it in mind, won't you?" Jackie asked. "Let's talk later." She gave Kenneth a quick glance. "I don't think I'll be back this evening."

"I might not be either," Brooke replied, squeezing Kenneth's hand. "My bed isn't really meant for two. Especially not when one is... so tall."

Kenneth smiled.

"Just think," Jackie said. "Maybe Kenneth could move in with you. You could ditch the two tiny beds and get one bigger one. It's a great apartment for a couple, less so for roommates."

"I wouldn't mind," Kenneth said.

"It's something to think about," Brooke said coolly, not convinced, "but my circumstances still don't let you off the hook."

"Noted." Jackie breezed out the door.

Brooke turned to Kenneth, eyebrow raised.

"She has a point is all," he said. "Why don't we pool our resources? It's easier for a couple to share a small space than two strangers."

"Kenneth," Brooke said dryly, "we're only a few weeks

away from strangers. Don't you think moving in together so quickly might strain our relationship rather than helping it?"

Kenneth stuck his lips out, thinking. "I don't know," he replied after a long, quiet moment. "I suppose if you think it will, you're likely to get the result you're expecting. On the other hand, remember how inevitable, how *fated* our relationship has felt, from the first moment. Despite all your logic, you couldn't hold back. I never even tried. I'd like to think it's because we're meant to be. Of course, I'll respect your wishes on the timing, but my feelings on the matter are... whatever we decide, it will be okay."

There's a lot of logic to what he's saying, her inner financial advisor reminded her. *Why spend money on two rents? He says things in ways I never thought of, and as usual, he has a point.* "I'll have to think about that too," Brooke said at last. "My lease is not up until summer. You?"

"July," he admitted.

"Then let's talk about it when you get back from Europe. That would be more sensible."

"Fair enough," Kenneth agreed easily. He lifted their joined hands to his lips and kissed her fingers.

The inner voice that took control of her relationship decisions cringed at moving forward so quickly. Even summer seemed too soon. *If we're still together, and he doesn't flit off to Kalamazoo or something, it's still only a few months.* Uncomfortable, she left the topic for later. *Probably in the middle of the night.*

"Do you want to go?" he asked. "Our reservation is in twenty minutes."

"Good idea," Brooke agreed. "I'd hate to miss out on dinner." Her stomach growled as if on cue.

"And do you have your bag ready?"

"I do," she agreed. "Just in case we do move in together

someday, is your bed yours, or did it come with the apartment? How much furniture would we hypothetically need?"

"It is mine," he told her. "My apartment was actually unfurnished, so my folks donated some used furniture as a gift."

"Nice," she replied, filing the idea away for the future. Rising, tugging Kenneth so their fingers could remain linked together, she crossed the room and retrieved a small satchel, along with her purse, from behind the curtain.

"Are you ready for a fun weekend?" he asked.

"That I am," she replied. "I've been working hard, and I'm looking forward to relaxing with my man for the Thanksgiving break."

"Sounds good to me too," Kenneth replied. "Did you arrange the food delivery?"

"Tomorrow morning," Brooke told him. "All we have to do is heat it up."

"Maybe someday we can go visit my folks for Thanksgiving," Kenneth suggested. "We all help out by cooking our favorite foods. Deep-fried turkey. Sweet potato casserole. Mac and cheese. Pumpkin bars. It's a bit of a hodgepodge, but so tasty."

"Sounds great," Brooke replied. Drawing her key out of her purse, she locked the apartment door and escorted Kenneth down the stairs to the lobby, where, as usual, tenants gathered around the mailboxes, gossiping.

"Girl, look at you," her favorite gay neighbor exclaimed, rushing up. His gelled, sandy hair didn't move as he hurried across the room, arms flapping. "What a stud. Nice."

Brooke laughed. "Kenneth, are you a stud?"

"I mean, I've heard worse," he replied, grinning.

"Could be *so much* worse," the man agreed. "Wish I could find me one of you..."

"He'd have to swing the other way," Kenneth pointed out.

"Well, yeah." The man grinned, stroked his tidy, tan goatee, and swatted Kenneth on the arm. "You two kids have fun."

"Oh, we aim to," Brooke said. "By the way, has there been any word on the sale of the building?"

"I hear there's been an offer. Maybe two. It wouldn't surprise me. For all the unlovely changes inside, it's a gorgeous building in a prime location. Someone's gonna want it. The only question is, what will that mean for the rest of us?"

"You got that right," Brooke agreed. "See ya later, Stanley."

"Bye, darlin'," he replied, waving as she headed for the door.

Kenneth trailed after her.

Together, they hopped into Brooke's car. For once, the rude neighbor's car wasn't encroaching on her space. However, a mid-autumn weather front had darkened the sky with low, threatening clouds.

"Do you think we'll have snow?" Brooke asked.

"Highly possible," Kenneth replied, opening the passenger door and letting himself in.

"I hate driving in snow."

"Better stay until Sunday, then," Kenneth suggested.

"Good idea," Brooke agreed, smirking. Her insides clenched. *Oh, so much fun is coming.*

"By the way," Kenneth added as Brooke revved the engine and backed carefully onto the street, "I spoke to your sister the other day."

"What?" Brooke braked hard to let a semi rumble along behind them.

"Yeah, sorry. I forgot to mention it. It was the night after we made love for the first time; you remember, when we were both so tired?"

"Sure," Brooke said cautiously.

"Your sister called. I tried to send the call to voicemail, so

116

the ringing wouldn't disturb you, but these big ole clumsy fingers... I picked up the call by accident."

Oh, God. What did she say? "I hope she didn't ask you any awkward questions."

Kenneth grinned, which Brooke took in at a glance as she checked around them, found a gap in the traffic, and maneuvered her way into it. *I miss the open roads and elbow room in Texas. This is like living in a sardine can.*

"Just the normal stuff," he said, and Brooke's tense shoulders sagged. "She wanted to be sure I would treat you right. Should I have told her I plan to... all night long?"

Brooke giggled. "She would probably approve."

"Is she really psychic?"

The light turned red. Brooke gently compressed the brake and pulled up behind a Mack truck, two sports cars and a minivan. *I wonder if we'll make it through on the next green.* "I'm not sure. She says she is, but she might just be a keen observer with a better-than-average intuition. But hey, she makes a living reading cards and palms and selling herbs and crystals. I'm not going to say whether she's actually reading these people's futures, but I'm quite sure she believes she is. Why? Does that bother you?"

"Not much," he replied. "I mean, Granny's pretty religious, but my folks, my siblings and I, we all kinda live and let live."

"Good. Um, Kenneth?"

"Yes, babe?"

Brooke grinned as the endearment warmed her down into the depths of her being. "I wondered something. In that painting of your grandparents, is your grandmother...?" She trailed off, not knowing how to proceed.

"Biracial?" Kenneth guessed.

"Yeah."

"Sure is. She wasn't supposed to be born, you know? Her

mother was white, very young, and her family had no interest in pushing any envelopes. Abortion wasn't much of a thing, back then, and Granny's mom's family had no idea how to procure one, so she went to a home for unwed mothers. Granny grew up in an orphanage and sang her way through college. Grandpa met her in a night club, and the rest is history. She's stronger than strong."

"I wonder if she... if they..."

"Would like you?"

Brooke didn't answer. She focused her eyes on the road ahead of her, where cars moved from one lane to another.

"What are you thinking, Brooke? Is that busy mind of yours finding a new objection to obsess over?"

"Not really," she lied.

"I wonder about that." He sounded amused.

"Well, I mean, I haven't ever..."

"Been in an interracial relationship?"

"No, not that," Brooke explained. "My ex-boyfriend is Korean. I've always been fairly omnivorous. There are many things more important to me than skin color."

"Clearly," he commented, that amused tone still lingering in his voice.

Brooke executed a tricky left turn, ignoring the honk of an oncoming car that had the right of way—and half a block of clearance—before making her way carefully into the far-right lane in anticipation of the turn toward the university. "I'm glad you thought of this idea," Brooke said. "You know, of leaving my car here at the university while classes are out for the break. I had no idea how to keep it near your apartment, with all the street side parking either crowded or restricted."

"It's a problem, for sure," Kenneth agreed. "There's my car, right where I left it before catching the bus to your apartment this afternoon. Pull into the next spot, okay?"

Brooke parked crookedly in the spot, grabbed her keys and reached into the backseat for her bag. Another shiver of excitement ran up her spine. She jumped from the driver's seat and circled around to Kenneth's SUV. Another chill shook her, this one generated by the growing chill of a late-November evening.

Kenneth turned the key in the ignition, and the SUV coughed, spluttered and reluctantly agreed to start. As he backed away from the divider and made his way out of the parking lot, the sky grew darker.

Brooke watched out the window as evening and an approaching storm conspired to drop the light level. "Looks pretty grim out there."

"That it does," he agreed. "I wonder if we'll make it back to my apartment before the storm breaks."

"Doesn't seem likely," Brooke replied. "Unless..."

"Unless?"

"Unless we change our reservation to a takeout order and eat it back at your place."

"That, my dear, is an excellent notion." He reached across the center console and squeezed her hand. "It's about a twenty-minute drive to the restaurant, so if you'd be so kind to call in our order, they might have it ready by the time we get there."

"I'm on it," Brooke told him, fishing her phone out of her purse.

Scrolling across the screen, she found the restaurant. "Before I call, what are we ordering?"

"As I recall, you owe me some pork ribs," he replied.

She smiled. "Darn, I had hoped you would forget."

"Not a chance. We were both eating that pile of brontosaurus ribs you ordered for us for days. Let's get something a little more refined. Check the menu, but I think they have a barbecue dinner for two with pork ribs, two sides and cornbread."

"I see it," Brooke agreed. "What sides?"

"You like okra?"

"Ugh, no. Sorry. Not to my taste. How's their potato salad?"

"Sadly, it tastes like the Midwest. No Southern flavor there."

"All mayo?" Brooke guessed.

"Yeah, and they did some kind of 'gourmet' experimenting with the seasonings."

"Ew." She wrinkled her nose. "Messing with the classics. Tsk, tsk."

Kenneth chuckled at her scolding as he turned left onto a wide, multilane street, already crammed with people racing about. The traffic slowed to a crawl as everyone forced their way into the far-right lane so they could turn into the grocery store.

"How about green beans?" she suggested. Kenneth set his blinker and merged to the left, creating room for the car behind them to move over, while simultaneously saving them from the snarl. "The menu says they have onion and bacon. That sounds good."

"I'm good with that. Green beans and... mac and cheese?"

"Sounds like that's a favorite of yours," Brooke pointed out.

"You got that right," he agreed easily, "but I'm a snob about it. Nobody makes it as good as my granny. These guys are tolerable, but..."

"But there's nothing like home cooking? I've heard that. I wonder if it has to do with how close a family is."

She found the little green phone icon and pressed it.

"Jack's," a cheerful voice that sounded strained spoke into the phone.

"Hi," she replied. "I have a reservation with you all in half an hour, and..."

"Under what name?" the nervous hostess interrupted.

"Hill," Brooke replied.

"Yep, you're confirmed."

"I'd like to change my reservation to an order for takeout," Brooke said fast.

"What?" The hostess asked into the phone. Then, her voice came through again, but muffled, as though she'd put her hand over the receiver. "How many? It's going to be about a twenty-minute wait. You can take a seat here, or head over to the bar." She spoke again, this time clearly. "Sorry about that. What did you say?"

"I said," Brooke replied, "that we would like to place an order to go and cancel our reservation."

"Oh, wow. That'll make some folks happy. It's crazy in here tonight. Okay, shoot. I'll put in your order right away.

"I'd like the pork rib plate for two, with macaroni and cheese and green beans."

"Great! See you in a few." The line went dead.

"That was weird," Brooke commented. "I guess they're super-busy."

"Makes sense to me," Kenneth said. "Tomorrow is a huge cooking extravaganza for a lot of people. Not making dinner tonight too sounds like a good trade-off."

"Ooooh, right. I didn't think of that."

"You didn't? The cooking in my family's household starts days in advance. Brooke, didn't you have any family traditions growing up?" Kenneth asked. "Who made y'all's Thanksgiving dinner?"

"Dad always had a housekeeper. Usually a cook too. He liked to work on Thanksgiving because it was so quiet at the office, so my sister and I had turkey sandwiches in front of some holiday cartoons."

"Christmas?"

"Same, except he gave the nanny the day off, so all our foods were laid out so we could get them ourselves. Cereal for breakfast. Sandwiches and salad. Pudding cups...."

"Ugh. No family to look after you kids at all?"

"Autumn and I had each other," Brooke told him solemnly, "and not much else."

"No wonder she's so protective of you."

"Right," Brooke agreed. "I wasn't able to protect her very well. I went off to college..."

"I get where you're coming from," he said. "It's tough being the oldest, isn't it?"

"It is," Brooke agreed. "I felt a lot of guilt when Autumn got pregnant and had to drop out of college. I felt like I had failed her."

"That's not true, you know," Kenneth pointed out.

"I realized that, finally," she replied. "Actually, Autumn insisted. She said it was insulting to her for me to take responsibility for her choices, good or bad. Besides, she went to community college, got her business associate's under her belt, and ended up opening a shop that has become quite... successful. She's happy, so how can I not be?"

"That's a better attitude."

From the tone of Kenneth's voice, Brooke could tell he was smiling. She glanced over and confirmed it. *I love his wide, open-hearted smile. I'm falling fast. Gee, I hope I don't get my heart broken. Universe, if you're listening the way Autumn always says you are, please work out the details so we can be happy together.*

For a moment, Brooke could have sworn that time paused. The car, stopped at a red light, made no detectable sound. The hum of traffic stopped as a rare break in the east-west flow opened up the road beside them.

In that moment, fat, puffy snowflakes came wafting lazily out of the sky. At the edge of the heavy cloud from which they'd emerged, a shaft of sunlight fell, bright and cheery, onto an evergreen tree. The golden light, green foliage and white snow together looked like joy brought to life.

There's my answer, she realized. *It didn't come the way I expected, and if I hadn't been looking, I might not have recognized it, but my request was heard.*

Lightness bubbled up in her heart. After years of stress, hard work and discipline, she had finally earned something good.

Then the traffic light changed. Kenneth's SUV rolled forward.

A surprisingly short time later, Brooke and Kenneth found themselves in his apartment, her overnight bag and their barbecue dinner in tow.

Just for fun, they sprawled on the floor in the middle of the apartment and dug into the tasty mess in front of them, laughing as sticky sauce spread across their fingers and cheeks.

"Now, tell me honestly, baby," Kenneth said, "isn't that better than a beef rib? It's so tender."

She shrugged. "Yes, it's more tender, but the flavor, Kenneth. This tastes like a pig. It's not beef."

"Them's fightin' words, darlin'," he drawled.

She sighed dramatically. "An interfaith romance. Think we can make it work against such terrible, terrible odds?"

"I don't know. We'll have to find a way."

"I can tolerate your barbecue if you can tolerate mine," she suggested.

"But what about the children?"

Brooke giggled. "I guess they'll have to decide for themselves."

"Will you try to influence their decision?" Kenneth quipped.

"Of course," Brooke replied without pausing. "After all, I'm clearly right, so..."

They both dissolved into giggles and then leaned forward for a sticky, barbecue kiss. As Kenneth's tongue delved into Brooke's mouth, the realization of what they'd just said dawned on her.

Kids? Oh, God. Do I want kids? Do I want Kenneth's kids? Unlike earlier, the sense of peace and rightness didn't arise, but rather a warm glow that told her the right answer would present itself at the right moment. *This relationship is surely teaching me to stop stressing myself.*

Kenneth released her lips. "Have you had enough to eat?"

"Stuffed," Brooke replied, and then her cheeks warmed as she realized the different ways that could be taken.

"Exactly what I had in mind. Shall we clean up a bit and then... retire?"

Brooke glanced at the bed and swallowed hard. "Um, Kenneth?"

He dropped his teasing demeanor immediately. "Is everything all right?"

"Oh, yes," she agreed, laying a soothing hand on his arm. "It's just... about those barbecue interfaith kids?"

He raised one eyebrow.

"Let's not conceive them yet. Between my sister and my roommate, I've had unplanned pregnancies on my mind for a long time. I'd rather not experience one myself."

"Condoms in the bedside table," he pointed out.

"Right. I'm good then."

"Great." He grinned. The barbecue sauce smeared across his face gave him a clown-like appearance.

She giggled. "You're a mess, honey."

He eyed her.

"I guess I am too?"

"Yes, ma'am, you are. Tell you what. Why don't you head into the bathroom and clean up? I'll put away these leftovers."

"Great idea!" Brooke jumped up and hustled into the bathroom. Over the roar of the sink, she could hear Kenneth rustling around in the other room. She washed the sauce from her hands and cheeks and then retrieved her overnight bag from where she'd stashed it by the bathroom door.

Brush and floss. No stringy meat kisses. She shivered. *This is so much fun. I almost forgot about fun. Maybe that's what Autumn was trying to tell me. It's all well and good to plan and work, but they're not a replacement for living.*

Brushing and washing completed, ready to shift gears, Brooke hopped out of the bathroom, passing Kenneth as he scooted in. "Hurry," she urged.

He laughed. "Believe me. I will."

In the few minutes he spent in the bathroom, Brooke stripped down and slipped under the sheets.

A moment later, Kenneth emerged, washed and brushed, wearing only his boxers.

Brooke grinned at the sight of her man, in all his soft, sexy teddy-bear glory. *Hard bodies and stacked muscles have nothing on a cuddly man. I wouldn't change a thing. He's not a bit fat, just wonderfully huggable.*

"Come here, baby," she urged, sitting up so the covers fell away from her breasts and reaching out to him.

"In a hurry, are you?" he teased.

"You'd better believe it," she replied. "See how much?"

He eyed her breasts, taking in her swollen nipples. "Yeah, I sure do. An eager lover is a wonderful thing. Scoot over, baby, and let me in there."

Brooke edged away from the side of the bed, and Kenneth joined her, sliding under the covers and taking her in his arms. They leaned together, capturing each other's lips in a kiss of mutual arousal. Brooke's body relaxed in Kenneth's embrace. The tension of the workweek melted away.

He eased her back onto the mattress and leaned over her, engulfing her in the wonderful warmth of his body.

"You feel so good," she murmured.

"You ain't seen nuthin' yet," he quipped.

"Show me," she urged, grabbing his hand.

He shifted his weight onto his side and willingly let her draw his fingers to her breast, where he stroked and plucked first one pink nipple, and then the other.

Pleasure shot straight to Brooke's sex in a surge of warm moisture. *Lord have mercy! I'm ready now.*

Kenneth leaned down and lapped at her nipple. The broad, wet stroke of his tongue made her whimper. When he contrasted the soft touch with a teasing nip, she squeaked in surprise. Then she moaned low as he settled in and suckled her.

"Oh, God," she murmured. Coherent words and thoughts fled, leaving her a creature of raw need.

The need to bring him the same pleasure he was bringing her took hold. Her hand slid down his body, reaching low. She found him fully erect, straining against his boxers, and she stroked him through the fabric.

"Aw, yeah," he groaned. "Touch me, baby. Please."

"Get that off you," she begged. "It's in the way."

He shifted and dragged off his boxers in an annoyed rush. When he returned, it was to straddle her, pinning her hips and letting her feel the fullness of his love as it covered her.

He's made of love. Nothing but love. And he wants to give it all to me. Awed by the realization, Brooke drew Kenneth down for another kiss. "I want you," she mumbled against his lips.

"Already?"

"Yes, please—now."

"But..."

"Later. We have days. Right now, I just need you."

"As milady wishes," he agreed, his expression serious, so close to her face. "Open, baby." He shifted, allowing her to bend and spread her knees.

Brooke made a blind grab at the bedside table and fumbled until she found a square packet. Then she nearly dropped it as Kenneth cupped her sex with one big hand. When his fingers pressed inward, testing her moisture and delving into her vagina, a cry of pure pleasure echoed from her throat.

"Like that?" he asked. "Let's see about this..."

She bit her lip as he withdrew, only to return with a second finger. When he eased in, gently imitating intercourse, and his thumb stroked directly onto her clitoris, Brooke groaned, "Oh, God. Kenneth!"

"Hush now, baby. You feel so nice and wet. Let me pleasure you."

"I... I..."

"I know." He kissed her but made no move to obey her spluttering request. "I want to be inside you. I will be. Just wait a minute, baby. You're so close. Let me feel you come."

Words failed again. Brooke collapsed against the pillow, muscles weak.

Kenneth, true to his word, claimed her sex with long strokes of his fingers. He continued to caress her clitoris with his thumb.

A long moment passed as pleasure built, coiled and drew

her inward until her entire being felt like one raw nerve. She poised at the brink of completion... trapped at a plateau.

Kenneth kissed her throat, trailing his lips up her cheek to her mouth. "I love you," he murmured against her, just as her release broke over her.

Brooke's back arched, drawing her mouth away from his as she released a wild cry. The condom dropped from her clenched fist onto the bed.

Kenneth scooped it up, rising to his knees. Somehow, he managed to tear open the packaging and roll the condom on with one hand. He moved quickly, withdrawing his fingers and easing his straining penis inside her.

"Oh, yes," she moaned. "That's so good."

"So good," he agreed, drawing back and returning with more force.

"Like that," she urged. "Please, baby. Take me hard. I need you."

"Oh, yeah," he growled. "Yeah."

He remained on his knees, grasping her hips to hold her in place as he surged hard into her, drew back and surged again. The power of his thrusts into the most secret places of Brooke's core sent her shuddering into another wild orgasm. The moment felt like pure oneness. Pure connection.

At that moment, only they existed, lost in a world of pleasure all their own. No other cares troubled them. Nothing else mattered. Only their love, which created a cocoon of safety where nothing could harm them.

She reached out, grasping his shoulders and drawing him down on top of her so she could kiss his full, beautiful lips. "I love you," she murmured, her voice rasping as spasms of ecstasy fluttered in and through her. "I love you, Kenneth."

"I love you, Brooke. Argh!" His back tensed under her

fingers. His thighs went rigid. His deep, plunging rhythm powered on, fueling itself as he also succumbed to orgasm.

Kenneth was far from awake when he heard the water hitting the wall of the shower. He smiled sleepily to himself. Sated and happy, he rolled over in the bed, breathing in the fragrance of his lover, of himself, of their mingled passion in the sheets. *Since Brooke got over her worries about our future, this has become quite a lovely romance,* he thought drowsily. *It's not really bedtime though. I guess we're both working pretty hard.*

A fragment of Beethoven drew him up from near slumber. Grumbling, Kenneth dragged his heavy limbs off the bed. When the melody intensified, he stumbled over to his coffee table where he had plugged his cell in. He made a wild grab, barely registering his mother's number as he pushed the button and lifted the phone to his ear. "Lo?"

"Hi, son. How's it going?"

"Not bad," he replied, moments before a huge yawn forced its way out.

"Long week?" she guessed.

"I suppose so," he said, not wanting to get into why he might be so tired at seven in the evening. "I gave an essay exam in my music arranging class, which I had to take home and grade. Then I had to input grades for my voice lesson students, and one was behind on hours. I'm not even a professor yet, and I'm already worn out."

"You'll be fine," his mother assured him. "Just remember how much paperwork I always have to do, and that's after wrestling kids in and out of their wheelchairs all day. You get through, son. You find it."

"I know, Mama. I just have to build up my stamina. I'm not used to it."

"You need a break," she told him. "I always look forward to my breaks."

"And I have the next five days off," he reminded her. "I'll be relaxing for sure." *Relaxing in bed with my girlfriend,* he added silently, a wry grin spreading across his lips.

"And then only a month or so until Christmas, right?"

I know what she's angling for. "That's right. Why do you ask?"

"You know," his mother replied, amusement in her voice. "I want to know if you can make it home for Christmas, of course. You're gonna be gone to Europe for months, and I haven't seen you in a year. Please tell me you're coming home, Kenny, at least for a while. I miss you."

Kenneth opened his mouth to answer when an idea sparked to life. *I wonder.* "You know, Mama, I just might. I wonder, though. How would you feel if I brought someone with me... someone special?"

"A lady?"

"Mmmm hmmm," he replied. "My girlfriend."

"Oho! You didn't tell me you were seeing anyone."

Kenneth sank onto the sofa cushions and lifted his legs up, so he sprawled across the entire length. "We haven't been together a very long time—just about a month—but it's moving fast. We're very close, and... and it seems like a good time."

"Well, goodness. Um, would she want the pull-out couch, or would the two of you be sharing your room?"

Always practical, aren't you, Mama? "I haven't asked her yet, but I suspect... my room."

"Oho!" his mother said again, this time with a knowing tone in her voice. "Well, I'll speak with your father, but sure. The more the merrier, and if she's that special to you, you're right.

We need to meet her. What does she do, this paragon of women?"

"She's a music teacher," he informed her, grinning even wider.

"Ah. A singer?"

"Yes, ma'am."

"That explains a lot. What's her name?"

Here we go. The moment of truth. "Brooke. Brooke Daniels."

"Oh." A long, heavy pause hung between them, and then, blunt as always, his mother blurted, "Kenny, that sounds like a white girl name."

"Good guess, Mama. Yes, Brooke is white... with brown hair and blue eyes. She's gorgeous."

"You do sound infatuated, don't you? Son... why? You know, I'm sure there are plenty of strong, black women up there in Chicago. Some might even be musicians..."

"And I hope," he interrupted her, "that each of them finds the man... or woman she deserves, no matter their race. I can't explain how it came about, but there's no doubt in my mind. Brooke is the one for me."

"This kind of thing didn't work out too well for your grandmother or her parents," she pointed out.

He glanced at the painting hanging over the table. "Yes, I know. But remember, that was over sixty years ago."

"And things really aren't better, are they, son? Are the police still following you around?"

"Some," he muttered. "I've gotten to know some of the officers, so mostly they just wave."

"And if they see you with a white woman?" Shayla pressed.

Kenneth rolled his shoulders, glad to turn the conversation to lighter topics. "They don't worry at all about that. Nowadays, people rarely give more than a glance at couples who are... different, and if they do, Brooke sets them straight."

"In public?"

"Always. She's not afraid to hold my hand in front of anyone or hug or kiss me. A few times, she's had to shut down busybodies who had some kind of opinion, and she never batted an eyelash. She's proud of me, Mama. Of us. Get this. *She* thought *I* was out of her league because I'm an opera singer, and she's a high school teacher. She truly sees me, Mama. I really think you would like her if you give her a chance."

He paused, waiting.

His mother sighed loudly into the phone. "Okay, Kenny. Bring your lady friend home. I'll give her a chance. It's not what I would have chosen for you, but you always did make your own way."

"That's as it should be, isn't it?" he asked. "I mean, you made your choices for your life..."

"And this life is yours. Okay, okay. I'll let everyone know that we might be having an extra guest for Christmas."

"Thank you, Mama."

"Talk to you later."

The phone went dead. Kenneth lowered it into his lap, staring sightlessly at the blank screen. *Well, what did you expect? You know how Mama feels about ensuring black folks get a fair shake in life, and it makes perfect sense for her to do so. Now, it's time for her to broaden her horizons. She'll accept Brooke in time, I'm sure.*

Slowly it dawned on him that the water had stopped running. A moment later, Brooke made her way out, wrapped in a towel, her wet hair hanging loose around her shoulders. He bent his knees, making room for her on the sofa, and she sank down beside him, pulling his feet into her lap.

"Feeling good?" he asked her.

"Oh, yes," she agreed. "I can't think of the last time I've been so relaxed. You're good for me, Kenneth. I'm so thankful for you."

Her words warmed him. Though he'd tried to put her initial reluctance behind him, he hadn't entirely forgotten. Every word of affirmation hit him in a good spot.

I still don't quite trust this—her—entirely. She's holding back. I can feel it. She's very loving and connected... and sexy, but deep down she doesn't believe in us. She won't until the whole picture comes together for her, and I'll always come second to her job.

That knowledge hurt. It hurt worse with each passing day. The more he got to know her, the more her reticence stood out in his mind.

We're connected. A couple. And yet, she'd think nothing of giving this up if her job demanded it. The reality presented a conflict he struggled with, but something about her told him it was worthwhile, and that it would be resolved somehow if he could just hold out long enough.

"Brooke?" he asked hesitantly.

"Hmmm?"

"What you said earlier... did you mean it?"

She considered him, her eyes shining blue in the dim light. "I did. Maybe that doesn't make sense. Maybe it's too soon, but I can't help it, Kenneth. I love you. I love you and I'm not sorry."

I wonder who she's trying to convince because she surely must know it's not me, and I don't even think it's herself. Whose disapproval worries you so badly, baby girl?

"Did you mean it?" she asked. "You said it first."

"Isn't that just our way?" he quipped.

"I guess it is. Well, if you want to be the keeper of my heart,

Kenneth, I won't object. You've more than earned the right by being so wonderful. I guess I don't need to ask, really, do I?"

"You don't," he agreed. "You knew I loved you before I said it, and you still know it, at least if you let your heart lead you instead of that busy mind of yours."

"I know," she replied. Her fingers squeezed down on his foot, seeking and massaging a tender spot. "I believe that you love me, Kenneth. Heaven only knows why. I've been a devil of a girlfriend, not nearly supportive enough, and I regret it."

"Hey now," he argued, sitting up and stroking his knuckles across her cheek. "No more of that. I know you had your reasons to be cautious. Let's just try to move past it. We're together, and I don't see an end to that. Come what may, if we make each other the priority, we'll be okay. Promise me?"

She nodded. "Somehow, the way will present itself. I have to believe that. My sister would say I have to manifest it. I miss her so bad sometimes. It's not good to be so far away, but what can I do?"

"I don't know." He leaned back, allowing her to massage his foot. "I miss my family too. I never planned to stay so far north forever." *Shoot. Why did I say that?* "Um, Brooke?"

"Yes, honey?"

"Um, how would you like to meet my family?"

Her eyebrows lifted and her big blue eyes nearly bugged out of her head. "What?"

"I'm not kidding. They want me to come home for Christmas. Would you like to come?"

"Oh, Kenneth, I don't know. What would they think of me?"

"They'll love you," he told her solemnly. "I love you, and we're great together. How else would they feel?"

"They're okay with you having a white girlfriend?"

"They'll have to be," he replied. "They don't get a vote."

"This isn't exactly filling me with confidence," Brooke admitted. "Be honest with me, Kenneth. Is someone you care about uncomfortable with interracial relationships?"

"My mother," he admitted. "She's not against you as a person, but she does have an interest in black women finding the best black men. I'm her son. Naturally, she thinks I'm the best, so..."

"So, she wanted you to find an amazing black woman? Create a strong, black family? Change the world?"

"Bingo."

"Honey, why didn't you?" Brooke asked. "Why me? I've seen the university, the chorale *and* the opera. There are *so* many gorgeous, smart, talented black women. Why me? Not only am I white, I'm a neurotic mess. You could have someone... more like you."

"Who can explain these things," he replied. "You and I, we have something special. If you're meant for me and I for you, the best any of those amazing black women could be is second best. They deserve to be with the person who's meant to be their number one."

"That's pretty metaphysical," Brooke commented. "I think you'd get along well with my sister. She's a big believer in fate."

"I'd love to meet her sometime."

"Well," Brooke said, tapping her chin with her fingertip, "if we meet your family over Christmas, maybe we can plan a long layover in Dallas. If we stayed there over one night, we could have dinner with her before going on..."

"Sounds like a plan," he said, smiling. *She wants me to meet her sister. Wonderful!*

"Great." Brooke beamed, but he couldn't help but notice a hint of uncertainty lingering in the corners of her eyes.

CHAPTER 9

"'oooooo-waaaaards meeeeeeeen!'" The drawn-out final cadence of the "Glory to God" chorus rang through the choir room with chill-inducing energy. Brooke's smile almost hurt. Rehearsal had gone from a pleasure to a joy.

It's so lovely to stop crushing on Kenneth and instead, to embrace him. Monday nights are rough because it just isn't practical to spend the night together when rehearsal ends so late, but there are so many other nights now.

"Excellent work, everyone," Dr. Davis whispered, his quiet voice cracking with emotion. "This is going to be the best concert ever. I'm so proud of everything you've accomplished." He cleared his throat, rubbed both eyes and continued, sounding much more normal. "Next week is the last rehearsal here in the choir room. In two weeks, we'll have our first of two rehearsals with the orchestra. One will be Monday, just like a regular rehearsal, to get all the excitement out of the way. Then, the dress rehearsal Thursday, and our concert will be Friday, December 3rd, at seven. Curtain call and sound check at six, as always. If you have any questions, email the symphony office or ask your section leader. I'm afraid I'll be out of town this week and not available."

He paused, regarding the choir. "Take care of yourselves. Wash your hands. Drink water. Try not to get sick between now and next week. You're dismissed."

A quiet roar of murmurs, like the sea rolling over the sand, broke out among the choir, punctuated by the stomping of feet as they made their noisy way down from the risers.

Over the din, Brooke barely heard Dr. Davis say, "Miss Daniels?"

Is he calling me? she wondered.

"Miss Daniels, may I speak with you, please?"

Huh. He is calling me. "Coming, sir."

She made her way down to the podium, where a swarm of people pestered the director with questions. He met her eyes and smiled wryly.

Shoot. Guess I have to wait.

Waiting turned out not to be onerous, because a moment later, Kenneth embraced her from behind, resting his chin on the top of her head. His palpable presence immediately drove all the day's tension from her shoulders, leaving her limp. *I want nothing more than to curl up in his arms and sleep.*

At last, the straggling chatters wandered off, leaving Brooke and Kenneth alone with the professor.

"Miss Daniels. Thank you for waiting. I have a request to make of you."

"What's that, sir?" Brooke asked, regarding the elderly man with tired curiosity.

"Our soprano soloist backed out," he explained. "She was diagnosed with vocal cord nodes and will need to have surgery and spend a considerable amount of time on vocal rest."

"Oh, dear," Brooke said. "That's terrible. Poor woman."

Then a niggling idea dawned on her, setting her heart pounding. "What can I do to help with that?" *Surely, he wants me to suggest a local student, right?*

Dr. Davis cleared his throat. "Mr. Hill suggested that, since you've sung the soprano solos from the *Messiah* many times, you might be able to fill in. Would you be willing to do that?"

Brooke's jaw dropped. "Me?"

"Yes, of course."

"But, we have so many excellent sopranos. Ones with more experience than I have, and..."

"You have the correct tone quality for Baroque music, Miss Daniels," he explained. "Yes, we have many fine sopranos, but most of them sing in the romantic style, with a heavy tone and large vibrato. While they're able to control it for choral singing, it seems likely they would struggle to resist letting their solo... wiggle, and the recitative sections would become muddy. You have a pure, clear tone, with minimal vibrato, which the piece requires. Would you consider it?"

"You should do it, Brooke," Kenneth murmured in her ear. His warm voice made an agreeable shiver climb up her spine. "You're a fantastic director, but don't you ever just want to sing? I doubt once-a-week rehearsals and four concerts a year satisfy you. Am I right?"

"You're right," she replied, "but..."

"But?"

Kenneth did this, she realized. *He planned it as a gift for you. He wants to make you happy.*

In that moment, she did feel happy. So happy it hurt, in her chest, where her pounding heart threatened to shatter her ribs. "Yes," she whispered. "Yes, I'll do it. Um, as long as I can still sing with the chorale too."

"Of course," Dr. Davis replied. "We'll position the microphone near your section. Step out for your solo. Then step back and join the choir again. We're doing the same for Mr. Hill, and our alto and tenor soloists will have the same option, should they choose to accept it."

"Works for me," Brooke said, trying to sound lighthearted, but her voice rasped.

"You'd better rest from talking. You sound a bit strained," Dr. Davis pointed out. "Drink some warm tea with honey and lemon, and please don't let too many teenagers breathe on you. I'm in no mood to find another replacement."

"I'll do my best, sir," she promised. "Good evening."

Dazed, she let Kenneth lead her away. Over by the coat hooks, she stood staring, unsure what she felt. Kenneth moved away from her, and the loss of his warmth left her shivering. He found her coat, one of the few remaining after almost everyone had left and wrapped it around her. The sound of the zipper broke the spell, and she jumped at him, dragging him into a tight hug.

"You did this!" she exclaimed. "Kenneth, you did this... for me."

"I did," he agreed. "I take it you're pleased?" Though the words sounded mild, a hint of *something* in his tone begged her to recognize the intent behind them.

"Thank you," she breathed, drawing him down for a kiss. "Thank you, honey."

"Anything for you," he vowed.

She kissed him again.

"You'd better head home," he suggested. "Remember what happens when we get kissing on a Monday night..."

"Yeah. Good things, mostly, but a tired next day."

"A tired *Tuesday*," he pointed out. "Don't you normally have late rehearsals on Tuesday?"

"Until seven," Brooke told him.

"Damn. Can I see you Wednesday?"

"Thursday," she told him. "I have no extra rehearsals on Thursday. There's a weekend workshop on Saturday, so it's Thursday or nothing."

"Thursday," he agreed. He kissed her again. "Off you go then. Good night, baby."

"Night."

Brooke's mind wandered as she drove, so badly that she had no awareness of anything between when she pulled out of the parking lot until she eased into her cramped parking space next to her usual, badly-parked neighbor. She struggled through the biting cold of the first of December and ducked into the lobby/mailroom. There, she saw her friend hovering, as usual, near the mailboxes.

"Stanley, is this all you do, loiter in the lobby?" she teased.

"It's where all the best gossip comes from, darling," he lisped with a flamboyant wave of his hand. "Better check your mail right away."

"What do you know about my mail?" Brooke asked. "I hope you weren't snooping. Disturbing the mail is a federal offense." She unlocked the box and drew out a pile of fliers, bills and one envelope with the management company's imprint on the upper left corner. She tore it open and stared at the missive with her heart pounding. *Surely not.*

"Cool your jets, Brookie," Stanley drawled. "I got the same mail as you. The sale just closed. They're evicting us all. We need to be out by the first of the year so they can begin renovations."

The cold from outside seemed to have slithered through the door, waiting for the right moment to attack. Once Brooke's guard was lowered, it wrapped her from head to foot, kissing her and eliciting a shiver that shook her frame. *Great. Now what?* she wondered. "We expected this," she said through numb lips.

"We talked about it, but who believed it would actually happen?" Stanley shook his head. "I had hoped the new owners would just take over and not raise the rent too much."

"So did I, but that was never likely, was it? It's a historic building that has been badly treated. It has beautiful bones."

"It does," Stanley agreed. "Well, what's done is done, and a month, right around the holidays, is hardly enough time to find a new place."

Oh, God. He's right. This is a nightmare. I'll surely have to find a temporary situation while I search, and I'm nowhere near ready to buy anything. Not unless I want to move two hours out of town and commute every day. "I have to go, Stanley. Good night." Unaware of what or even if he answered, she floated away. Floated, because she couldn't feel her feet, the floor or anything else. She was numb but for the tingling in her fingertips.

Heedless of the 'rules,' she unlocked the door and threw it open with a noisy bang. No protesting shout responded, and Brooke flopped gracelessly on the couch, her arm over her eyes. "Okay, Universe, what are you doing to me? What does this mean?"

She considered calling her sister, but then rejected the idea. "It's late. The sound of the phone might disturb River. That wouldn't be kind. Besides, what if she's resting?"

Agitated, Brooke jumped to her feet again and meandered aimlessly around the apartment. The walls of the compact space seemed to close in on her. "Nowhere to go, but I can't stay here. Jackie will be happy she's off the hook, but... what will I do?"

She passed the bathroom and ducked in, distracted herself for five minutes by brushing her teeth and washing her face, though her restless mind never truly released the problem.

"I *hate* it when other people's decisions interfere with my plans. I hate it. It's one thing to consider the options, discuss and make adjustments. It's another altogether to rip the rug out from under people."

She stepped out of the bathroom and shut off the light. Again, she walked around the room, one way and the other as worries assailed her. Carelessly, she made her way on her journey to nowhere, until her purse strap caught between her feet, tripping her.

"Damn it!" she snarled, righting herself and grabbing at the offending strap. The weight of her bag had her digging inside through a growing collection of unneeded receipts and chewing gum wrappers until she found her phone. Without thought, she activated the screen and pressed her top speed dial number.

"Hello?"

The beautiful, low tone of Kenneth's beloved voice wrapped around her and sank into her, taking the edge off her distress.

"Baby, are you there? Did you butt dial me?"

"No, I'm here," she replied. "Sorry. You just have such a beautiful voice, I got distracted."

"Thanks." Now, Kenneth sounded bemused. "Did you need something?"

"Yes. I hope I didn't wake you."

"You didn't," he replied. "I was wrapping up the last round of edits to my opus."

"Oh, I'm sorry I disturbed you."

"Don't be," he urged. "It's boring. I'm glad for the distraction. Besides, you sound upset. What's wrong, baby?"

"My building's been sold," she blurted. "I have to be out by the first."

"Of January?"

"Uh-huh."

"Damn, that's fast. Is that even legal?" Kenneth demanded.

"Thirty days? It can take that long just to get an application approved."

"I know," she replied, distress rising. "I'll surely have to get a room in some cruddy, long-stay hotel, at a pirate's premium, wasting money every week until I can find something. *Then* I have to put down first and last month's rent and deposit. Do you know what a terrible bite this will take out of my savings? Not to mention the time it will take to get all this done right around Christmas with a concert to direct, another to perform in, solos, finals and grading."

Overwhelmed, Brooke threw her hands into the air and asked, "What am I going to do, Kenneth?"

"Hey," he said, his voice low and slow as molasses. Dark and sweet. "Easy, Brooke. Be easy. There's a solution. We'll think of it. It'll be simple and painless."

"How do you *know*?" she demanded. "What can I do?"

"First of all," he urged, "you need to stop panicking. Moving apartments isn't *that* scary. I get that it's not what you wanted but worrying yourself sick won't help a bit. Then, you remember that you don't have to do this on your own. I'm here. I'll help you. You'll never be homeless, and you won't need to stay in any trashy hotels. I promise."

Oh, of course. Of course, he'll let me crash with him until I find a place. How nice that would be anyway. Brooke relaxed a little. *Still a hassle and a hit to the finances, but no weeks spent in transition. It'll be okay.* She took in a deep breath and released it slowly. "Thank you. You really are the best, Kenneth."

"Do me a favor, okay? Are you ready for bed?"

"Just need to change."

"Then change, honey. Put on your most comfortable pajamas."

She pushed the button to put the phone on speaker and pulled out a flannel nightgown. "Done."

"You had a big day and you're overtired. That's why you're panicking, but you can't let this keep you up all night. You'll get sick, and you have a big solo to sing. Are you lying down now?"

"Almost." She quickly circled the apartment, turning off the lights. Then she slipped under the covers. "Now I am."

"Good. Think about where your body is tense. Shoulders? Relax your shoulders. Unclench your fists and jaw. Imagine you were about to sing "Queen of the Night." What would you need to do with your body to be ready for such a challenging aria?"

On cue, her body fell into singing posture, forcing the tension to release. Fatigued engulfed her. She yawned.

"You're going to be fine," Kenneth reassured her. "Everything is going to be fine. You're going to have a good night's sleep, and tomorrow—yes, tomorrow—the solution will present itself, and it will be easy."

"But how can you...."

"Stop," he urged. "Stop panicking. Just trust me. Do you trust me?"

"Yes."

"Then relax. Worrying won't help. Relax. Sleep. I love you, Brooke."

Again, she forced her muscles to release. *He's right. Worrying just wastes energy. It doesn't solve problems.* Exhaustion crept up, overtaking the lingering stress. "I love you, Kenneth."

"I can't tell you how I love to hear that. Sleep, baby. Good night."

"Good night," she slurred. Barely awake, she fumbled at the phone until she pushed the button, and then she dropped it on the bedside table. Sleep claimed her a second later.

Kenneth hung up the phone, an irresistible idea gelling in his mind. Without pausing for further reflection, he searched through his phone and made another call.

A sleepy voice fussed into the phone, "If this isn't an insanely gorgeous man with chocolate, I'm hanging up."

"Um, okay?" Kenneth said. *Is it really that late?* He glanced at the screen. *9:37. Not that bad.*

"Who is this?" Autumn sounded awake now.

"It's Kenneth. Sorry if I woke you."

"Kenneth? Brooke's Kenneth? Oh, hi."

"Yeah, hi. Um, I have a question for you."

"Shoot," she suggested, not as an epithet, but as an invitation.

"I need to ask Brooke a question, but I'm concerned what her reaction might be."

"Oh, God. Are you going to propose?"

Kenneth choked. "No. I mean, yeah, probably, someday, but not now. That would be insane. I'm not going to propose marriage at this point. We've been a couple for less than two months."

"Okay, that's probably wise," Autumn said. "Some people would be okay with moving that fast, but not Brooke. Definitely not."

"Right."

"Then what are you asking and worrying about, Kenneth?" Autumn sighed, and her sigh turned to a yawn.

Right, Hill. Get to the point. "So, um, Brooke's apartment building has been sold, and all the tenants will be evicted. She's panicking, of course, but it shouldn't be such a big deal. I want to invite her to move in with me, but she's so skittish. Do you think the invitation would help or panic her more?"

"Ooooh." Autumn exhaled. "I get where you're coming from with that question. Good on you for being so sensitive."

He sighed. "Can you tell me *why* she's so scared of everything? The connection we have is... indescribable. I love her. She says she loves me, but..."

"But she's always holding back?"

"Exactly. Does this have something to do with y'all's father? She's mentioned a few times how controlling he can be..." he trailed off, not wanting to offend.

"Yeah, that's a big part, I'm sure. Dad's never acted right where Brooke is concerned. He's harder on her than he has any reason to be, and it's often ugly. It's like, no matter what she does, it's not enough for him. He finds reasons to be disappointed in her. You should have seen him when she told him she was changing her major to music. You would have thought she pulled out a gun and shot him."

"For living her life? For not letting him dictate her career path? That's really not okay."

"I know," Autumn agreed, "especially when you consider that he *never* gave me a hard time about anything. Not when I got pregnant and dropped out of college. Not when I opened an occult shop. Hell, he gifted me the down payment on my storefront, and he lets me rent the guest house on his property for below market value so I can save money."

"What the hell? No wonder she has issues."

"Yeah, Dad's an ass to her. That's a big part of the problem. She keeps trying to win his approval, but I don't honestly think there's any way she will ever be able to. She should just put up boundaries on his bullshit and be happy."

"Sounds like a good plan."

"You can help her with that," Autumn suggested. "Show her what self-acceptance looks like. Affirm her every chance you get. From what she's told me, you do it without thinking."

"Well, yeah. She deserves to be happy just like me or anyone else."

"Okay, good. Then you should definitely invite her to move in. It's time for her to challenge her status quo again, and the universe has forced it on her. It's practical for you two to save money by living together. That argument should sway her at least a little."

"But will she agree?" Kenneth demanded. "Her reticence about our relationship surely has more to it than an overbearing father."

"It does," Autumn agreed. "I think Dad is at the root of Brooke's issues, but... Okay, listen, this isn't really my story to share, but I doubt she'll be forthcoming about it. She's still hurt and humiliated. I know she's not trying to hurt you, but... baggage is a bitch."

"I'm listening," Kenneth replied.

"So, not only did Dad try to choose Brooke's major for her, he also introduced her to his intern, Jordan Hwang."

"Oh, God. He picked her boyfriend too?"

"More than that." Autumn sounded weary. "I think he saw it more like an arranged marriage. The only time Dad showed even the least bit of approval was when Brooke was dating Jordan and studying finance. She was following his path exactly as he laid it out for her, and she was miserable, but he was happy."

"It seems so archaic to arrange relationships for other people," Kenneth said, knowing the comment to be inane, but not sure what else to say.

"It is," Autumn agreed sadly, "but Brooke was so eager to have Dad's blessing. She even thought she loved the guy."

"Not surprising, under the circumstances," Kenneth replied. "She must have been desperate for someone's approval."

"You're not wrong."

"So, what happened?" Kenneth asked. "Did the relationship sour after Brooke changed her major?"

"No, I'm afraid not," Autumn said. "It would have been better if it had, especially since they'd only been dating a few months at that point. Instead, they lived together for two years. She believed—we all believed—that he was just waiting to finish school, and then he would propose."

"He didn't?" Kenneth guessed.

"Nope." Autumn sighed. "A few days before graduation, he told Brooke he was moving away to go to graduate school. She was surprised but asked where he was headed so she could apply there too. He told her..." She cleared her throat, and when she continued, her voice wavered. "He told her it was time to go their separate ways. That their college fling was over, and he planned to move on *without* his *roommate*. She was crushed. She had planned to marry him, and he only ever saw her as a fuck buddy."

Her blunt, teary words hit Kenneth like a punch to the guts. *That explains so much.* "Lord have mercy," he said, echoing his granny's favorite oath, "What did y'all's dad say? Didn't he get mad at his intern for not living up to expectations?"

Autumn snorted. "Dad? See reality? Hell, no. He blamed Brooke for losing such a 'good prospect' and told her it was her fault Jordan lost interest. She was crushed. I was amazed she made it through her master's program after that."

Kenneth's stomach churned into nausea as he imagined how that must have felt. *It's amazing she took the chance at all.* "So, would it be a bad idea to ask her, even though it would fix her housing problem altogether?"

Autumn paused. "I still think it's a good idea," she told him at last. "You should invite her, but somehow you need to help her know that this isn't a convenience or temporary... without her getting freaked out about the pacing. It's a bit of a minefield. I wish you luck."

"Thanks. Sounds like I'm going to need it. Thanks also for telling me what I needed to know."

"You're welcome. Please take care of my sister. She needs it. She deserves it."

"But will she allow it?" Kenneth asked.

"Fair question," Autumn replied. "Okay, never mind. I'll just go do some visualization exercises."

"Is that the New Age version of offering to pray?"

"Nah, I pray too," Autumn replied. "In fact, that's a good idea. Good night, Kenneth. Thanks for calling."

"You're welcome. Bye."

He hung up the phone and stared at it. *As usual, answering one question only brings up a pile more, each of them more unanswerable than the last.*

CHAPTER 10

*B*rooke yawned hugely as she turned the big key in the choir room door, bringing rehearsal with all its lingering questions to a decisive close. "Yes, I can write a letter of recommendation," she muttered under her breath. "Yes, we will be going to several competitions in the spring. Yes, spring break camp is happening this year. Yes, everyone still needs to audition for senior ensemble, even if they're seniors."

"Long day?" Nancy asked, popping out of her office.

"A bit," Brooked replied. "We're at that awkward part of the year when, although we've learned the notes, the students have to overcome inertia and work on the style and *pay attention.* They've got turkey making them sleepy and Christmas on the brain."

"And the concert is next week."

"And the concert is next week," Brooke agreed. "They'll be fine, I have no doubt. They're just not as ready as they think they are. It happens this time every year."

"It does," Nancy concurred. "Are you okay, Brooke? You seem a little agitated."

"I'm okay," she said instantly. Then, in the interest of honesty, she added, "I'm going to have to find a new apartment. My building has been sold. Merry Christmas to me, eh?"

"Oh, that stinks," Nancy replied, patting Brooke on the shoulder. "Do you have anywhere in mind?"

Brooke shook her head. "I'm at a bit of a loss, and I've been too busy all week even to begin looking."

"Oh, dear. And we have a rehearsal on Saturday as well. Maybe you should let me handle it so you can tour some apartments, honey."

"Oh, I couldn't," Brooke replied. "You all are counting on me, and it's way too many kids for just you plus the accompanist. I mean, they're all good kids, but..."

"Another set of eyes wouldn't hurt."

"Right. Don't worry, Nancy. I'm sure I'll figure something out."

"Maybe this afternoon? Since it's only four, you could make some phone calls..."

"That's a good idea," Brooke replied. "I'm heading over to my boyfriend's place. I'm sure he'll help me look."

"Oh, are you seeing someone?" Nancy's eyes widened behind her bifocals. "I'm not sure I knew that. You haven't mentioned anyone. What's his name?"

"Kenneth..."

"Kenneth Hill?" Nancy clapped her hands together and squealed like a teenager. "That adorable opera singer is your boyfriend? Oh, Brooke, that's wonderful!"

Brooke smiled, though it still felt stretched and thin. "Thank you. He's really just as nice and sweet as he seems. I'm incredibly blessed."

"So is he, honey," Nancy reminded her. "Hurry, now. Shoo. Go see him."

"I'm going, I'm going." Brooke zipped into her office and

scooped her heavy jacket from the back of her chair, shrugging it on despite the nearly-tropical heat in the office. Grabbing her purse from inside the desk drawer, she made her way back out. Nancy had returned to her office.

"Um, Nancy?"

"Yes, hon?"

"Have you heard anything on the head director position front?"

"No, I sure haven't," Nancy replied. "I don't think they're keeping me in the loop, but I'd be surprised if they say anything before the posting window closes in January."

"Oh, right. Want me to lock the hallway-side door as I go out?" she asked.

"Sure," Nancy replied. "Just let me make sure I can find my keys—yup, here they are. See you tomorrow."

"See you," Brooke replied.

As she shoved open the doors and stepped out into an early-December afternoon, the blast of cold took her breath away. Shivering, she made her way quickly down the sidewalk toward the teacher parking lot. She could see her vehicle near the rear. It seemed to withdraw as she approached, her breath puffing around her face and obscuring her vision.

"Northern winters," she muttered, remembering the 'cold' in Texas. "Fifty degrees and sunny. How tropical that sounds now. I miss the south."

A gust hit her square in the face, stealing her words and reminding her that, while winter had nearly arrived, even colder cold was likely in the months to come. "Ugh. I'm already over winter, and it hasn't even started yet."

Grumpy and frustrated, Brooke increased her pace. Despite the vigorous exercise, she grew colder as she walked, and more out of sorts than ever. "Damn this place," she murmured.

At last, she reached her vehicle, only to discover that a thin film of ice had formed on all the windows during the day. Cussing at another delay, she cranked the engine and set the defrost, before yanking on the gloves she'd forgotten in the car that morning. They were frozen and chilled her hands further before grudgingly accepting her heat. Ignoring her aching fingers, she reached behind the driver's seat and claimed the scraper, quickly grinding the frost off her windows in a haphazard pattern of long, erratic scrapes that left bits clinging here and there.

By the time she'd rendered her windows transparent, the car had warmed to a tolerable temperature, and she flopped on the seat, tossing the scraper aside and leaning her head against the headrest. As her body warmed, her uncomfortable feelings came to the forefront. "I hate winter a lot more than I expected to. I thought it would be an adventure, but it's just a nuisance. Golly, I'm a grouch today, but I just can't muster up any pleasant thoughts. Poor Kenneth. He's getting sour Brooke this time. Maybe I should cancel just so I don't inflict my bad mood on him."

Her phone chimed.

Waiting for her frozen fingers to thaw enough to grip the wheel, she fumbled numbly in her purse and drew it out, seeing a text from Kenneth. Instantly, a sense of warmth and calm flared in the center of her chest, radiating out toward her chilly extremities. She opened the text and saw it was a picture of him holding a bottle of Kahlua. Beneath, a brief message said, **It's been a long week. Let's celebrate making it to Thursday.**

I couldn't agree more. On my way, she sent back.

He replied with a thumbs up and several smiling and kissy-face emojis, along with a couple of hearts.

Brook's grumpy mood evaporated. She shifted her car into drive and made her way out of the parking lot. Between the school pickups and the folks who left work early, the streets were crammed and crawling. She inched her way along, trapped behind a city bus, unable to get around it because the traffic in the left lane never thinned.

The sky, surprisingly dark for the early hour, billowed with heavy, undulating clouds. As Brooke drove along, they seemed to swell and retreat, pulsing against the sunset. A splat hit the windshield, and then another, and a third; fat, heavy raindrops with ice in their cores.

Oh, great.

The traffic slowed even further until Brooke was only able to move forward a couple of painful inches at a time. The fifteen-minute drive across town took nearly an hour, and by the end, the road grew slick. Her car began to fishtail at turns.

At last, she reached the park across the street from Kenneth's building and happened upon a spot, almost too small for her little car and nowhere near where she wanted to be. Still, she eased in, awkwardly parking at an angle that wasn't really parallel to the curb at all, though she didn't poke out into traffic.

"Good enough," she muttered, examining her alignment. Then she turned away and trudged half a block in an obnoxious wind that drove splats of slush into her face.

Her flat work shoes slipped and slid on the sidewalk, and her feet nearly went out from underneath her. She grabbed the trunk of a slender, leafless sapling to steady herself before struggling forward to the crosswalk that traversed six lanes of zooming, out-of-control traffic.

I don't want to cross that, she thought.

Another blast of icy wind shoved her back from the edge as though protecting her.

On the opposite side, a tall figure in a bright blue puffer coat stepped up to the curb. Though the wind buffeted him, he didn't get blown off course the way Brooke did. He stepped confidently into the crosswalk, eyeing the cars as though to still them with the force of his will.

They didn't encroach on his space.

Kenneth reached the opposite curb and extended a hand, drawing Brooke against him. "I was worried."

"Traffic was a disaster," she muttered into his coat. "I got stuck behind the bus. I think I inhaled a whole tank full of diesel exhaust."

"I figured something like that," he replied. "Traffic is always rotten this time of day, and the weather makes it worse. As a fellow southerner, I wasn't sure how you were navigating it all." He waved a hand at the offending precipitation. "Wintery mix is such an innocuous name for this devil's slush."

"I know it," Brooke replied. "I won't lie. It was pretty scary driving."

"I can tell. You're shivering. The light is about to turn back in our favor. Let's hurry inside."

Brooke didn't respond. Instead, she nestled deeper into Kenneth's jacket, letting him guide her forward, into the street. He made another decisive crossing and ushered her into the lobby of his building.

"She okay?" a random voice asked.

"Yeah, just cold. She's so tiny, and it's nasty outside," Kenneth replied. "I was afraid she would blow away to Wisconsin. I don't want to lose my girlfriend."

She giggled, stepping back from his coat. "You weren't wrong to worry. I had some doubts about my ability to make it across on my own." Biting her glove, she dragged her hand out and laced her fingers through Kenneth's. "Thanks for rescuing me, babe."

"Any time. Shall we go up?"

"Let's."

Kenneth waved to his neighbor and stepped away toward the elevator. Once the doors closed out the view of the lobby, Brooke threw her arms around Kenneth and tugged him down.

"There's a camera, you know," he murmured against her lips.

She shrugged. "I'm sure the security guard has seen people kiss before. I'm not proposing anything more vigorous."

"Aww." He stuck his lip out in a showy pout.

"In the elevator, silly. Once we're alone..."

"Aw, yeah."

They looked into each other's faces and burst out laughing.

A moment later, the elevator bounced to a stop, and the couple lurched out, hurrying down the hallway to Kenneth's apartment.

"Isn't this ridiculous?" Brooke asked with a chuckle.

"Madness," Kenneth agreed. "Feels like high school all over again."

"Tell me about it." Brooke tapped her toe impatiently as Kenneth fumbled his key out of his pocket and fitted it into the lock.

"Are you in a hurry, babe?" he asked.

"I could be."

Kenneth dropped the keys on the floor. "Oops."

"You know, if you play tricks, you get to have fun teasing me, but you're also delaying *us*." She knelt and scooped up the keys, handing them back to Kenneth.

"Oh!" Chuckling, he opened the door and stepped inside.

"You're in a good mood," she pointed out.

"Well, you're finally here," he told her. "I missed you. I'm also nervous as hell."

Brooke raised one eyebrow. "Why?"

"I have something to ask you," he said. "It's kind of a big deal, and I don't know how you're going to react."

"That sounds ominous. Maybe you should get it over with and put us both out of our misery." Despite her flippant tone, a queasy sensation began swooping in Brooke's belly.

"I agree. Set down that bag, and come sit with me," he suggested.

Brooke dropped her purse and overnight bag near the door, and let Kenneth lead her to the left-facing loveseat. Her heart began pounding.

Please don't be dumping me now, she willed. *Please don't be ending this now that I'm hooked.* That her thoughts didn't fit the context of his comments didn't even dawn on her. Blind panic welled up, and she squashed it down as best she could.

He turned partway to face her, grasping her hand and laying their laced fingers on his knee. He took a deep breath. "I need to ask you something," he said again. "I don't want you to take this the wrong way. I mean, to be honest, I talked to your sister, and she told me a little about... about your ex, and I don't want any of that bullshit getting tied up in this."

Confusion did nothing to assuage Brook's mounting panic. "Jordan? What does he have to do with anything?"

"Maybe I should get to the point," Kenneth said. "Brooke, I want you to move in with me. Are you willing?"

More confused than ever, Brooke lowered her eyebrows and stared at Kenneth. His warm, brown eyes looked tender... and worried. "Yes, I really appreciate it," she said. "It's great to have somewhere to stay while I look for a better place to live. I hated the idea of wasting money on some fleabag hotel."

"No, not that. I mean, if it's important to you to live separately, of course that's your choice, but I'm not talking about you crashing here temporarily. I want us to move in together... as a couple."

"You mean, long term?"

"Exactly."

Brooke swallowed hard. "I don't know, Kenneth. Isn't it kind of fast? We've been a couple since October, but it's barely December. Less than two months."

"I know," he agreed. "Normally I would have waited a few more months, but the thing with your apartment building..."

"I know." She bit her lip. "It's a sensible option, but..."

"But?"

"But I need a minute to think."

"You knew I would be asking eventually. Under the circumstances, why does it surprise you?"

Brooke regarded Kenneth's face, taking in each beloved feature. Short, dark hair curled close to his scalp. Wide, warm brown eyes fixed on her with undeniable heat. Broad nose and full lips peeked from under a neatly-trimmed beard. He looked so appealing and sweet. It tugged at her heart.

Why fight the inevitable? she asked herself. *Kenneth is it for me. He's just it. There will never be anything like this again. He loves me back. Loves me enough to tolerate all my waffling and overthinking. Willing to limit his job search so I can build my career. All he wants is for us to be together. To spend our nights together, even when we have rehearsal. To come home to each other.* The thought was undeniably compelling.

"It would be practical," she said again. "I think we're going to be pooling our resources more and more in the future. Why pay two rents when we only need to pay one?"

"Two sets of utilities..."

"But my car..."

"This building actually allocates two spaces per person, but both cars have to be registered to tenants. Didn't want you to get towed."

"Ah, thank you."

He smoothed her hair back from her face. "It's practical, but that's not why I want to."

"I know that," she said. "One thing I've learned so far is that I can trust you, Kenneth."

His smile grew from a wistful expression to a tender grin. "That means a lot to me, Brooke."

"I never thought *you* weren't good enough for *me*," she reminded him. "I was only ever concerned about holding you back."

"Like you could," he scoffed.

"Tell me one more way it's practical," Brooke urged. "I'm almost convinced."

"I have to go out of town for a few months in the spring. The lease isn't up until June. I hate the idea of paying for an empty apartment, and..."

"Sold," she said.

He grinned. "So, you'll move in?"

"I will," Brooke agreed. "When?"

"You said you had a rehearsal this Saturday, right?"

She nodded.

"Sunday then. I'll help."

"Perfect." Brooke shivered, unable to keep a smile from her face. "I'm happy."

"Me too."

"Kenneth?"

"Yes, honey?"

"I'm also still cold."

Kenneth sank back against the cushions of the sofa. "Well then, baby, why don't you come over here and see if I can warm you up."

Brooke grinned, rising to her feet and tugging her sweater over her head.

By the time Kenneth finished with her, she no longer felt any chill or stress. She lay collapsed against his chest, her head on his shoulder, limp as a well-fed kitten and just as content.

CHAPTER 11

Though she'd walked onto the stage more often than she could recall and she'd long since stopped being nervous about it, this time, the lights made Brooke sweat in her concert-black dress. To her right, the alto soloist glittered in a blue sequined dress, her hefty body tottering on pencil heels. The tenor soloist, a slender whip of a man, had added a wild red tie. Directly across from her, Kenneth caught her eye, looking handsome in his tux and freshly trimmed beard.

He winked.

What was I thinking, agreeing to this? she fretted. *I haven't soloed in years. Not since college. Do I* want *to do this?*

The time to protest had passed, so Brooke steeled her spine and turned forward, intentionally ignoring the audience she couldn't see in the darkened concert hall.

Dr. Davis stepped up onto his podium. He lifted his baton and directed the concertmaster to sound his string so the orchestra could tune.

Brooke let her gaze wander over the violins, then the woodwinds, and last the brass and low strings as they all aligned their pitches. She inhaled slowly through her nose and exhaled. *Shit. Here we go.*

The orchestra played a long, low chord. Then a short one followed by another long one. Another short chord. A running melisma. They crawled slowly through the first portion of the *Messiah* overture.

Brooke slowly shifted her weight from one foot to the other to prevent herself from locking her knees. Her heart thudded in time to the rhythm. Slow but heavy, pounding in her throat.

The second section of the overture began with the violins tripping quickly over a playful run. The violas and the lower strings chased after them. Then the winds joined in, and the tympani pounded. The oboes quacked while the clarinets tooted. Somehow, beneath the cheerful melody, a mournful tension took hold and grew. At last, they ended on a pleasant chord.

The tenor soloist stood up.

He's so slight, Brooke thought. *I wonder how much power he has.*

He answered by drawing in a huge lungful of air and singing, "'Cooooom-fort ye.'" Though gentle, his tone had more strength than she'd expected. She smiled as he moved confidently through the "Comfort Ye" recitative, and then flew into the "Ev'ry Valley" air. He played with the melismas, making them his own and savoring each turn and trill.

Gee. I hope my ornamentation doesn't clash. It's so much simpler and more traditional. I wish we'd had time to confer before the dress rehearsal.

He finished the aria, and Brooke stepped back into the midst of the soprano section for the choir's opening chorus, "And the Glory of the Lord." The familiar music helped soothe her jangling nerves.

This is good, she thought as the adrenaline of terror and the

joy of performing blended together to create a high no drug
could ever match.

The short chorus didn't take long, and then another solo
section began.

This time, it was Kenneth's turn to wow the audience,
and he did. His full, rich bass took hold of every molecule of
Brooke's body as he moved through the "Thus Saith the
Lord" recitative. As this narrative portion came to an end, he
glanced Brooke's direction, caught her eye, and winked.
Then, like the tenor, he dived into his aria, "But Who May
Abide." He put his own unique stamp on the challenging
melody, taking it to an even greater level of technical
demand.

I'm dazzled, Brooke thought. *It's so hard for the lower voice
parts—the alto and bass—to match their tone to the facile
mobility required for a piece like this, and yet, he touches each
note as lightly as a feather. Oh, I'm so in love with him.*

She fought to focus, because the next chorus, "And He
Shall Purify," was one of the most difficult they would be
performing, and it had several blind entrances that could not be
felt, only memorized. *It's not my favorite, but it's really showy.
Savvy listeners will appreciate how hard we've worked to
prepare it.*

It would seem they did. Subtle shifts in the shadowy figures
beyond the stage suggested they had leaned forward in
anticipation. Despite the difficulty, Brooke didn't struggle to
properly count, nor to make note of her entrance pitches.
Muscle memory had taken over.

The next section went to the alto soloist, who put a
different, special spin on her recitative and aria. She passed the
torch to Kenneth with a simple cast of the eyes. He took it up
with gusto, setting the stage for one of the most popular
choruses in the entire piece, one Brooke was sure many

members of the audience had particularly come to hear. *One I've been looking forward to singing.*

The orchestra set them up by playing the lines leading up to the entrance of the entire soprano section. "'For unto us a child is born...'" she sang, relishing the long, complicated patterns of running notes that sounded so much more difficult than they were.

The pastoral symphony passed in a blink of peaceful, orchestral lines, and then it was finally Brooke's turn.

Oh, crap. It's me. Trying to breathe slowly, she stepped forward, approaching the microphone, and closed her eyes for a moment. *Center and breathe. Breathe. You can do this.* The light illuminated her face.

"'There were shepherds abiding in the fields,'" she sang, noticing her tone sounded a little thin. With all her concentration, she forced her attention to her gut, powering her voice so that she could fill the hall with sound. "'Keeping watch over their flocks by night.'"

The orchestra came in.

"'When lo, the angel of the Lord came upon them. And the glory of the Lord shone round about them. And they were sore afraid. And the angel said unto them, 'fear not, for behold I bring you good tidings of great joy, which shall be to all people. For unto you is born this day in the city of David, a savior which is Christ the Lord...'" As Brooke settled into singing, her nerves faded, and her concert high ratcheted up until it drowned her fear and put her into a dreamlike state.

More arias, recitatives and choruses passed. Brooke's longer solo, "Come Unto Him," flew by in a blink. Still, awareness didn't begin to return until halfway through the Hallelujah chorus, but even then, her dreamlike state persisted. The candlelit carol-sing nearly put her into a trance.

Then, applause thundered through the room

Brooke blinked, realizing her legs and back ached.

More applause. Lights. Brooke blinked as the dreamlike state retreated, leaving her exhausted. When the director indicated her, she bowed. Then, she bowed again with the choir.

The orchestra bowed and began to make their way off the stage. The house lights clicked on.

She stood blinking as the singers withdrew.

"Come on, baby," Kenneth urged. His voice startled her. He took her arm and led her to the back. "Are you okay?"

She shook her head. "Concert high," she muttered.

"I hear ya. I'm flying. Tell ya what... when I was younger, my folks used to buy me ice cream after a performance. Wanna wake up with some sugar and then head home... to our apartment?"

His big grin drew her back toward the real world. "I'm glad you're driving. You're more used to this than I am."

"You'll be okay," he said. "But don't be surprised. The high is addictive. You'll want to solo again. I guarantee it."

"As long as you're with me," she replied.

The bleachers in a college gym felt just as lovely as the ones in the high school gym where Brooke had attended many pep rallies. She arched her aching back, digging a knuckle in and wishing for chairs with backrests. The roar echoing off the high ceilings made her ears ache. The bunting hanging from every corner did nothing to muffle its intensity, though it did add a touch of elegance to the otherwise mundane surroundings.

On the floor, row upon row upon endless row of graduates shuffled and squirmed in folding chairs, waiting for the president of the university to stop chattering on, so *their* moments could commence. As expected, they started with the graduate students.

"Receiving a doctor of musical arts degree, Kenneth Tyrone Hill. Mr. Hill wrote a gospel opera called 'Jimmy at the River,' which the Chicago Children's Opera premiered in November. Congratulations, Dr. Hill."

Brooke's two-fingered whistle contrasted with the polite pattering of applause as Kenneth mounted the stage in his funny, floppy hat and long-sleeved robe in the university's colors. He glanced up at her and winked before shaking hands with the president and collecting his diploma.

Brooke's mind wandered immediately thereafter as dozens of master's students, followed by hundreds of undergraduates traversed the stage. She vividly recalled her own college graduations—both of them. The thrill of receiving affirmation of her hard work and sacrifice. The joy. The disappointment that no one had come to witness her moment. The memory of that maelstrom swirled around her, leaving her even more uncomfortable than the bleachers on which she sat.

At last, Zuniga, Angie, accepted her Bachelor of Science in Nursing, and the graduation ceremony ended. Brooke made her way, in a suffocating crowd of well-wishers, to the door through which grinning graduates streamed into the arms of their friends and family. They found positions around the spacious lobby to pose for photos, as the snowstorm outside provided a less-than-appropriate backdrop.

This must be a lovely ceremony in May. Much bigger though. What a trade-off. I graduated in December, and it was packed as hell, but at least we could go outside into tolerable weather and take pictures with a park and some trees in the background.

"Brooke!" Kenneth's glorious basso shouted her name over the din, and she met warm brown eyes, nearly overflowing with

166

joy. She shouldered aside a teenager who was staring at her cell phone and flew into Kenneth's arms. He squeezed her.

"You did it," she whispered. "I'm so proud of you!"

"It's so awesome!" he punched the air with his free hand. "I did it!"

"You sure did, Dr. Hill." She smiled.

He kissed her. "I'm so glad you're here, baby."

"Of course. Where else would I be?"

"I thought you might have rehearsal. Isn't there a concert soon?"

"It's the day after tomorrow," she explained, "so of course there's a rehearsal, but I requested the time off. I have been to every rehearsal this year, no matter the time. Nancy didn't mind. She was worried I wouldn't be *here*. As if there was any choice. The man I love is receiving his doctorate. Where else would I be?"

"I'm glad you came," he said softly, so softly she almost couldn't hear him.

"So am I," she replied. "So very glad."

He leaned in and laid a warm kiss on her lips. "So very, very glad."

CHAPTER 12

"That was some landing," Brooke commented, pulling her carryon out from under the seat in front of her.

"Well, it's windy," Kenneth pointed out. "I'm glad it wasn't worse."

She glanced at him. "I had no idea someone with such a dark complexion could turn green."

"Brooke, please," he muttered, swallowing hard.

Brooke stroked his cheek, enjoying the sensation of coarse stubble beneath her fingers. "I'm sorry. I didn't realize you would get airsick."

"Yeah, well, I did." He swallowed again.

"Look, we're moving," she said, urging him to his feet. "Let's get out of here."

"I think that would be a good idea," Kenneth agreed. He hoisted himself to his feet with a noisy groan, tugging his backpack out from under the seat in front of him as he went. "I'm getting old," he commented.

"I don't think so. You look great."

"I do? Look at these grays." He ran his hand over his hair.

"I don't know. I can't see the top of your head. You're tall. I'm short. What I see looks damned sexy."

"Oh." Kenneth shook his head, and when he stilled, his ashen color had returned to normal. He leaned down and dropped a quick kiss on her lips. "Thank you, baby."

The people ahead of them started moving forward, and Kenneth ducked out of the seats into the aisle, dragging Brooke behind him. She clung to his fingers. Together they hustled out of the plane and into the busy Dallas-Fort Worth International Airport.

Once clear of the jetway, Kenneth guided Brooke out of the hustling mobs of people racing from gate to gate. "When is our flight?"

"Tomorrow at ten," she replied. "Time to have dinner with my sister and nephew, and then cuddle up at their house for tonight before..."

"Before we face the onslaught of my younger brothers and sister, Mama, Dad and Granny?"

"Yes, that."

"You're not nervous about this, are you, honey?"

"A bit," Brooke replied. "I mean, I know your family means a lot to you."

"And so do you," he reminded her.

She smiled, though it felt more like a tense stretching of her facial muscles than an expression of happiness. "Thank you. I'm also a little nervous to be here. I'm glad to see my sister, but I hope my dad doesn't get wind of it. He'll ruin everyone's Christmas."

"Ouch. Is he that bad?" Kenneth asked.

"Worse," Brooke replied. Then, not wanting to get into more detail, she grasped Kenneth's hand and led him toward the exit. "Come on. Autumn said she would pick us up by the American Airlines ticket counter. That's a bit of a hike from here."

"After that flight, I don't think I'll mind. I need to stretch my knees."

"Stretch away, babe."

They hurried through the airport, past stores and restaurants from which the scent of old grease wafted horribly. "Smells like french fry time," Brooke commented.

"With frozen fish," Kenneth added.

Brooke wrinkled her nose. "Lovely."

"Isn't it, though?"

They found their way to the ticket counter and out the door. The gust of wind that met them beyond the sliding door felt like... *home*.

"That's so great!" Kenneth murmured.

"Nice," Brooke agreed. "What do you think it is, about 60?"

"At least," he agreed. "Is winter in Texas usually so pleasant?"

"It can be. We get cold sometimes, but not Chicago cold."

"50s?"

"Or less," Brooke agreed, "but snow is rare and when it does happen, it's a dusting."

"Sounds tolerable. You know, this might be a mistake."

"What?" Brooke asked as she scanned the pick-up area in search of her sister's car. *I wonder if she still drives the same Camry.*

"Coming south in the winter. It was already way too cold and wet for my taste, and we can't really expect anything better until April. Now, we're going to get a taste of southern winter and then go back."

Brooke frowned. "You have a point. I do miss southern winter, that's for sure." Though the conversation seemed idle, it struck Brooke in a weak place. *If not for me, Kenneth would be headed south come summer. He's staying in a cold, wet climate he doesn't like... for me.* The unfairness of what she was asking him struck her again.

He volunteered for it, she reminded herself. *I didn't ask him to do anything. He chose it. He chose me.*

Somehow, the thought didn't soothe her. *He's always been better to me than I deserve.* Since she still didn't know how her career goals, Kenneth's career goals and their relationship fit together, she shoved the idea away, but the lingering sense of wrongness wouldn't be dismissed. It hovered in the background of her mind, making her anxious.

A car honked, and Brooke looked up to see a small Chevy pickup. The window slid down and Autumn's mane of dark blonde, wavy hair swung forward as she leaned out. "Hey, guys. Get in!"

Brooke opened the passenger door and slid into the center seat, setting her bag on her lap. Kenneth scrambled in beside her, tossing his duffle at his feet.

"How was your flight?" Autumn asked as Brooke slid an arm around her sister for a sideways hug.

"Bumpy," Brooke informed her. "I still feel a little green. I hope our flight out tomorrow is better."

"Sorry to hear that," Autumn apologized. "If you want, I can do an aura cleanse and meditation with you, to help you let go."

"I might take you up on that," Brooke said.

"Sounds interesting," Kenneth agreed.

"Sorry about the abrupt greeting," Autumn said. She eased the car into the line of vehicles that constantly flowed past. "I'll take some more time when we're home and out of this mess. No matter how enlightened I get, the traffic around the airport still gives me anxiety."

"I can understand why," Kenneth commented, regarding

the snarl of cars. "We haven't even entered the freeway yet. What's that like?"

"A nightmare," Brooke informed him. "It's like Chicago, but with much less public transportation. I mean, there are busses, and also the DART, but... most Texans prefer to drive themselves."

"So I see." He turned to the window.

Brooke could see his shoulders tense as Autumn made her way out of the airport and merged onto the freeway. There, a steady stream of cars flew by, bumper to bumper, at top speed. "Isn't Atlanta similar?" she asked.

"It is," Kenneth agreed, "but my folks teach in a suburb, and apart from the occasional concert or shopping excursion, we stayed in our little corner and away from the congestion."

"I suppose all city dwellers try to do the same. All but the taxi and bus drivers, who don't have a choice," Brooke commented.

"Most likely," Autumn agreed. "I know I do. My everyday world exists in about fifteen square miles between my place, which is on Dad's property, my shop, my ex's apartment and my son's school. I try to stay inside that area as much as possible. By the way, my ex decided he needed River for Christmas this year. He won't be home until after New Year's... unless he actually needs someone to *parent* him." She rolled her eyes.

"Aw, shoot," Brooke complained. "Your ex is still a butthead, Autumn."

"I agree, but what's done is done. It was fun while it lasted... some of the time."

"Um, Autumn, speaking of Dad," Brooke asked hesitantly, "are you sure he isn't going to burst in? You know I'm not comfortable seeing him."

"I know, honey." Autumn released the wheel with one

hand and gripped Brooke's shoulder in a gentle squeeze. "I didn't tell him I was expecting you, and he's always been very respectful of my privacy. I mean, the one and only time he tried to burst in without permission, he caught me in bed with my flavor of the month. I don't think he ever wants to see that again."

"Weren't you embarrassed?" Brooke asked. Her own face felt hot at the thought. *Lord, if someone burst in on me and Kenneth, I'd die.*

Kenneth's hand slipped into hers, as though he had heard her thought. He squeezed gently.

"I'm not embarrassed," Autumn replied. "It was him invading my privacy, not me doing something wrong. He tried to guilt me about my behavior, but I reminded him about his manners, and he left me alone after that. He now calls before he comes over, and respects me if I say no."

"He's always respected you more," Brooke muttered.

"You're right," Autumn agreed. "Dad's an asshole. I know that, you know that, everyone knows that. No one wants you to subject yourself to his terrible behavior, and no one will on my watch."

"I appreciate that," Brooke said softly.

Kenneth squeezed her hand again.

Silence fell in the cab of the pickup as Autumn focused on the traffic. Kenneth watched the snarl in palpable agitation, and Brooke sat stewing in her anxiety.

The city flowed by, skyscrapers and apartment complexes gradually transforming into urban sprawl. First, tightly packed neighborhoods of sloppy, tumbledown houses. Then friendlier neighborhoods with lawns and oak trees. Last, suburban cookie-cutter subdivisions gave way to semi-rural ones with quarter-acre or bigger lots. Here, chickens roosted in yards, and the rare horse stuck its head out of a field to watch them pass with solemn eyes.

Autumn turned into a long gravel driveway marked with an ostentatious wrought-iron fence.

"This is where your dad lives?" Kenneth whistled, eying the quarter-acre front yard. Behind it, a sprawling, single-story house in golden bricks seemed to glow in the sunlight. Front windows, washed daily by the housekeeper, posed a threat to the grackles and mockingbirds in the mesquite trees that lined the sidewalk leading up to the door. The green metal roof gleamed. In fact, the whole building had the appearance of money brought to life.

It made Brooke ill to look at it. "Don't get excited," she replied. "I haven't been inside the house since I changed my major to music."

"He disowned you?" Kenneth's eyes widened.

"Nah, I'd be welcome to visit if I wanted to," Brooke explained. "It's just that he's so rude and sarcastic. I don't have any patience for it. He ruins every visit by trying to force me to admit I made a mistake."

"I don't think you did, for what it's worth," Kenneth said. "You're a talented musician, which is objectively verifiable since you not only auditioned your way into the symphony chorale, you even managed to solo for them. You're also a gifted teacher, as evidenced by how well your students—many of them freshmen, by the way—win competitions. You clearly found your niche, and whatever's stuck in his craw has more to do with him than you."

Though the words were right, the pall cast over Brooke's senses as they entered the shadow of her childhood home dampened even Kenneth's irresistible warmth.

"He's right, you know," Autumn said.

Brooke noticed that her sister's voice and Kenneth's held

the same affection. *People do love and respect me; people who truly know me and people who want to know me.* She filed away the realization so she could think about it later.

Autumn continued speaking soothing truths. "Dad's issues are his own, and the sooner you embrace that and stop expecting him to be some kind of... anything positive to you, the better and healthier you'll be. Please, don't let his hang-ups become your problem."

"You make that sound so easy," Brooke commented bitterly. "He's my *father*. Who doesn't want their father's blessing on their life choices?"

"Everyone wants that," Autumn agreed, "but not everyone gets it. It's okay to mourn the father you didn't have and move on. Don't you have love and support in your life?"

"I'm starting to," Brooke said, squeezing Kenneth's hand again.

"And for that, I'm thankful," Autumn said. "Thank you, Kenneth."

"For what?" he asked.

They passed beyond the house into the Texas sunshine beyond, and immediately, Brooke felt lighter.

"For putting up with Brooke's porcupine quills. She doesn't want to be so prickly. I know it, but..."

"Hey, I'm right here," Brooke protested, thankful her laugh only sounded moderately brittle. "Can we save the love-fest for a bit? You two are making me sound pathetic."

Autumn laughed. "Okay, okay. I'm sorry I got so heavy."

Brooke looked at her with a raised eyebrow that Autumn, navigating the long driveway didn't see.

"It's good to see you," Brooke said, trying to steer the conversation back toward neutral territory instead of an analysis of her personality flaws.

"Same, sis. I miss you so much. I wish you could have found

a job a bit closer so I could see you more than once every five years, but then again, getting away and making space was probably good for you."

Brooke nodded. "Chicago is great, except for the weather... and the traffic. But I love my job and look at what else the city brought me." She leaned against Kenneth's shoulder. A touch on the top of her head suggested a kiss. She smiled.

Autumn pulled the car to a stop beside the guest house, a two-story structure fronted with white plastic siding, black shutters around a prominent bay window, and cheerful bougainvillea blooming in the yard. A massive oak-shaded the driveway. "Well, this is it," she announced.

"I think this is about the same size as the house my entire family grew up in, up until a few years ago, and there are eight of us, including my grandmother."

"There's nothing special about a big house," Brooke said. "It's what's inside the rooms that makes a place cozy or cold."

"Now that I agree with," he said. "Shall we?" He opened the door and hopped from the cab, stretching his arms up over his head and releasing a groaning roar.

"What a hunk," Autumn said with a giggle. "Sure you don't want to overshare just a little... pretty please?"

Brooke turned to her sister and raised one eyebrow.

"Okay, okay. Never mind. Scooch on out and I'll show you where to put your stuff."

"Will we be staying in River's room?"

"I doubt you'd want to. He has so many Legos on the floor. I set up the guest room."

"A guest house with a guest room? What next?" Brooke shook her head.

"Dad likes the finer things," Autumn explained. "I'm damned lucky. Rent on a place of this size would bankrupt me. I'm spoiled."

"Is it worth the tradeoff though?" Brooke asked. "I mean, I'm far from flush financially, but I pay my own way, and I don't have to put up with anyone's bullshit."

"But that's the thing," Autumn explained. "I don't put up with it. I call him out on it, tell him to shut up, kick him out if he acts like an ass. He can only control me if I let him, and I don't let him."

"Well, I don't have the time or energy to deal with that," Brooke said.

"You don't have to," Autumn replied. "If someone is bad for you, it's up to you to decide how to deal with them, and not dealing is a perfectly legitimate option. If it's for your own greatest good, never explain or apologize. Just do what's best for you."

"That's also not easy," Brooke commented, "but, hey, Sis, can't we save the metaphysical counseling session just for a little while and have some fun together?"

"Of course, of course." Autumn jumped out of the car, grabbing her purse from behind the driver's seat, and made her way up to the house, fitting the key into the lock.

"This is already a bit tense," Kenneth commented, stepping up behind Brooke and sliding his arms around her waist.

She leaned back against his chest, enjoying the softness and the warmth.

"Come on, lovebirds," Autumn called. "It's open."

Brooke smiled and stepped forward, letting Kenneth's hands slide down her arms until she could lace her fingers through his. "Best to get inside," she said. "We don't want any of *his* spies to tattle on us."

"Lordy, I'm stuck in a thriller," Kenneth quipped.

Brooke glanced over her shoulder to see him roll his eyes skyward. She made a face and poked him in the ribs.

"Hey!"

"Silly guy."

She led him in and stopped dead, staring up into the spacious, two-story living room. "This is a guest house? This was built in the last five years? Be honest, Autumn. Did Dad build this just for you and River?"

"He did," she said. "It sometimes embarrasses me, but... my son is worth it. I can't afford to give him a life like this. Come on, let me show you to the guest room."

Brooke held her bag with one hand and Kenneth's fingers with the other as they followed Autumn through a living room with brown furniture and sunset golden walls decorated in shades of yellow, red and orange. Along the wall, a stairway with polished wooden treads and white risers led to an open loft with a sitting area filled with toys. Four doors lined the rear wall. The ones on either end were closed, suggesting occupied bedrooms. In the center, open doors revealed a bedroom with a brass bed and white comforter, and a bathroom with a dinosaur footprint bathmat and a shower curtain with jungle foliage on it.

"Just leave your stuff in here," Autumn suggested, "and feel free to take over the bathroom for the night. River won't be back for another week, sadly."

"I'm so sad I'm missing him. I feel like the worst aunt ever."

"Hey, I get it," Autumn said. "It goes along with being a teacher. You get great breaks, but not any time you want them."

"Right," Brooke agreed. "Please tell him Auntie loves him and was so sorry to miss him."

"I'll do that."

"Do you all mind if I take a shower?" Kenneth asked. "I hate the way airplanes make me feel, like germs are climbing all over me."

Brooke looked at her boyfriend with an amused half-smile curving her lips. She raised one eyebrow.

"Yes, I have issues. I get airsick, and I'm a bit of a germophobe, okay?"

"Also defensive," Brooke teased. "I guess I'm not the only one who overthinks things, eh?" She stepped up to Kenneth and wrapped her arms around him. "I love you more because you're not perfect. Remember that."

His tense expression eased a bit. "Thank you, Brooke." He leaned down and kissed her forehead before ducking into the bathroom and shutting the door behind him.

Brooke began to giggle. Making her way down the hall, she stepped into the bedroom and tossed her pack onto the bed, sinking to a seat on the mattress.

"Do you want to rest?" Autumn asked.

"Nah, I'm kinda wired," Brooke replied, bouncing back to her feet and crossing to the window that looked onto the yard... and across it to the big main house where she'd grown up. She shivered.

"I can help with that," Autumn suggested.

"By combing my aura?" Brooke asked, half-joking to distract herself from her nerves.

"Boy, you're full of teases today, aren't you?" Autumn commented, tossing her heavy blond hair over her shoulder. "Don't laugh. I make good money doing this for people, and they love it. I promise, if you let me, I can make you feel more relaxed and happier."

"You're welcome to try," Brooke replied, "but I'm probably the most anxious person you know."

"You might be surprised," Autumn replied. "Lots of people feel anxious about lots of things, real or imagined. I can help if you want to be helped. What do you say, Brooke? You left home five years ago, and it was absolutely the right thing to do. You weren't able to separate your feelings from Dad's expectations, so you needed physical space to make your own way. I don't see you making huge strides, though, to leave his bullshit behind. You act like you're still trying to prove something to him."

"What do you mean?" Brooke asked, immediately defensive.

"You haven't stopped treating your job like it's your identity. I haven't forgotten that you almost let Kenneth go in case there might possibly be a choice to make between him and your job, as if you couldn't get another job. Brooke, you could work anywhere. Like literally any state or major metropolitan area—not to mention a wealth of small towns across the nation —would be glad to have you, especially now that you have five years' experience."

"None would have the prestige," Brooke pointed out. "This is a charter school for the arts. Those are rare and special."

"And Kenneth isn't?" Autumn asked. "Wouldn't it be just as cool to create a prestigious program out of nothing? Or to find a high-powered public high school program? Texas takes its all-state choir *very* seriously. There's literally a thousand career opportunities out there. Why is this one job worth more than your soul mate? You're not going to deny he is, are you?"

Brooke shook her head. "Kenneth is amazing. I love him, and I'm so very glad he loves me too. He asked me to move in with him."

"What did you say?" Autumn demanded.

"I moved in three weeks ago."

"Shut up! You're living with him? Oh, my God. Way to go! I was so afraid you would chicken out."

"I didn't chicken out. I don't want to be apart from him, and we were both losing sleep trying to get home to our separate apartments. Besides, my building was sold, and I needed a new place to live. It was time to pool our resources, so we did."

"You made a decision without me? I'm so proud of you!"

Autumn grabbed Brooke's hand and hurried her down the stairs to the main room where she flopped down on the sofa, dragging her sister behind her.

"Yes, I'm a real grown-up now," Brooke said dryly.

"Good!" Autumn said. "Please, please let me cleanse your aura. You're in better shape than I realized, Brooke. All you need is to move past your stuck thinking, and you'll be on the right path. From there, all your meditation, grounding and manifestation will be sooooo much more open. You want that, don't you? You do meditate, don't you?"

"Um..." Brooke bit her lip. "I'm out of practice."

Autumn pursed her lips. "No wonder you're stuck. I can clean you up, but you need to make choices to take care of your soul, not just your job. I'm glad you've moved in with Kenneth, and y'all are happy together, but that's not the same as taking care of yourself. You and he deserve a healthy relationship, but you can't have that until *you* are as healthy as possible."

"I get that," Brooke said. "Kenneth has made me reevaluate my whole life plan."

"Has he?" Autumn challenged her. "Has he, or have you forced him into your life plan?"

"I didn't force anything," Brooke protested. "He offered..."

"And why was that the only option? Why is it so damned impossible for you to make any alterations to your plan for him? Isn't he worth it?"

"He's worth anything," Brooke breathed.

"See, you sound in love, but you're holding back from fully committing. That's why I want to help you out. You need to let go of some unhealthy attachments and make your own path."

"Golly, you're pushy. Talk about the hard sell." Brooke rolled her eyes.

"Only because it's you. I love you, and I hate to see you tied up this way."

"Okay, do it then," Brooke exclaimed at last, exasperated by her sister's pestering. "I didn't expect to come and see you and get a New Age pounce right through the door, but I can see I won't get any peace until you've done your thing."

"Great!" Autumn swiveled to open the drawer in her coffee table and drew out a small velvet pouch.

"Someone got a new toy," Brooke commented. "I will never forget how excited you get over a crystal. What is it this time?"

"Aqua quartz," Autumn proclaimed proudly. "It's got all the benefits of clear quartz, but it's been treated with gold. Look at this beauty!" She upended the pouch into her hand.

"Wow, that *is* pretty," Brooke said, examining the shimmering blue-green stone. "Can I see it?"

Autumn grinned and handed her the stone. Brooke couldn't help but smile, looking at the smooth, shining surface. "I like this thing. What will you do with it?"

"It's good for your upper chakras. I have other great stones as well. I think if I started laying out a grid, you'd roll your eyes, but there are a few things I have that can help you."

"Chakras?"

"You haven't forgotten, Brooke, how we used to explore all these things. You gave it up when you went to college, but you remember, don't you?"

"I remember," Brooke replied. "I never felt able to relax there no matter how long I sat in the lotus position, and eventually, I stopped trying."

"You weren't listening to your higher self," Autumn informed her. "Here, let me have that back. I have a different one for you to hold."

Brooke surrendered the aqua quartz with regret, but then Autumn brought out something purple with white veins. "Here, hold this in your left hand."

"Why left?" Brooke asked, memories nibbling at the edges

of her awareness.

"It's your non-dominant hand, your receptive hand. Here."

Brooke accepted the stone. Its polished circumference fit her palm, and she couldn't stop herself from stroking it with her thumb. "What is it?" she asked.

"Lepidolite. It will help you receive the feeling that you are worthy of healthy relationships. If you can cling to and prioritize them, you won't have time to waste trying to please *anyone* who is taking advantage of you. Just hold it. Play with it or stroke it if you want. Also, kick off your shoes. It's important your feet are in contact with the floor tiles."

"Okay." Brooke had no problem with the request, though it felt strange to be barefoot, as she'd been wishing for more coverings for her feet for months. "I don't know that stones actually do anything."

"I know," Autumn agreed. "Sometimes you just need a worry stone to keep your hand busy, right?"

"Right," Brooke agreed, glad to have a sensible reason why the lepidolite pleased her so much. She traced a white vein with the tip of her thumb. "So, what do you mean that I wasn't listening to my higher self?"

"When you went to college, you let yourself become Dad's puppet for a while. You studied what he told you to study. You dated who he told you to date. How did that work out for you?"

"Badly. I still have a hard time thinking he meant to do me harm though."

"The unintended harm is the most insidious," Autumn told her. She lifted the aqua quartz and slowly circled it round and round above Brooke's head.

"For over a year of your life, you shut down the possibility that there could be more for you than what Dad wanted. You shut down the possibility that there could be more than work and money," she said, "and, in his world, work *is* money. It is the job, it is the purpose of work and it is the purpose of life. He will have his own consequences for those choices, but they were never meant to be yours."

Autumn pinned her sister with a meaningful stare. "There is more for you, Brooke. There is more than the mere earning of money. There is spiritual health. You realized part of this on your own, but the rest got stuck. Your work, your love, your very self is more, higher and better than earning money."

Brooke nodded. "I know that."

"You know it, but you don't believe it, hon, or you'd be living in better balance. Recognize your work as a means to an end. Yes, you work because you enjoy it, but you're still hoarding the money, not saving to achieve a higher goal, but to prove something to a sour old man who can't understand anything better."

Brooke inhaled deeply and released her breath. When she did, she felt lighter, though she couldn't honestly say what had changed.

Autumn moved the quartz lower and traced a slow figure-eight over Brooke's eyes. "Because of your obsession with trying to make Dad proud of you, you let yourself be drawn in directions that did not serve you. Even though you eventually rejected his plans for you, you've lacked wisdom about how to engage along your new path. Your life is entirely out of balance. Only now, years later, have you begun to pull back from making work the center of your life instead of just one of many aspects you can draw meaning from."

Again, Brooke took a deep breath. This time, she let it out slowly. Her exhalation seemed to push Autumn's arm lower. She continued making her figure-eight motion, but now over Brooke's throat.

"You love to sing, but you almost stopped singing altogether because you were so busy working. You almost seem to have guilt about your music, and only focus on the work and the money. You teach people to make music, but you almost lost your own."

This felt true to Brooke. She recalled the euphoria of her most recent performance; a joy she'd used to comfort herself in school but had scarcely experienced since. *Kenneth is bringing this back to me. He's giving me back pieces of myself. It's how he loves me... but how do I love him?*

The aquamarine stone moved lower again, slowing tracing arcane symbols in the air just beyond Brooke's breasts. "You give your love to your students. You've given them what you denied yourself, but, Brooke, you don't have to hand it all over and leave your own cup empty. Love is for you too. You deserve to receive it. You can receive it. You can and you should. The supply is limitless. You still hesitate to accept even Kenneth's love, don't you?"

"Uhhhh..." Brooke didn't know how to answer that.

"You think he'll eventually leave to pursue his dreams, and you'll be stuck where you are, and you'll lose him and it will all be normal, don't you?"

Brooke swallowed.

"If you remain stuck, and he remains with you, neither of you will have your best. Allow love to enter your heart, Brooke. Feel the stone in your hand. Feel the energy moving down your body. It's been trapped and stagnating, but it's growing freer. Here, take this." She placed the aqua quartz in Brooke's other hand. "You have more to give than the sweat of your brow. You have more to offer than your labor. You can offer love, passion and many other good things. You can be a balanced lover or even a friend, though I imagine you haven't made many connections, have you?"

Brooke shook her head. Her power of speech, for the moment, had fled.

Autumn claimed another stone, this one black with a reddish tinge to it. She slowly waved it over Brooke's belly. "You're too overactive here. All your energy comes from your work and your drive for financial success, but with no channel to move it up to higher things, and with no grounding to send it to the earth, it leaves you agitated. You don't have to feel so anxious all the time, but it means you'll have to release the idea that financial success is anything more than a means to an end. You should not tie your sense of yourself and your self-worth to your work. You're much more important than that."

Something tight and ugly in Brooke's belly eased. It hurt like a blow to the middle, and then a rush of warmth rolled up her body and back down before crashing around her waist and pooling.

Again, the stone moved lower. "Your sacral never truly shut down. You allowed your creativity to remain because you needed it to power your work. That's why you were able to connect to Kenneth. I'm fairly sure every time you have sex with him, it heals you a little, but it's not enough. Sex alone is not love, any more than work alone is life. Yes, enjoy your work, and yes, enjoy sex, but recognize that without integration, you can only have a pale shadow of what is possible."

A tingling sensation crept up Brooke's spine.

"Soon, you'll be ready to move into that plane again. You've been ready for years, but somehow, you never believe it was a possibility for you. You still don't, but you're trying. Keep trying."

The pooling energy crashed and rolled against her lower extremities until Brooke felt quite ill.

"The blockage here may be worst of all," Autumn said. "Dad did this to you when you were a small child. He made you lack confidence in yourself at the deepest level. He tried to destroy your sense of self so he could make you into what he wanted—a puppet whose strings he controlled. I don't know why, but sometimes I hate him for it. You should too."

Brooke clenched her fists. When she opened them—palms up so the stones balanced on the center of each—they felt warm and they tingled. Golden light sparkled behind her eyelids.

"Acknowledge the hate so you can release it. Acknowledge the anger and hurt of a motherless child whose father relished control more than he loved her. A father who could never see her for who she was and tried to impose shallow values on you in place of your intrinsic worth. It was sick and wrong."

"Yes, I do hate him," Brooke breathed. "So help me, God, I do." *Who else am I angry with? With Mom, for leaving before I could ever know her? It makes no sense. She didn't choose to die, but that doesn't matter. She left me alone with him. And even Autumn... she didn't know, but she took my mother away.*

Those little sparks of anger and grief flew upward, out of the conflagration of rage that formed the core of her psyche. The source of her power and of her torment.

Again, the energy rolled and crashed, but this time, when it hit the blockage at the base of her spine, it burst through. Straight down her legs and out the bottoms of her feet into the cool tiles beneath.

"There you go," Autumn said. "Now, we need to cut away this cord he uses to draw energy from you."

Vaguely, Brooke saw her sister draw a silver knife from the drawer and circle behind her.

"What in the Sam Hill are you doing?" Kenneth's voice cut into the rolling energy Brooke was pouring into the ground, drawing up, and releasing again.

"Don't be alarmed," Autumn said, and her voice sounded distant and cool, as though the moon itself could speak. "I won't harm her. She has a negative attachment, a cord if you will, to our father. It doesn't serve her, and so it must be cut away.

She'll be less panicky overall without him in her head all the time."

Brooke could sense movement behind her, and then Autumn circled around, the knife still clutched in one hand.

"You're free now," Autumn said. "Concentrate on placing a boundary between him and you. You've given him too much power over your life and choices, but you don't have to do that anymore. You are free. You are perfect, just as you are, and you are worthy to love, to give and to receive. No need to turn yourself inside out or define yourself as a fat bank account and a house in the suburbs."

Unable to move or speak against the energy rushing through her, Brooke closed her eyes.

"What's that now?" Kenneth asked.

"Selenite," Autumn replied. "It will draw the last of the negative energy out of her aura. She's going to feel funny for a while, but in the end, this will be very good for her. You'll see. Brooke? Honey? You should drink some water."

Brooke blinked at her sister. Her whirling thoughts began to clear. "Water sounds good," she croaked. "What the hell just happened?"

"Nine years of trapped energy just broke free," Autumn explained, still gently waving what Brooke now recognized as her sister's favorite crystal—a slightly bent rod of luminous white—slowly up and down a few inches above her body. She reached out and plucked with her free hand, as though pulling a worm from the earth. "Kenneth, hon, could you pour Brooke a glass of water? Cups to the left of the sink, filtered water and ice in the fridge door."

"Sure thing," he replied.

In the background, Brooke could hear the rumbling of gears as the machine spewed out crushed ice and then a soft hiss as water flowed over it.

Autumn plucked again.

"Now what are you doing?"

"Dead cords," Autumn replied. "Attachments that no longer serve you. Possibly college acquaintances, former students, anyone who's not currently part of your life. They don't harm you, but they do take up some space and energy, so it doesn't hurt to remove them."

"You say things I don't understand," Brooke muttered.

"You say things I don't understand too, hon," her sister reminded her. "Your chords are nothing like mine, and cadences and crescendos and sforzandos. Remember when you were working on your master opus?"

"I know all those terms," Kenneth pointed out. He appeared out of nowhere at Brooke's side and handed her a glass of water.

"Thank you, baby. You know more musical terms than I do, for sure."

"Well, if you're worried, there are more doctoral degrees to be had, and plenty of schools to offer them."

Brooke immediately opened her mouth to refute his words, and then slowly closed it. *Why not?* her mind, now bubbling with energy, demanded.

"It was never part of the plan," her logic pointed out.

So what? her intuition argued. *Plans are roadmaps, not contracts. You can always decide on a different route.*

"Do you actually *want* to go back to school?" reason demanded.

Who knows? intuition snapped back, *but why should I refuse to consider it just because I never have before? Life doesn't stop after graduation. Kenneth's older than me and just graduating. Look how exciting it is for him to plan his career, to make choices, to follow his dreams wherever the wind takes him.*

Realization dawned. *I'm limiting myself to only what's in*

front of me, and even if I stay in this job forever, nothing says that's all I can do. I can live. I can sing. I can fall in love. Marry. Have children, or not. Adopt a ferret. Or go to graduate school. There's nothing wrong with any of that.

"Stop," she said out loud to the two voices arguing in her head. She took a sip of water and settled back against the cushions of the sofa.

"Stop what, hon?" Autumn asked.

"Nothing," Brooke replied. "Just thinking too hard, as usual."

Kenneth sat down beside her and adjusted her sideways, so she leaned against the arm of the sofa with her feet on his lap. "Cut that out," he ordered. "Just relax and be, baby. You don't have to answer all the questions at once."

Brooke tipped her head back. "I can feel your energy," she mumbled. "I could feel it from across the room. I could feel it from across the parking lot. It calls to me. That's why I can't resist you." She closed her eyes. A moment later, sleep claimed her.

"That sure was interesting," Kenneth said idly, patting Brooke's bare foot and admiring the silvery-green paint on her toenails.

"Wanna try it?" Autumn offered.

He laughed. "You sound like you're selling drugs. Is aura cleansing addictive?"

"Like exercise is," Autumn replied. She perched on a plush rocking chair at right angles to the sofa. "It makes you feel... healthy. Relaxed. Free. At least, that's how I feel."

"Is this a common reaction?" He indicated Brooke's prone form.

She shook her head. "Poor baby. If she doesn't turn loose of

Dad's judgment soon, she may become trapped in bitterness. She's too good a person for that. She deserves to be happy, but she doesn't know how to let herself be."

"I'm working on it," he pointed out.

"It's not yours to do," Autumn replied quickly. "Brooke's happiness lies in her own hands. She can choose to set up boundaries against intrusive people and live in peace, or she can choose to keep people-pleasing and wear herself out. There's nothing you can do for her, Kenneth, except to love her for who she is... and set up a few boundaries of your own."

Kenneth lowered his eyebrows and regarded his girlfriend's sister with a glower. "What do you mean by that?"

"You didn't have to let Brooke push you around with her ultimatums and silly demands. You can tell her no or tell her how you feel. She'll be okay making compromises and adjustments. That's how relationships work."

"You are the most uncomfortable person I've ever met," he said.

"I get that a lot," Autumn replied, flipping her long blond hair over her shoulder. "Don't get me wrong; Brooke told me a fair bit and I know how stubborn and set in her ways she can be. For an artist, she's nothing like a free spirit. But I can see something around you too. You're nervous. Why is that?"

"And why should I tell you something so personal?" he demanded. "I barely know you."

"I'm not asking you to tell me your secrets, but anything that concerns my sister concerns me. She sucks at taking care of herself, so I'm always on the lookout... when I can be. I'm asking for two reasons—one, to be sure you're not enabling her to stay stuck in her anxiety and her comfort zone."

Kenneth nodded. "That makes sense. No, I don't want her to keep on being nervous forever. I try to encourage her to view her options more broadly. What's the other reason?"

"Because one of you needs to be healthy. If you have hang-ups and problems ..."

"I see your point," Kenneth said. "I guess I have some things, like everyone else, but I don't think I'm too screwed up."

"Okay, then why did you hold out so much hope for Brooke while she was freaking out over her plans and trying to push you away?"

He shook his head, struggling to put into words something he'd never fully articulated. "Intuition, I guess. My mama and my granny always taught me to listen to myself. If something felt wrong, to run like hell, no matter what it looked like on paper. The flip side is, sometimes things just feel... right. Also, keep in mind the timeline. I met Brooke, we went on a few dates—really promising dates, mind you—where we found out we had amazing chemistry, multiple interests in common and a comfortable easy way of interacting. It felt like a future."

A hint of a smile crossed Kenneth's lips. "She startled the hell out of me when she backed off just as I was ready to move things forward, but the amount of time she took to 'think' was only about two weeks. I was finishing my degree. That kept me busy, and the next thing I know, she practically jumps me in the parking lot." He chuckled softly. "Apart from one tense conversation, we might not have seen each other during that time anyway. I know she went through a lot, but... well... she came right back."

"And you gave her a second chance," Autumn pointed out. "After she basically dumped you over nothing."

"You're looking at it wrong," Kenneth told her. He paused again. "Do any of those magic stones of yours help with being able to express myself better?"

"I'd offer to balance your throat chakra," she said. "Brooke dropped my aqua quartz, but it would be perfect for that. I can see it under the sofa there."

Kenneth shrugged. "Ask me another time. I guess I don't see it as her dumping me. It was a really intense start to a relationship, and she did have a valid point about us and our places in life. She took some time to think, and then she came back. Now we live together. I didn't *enjoy* the separation, but it's important to take your time and think when something's intense. She wanted space to do that. It's okay for her to take that space."

He glanced at Autumn and found her scrutinizing him with a quizzical expression. "What?"

"I'm not sure yet. Ask me another time."

"Fair enough," he agreed.

"Are you hungry? I bet when Brooke wakes up, she'll want something to eat right away. She's processing a lot, and it's stressful for her to be here."

"I could eat," Kenneth agreed. "What do you have in mind?"

"I could order delivery. Burgers? I know a great place..."

"What, you're not a vegetarian?" Kenneth raised his eyebrows.

"Usually I am," Autumn replied, "but I make the odd exception for a special occasion."

"Tell ya what, then," Kenneth suggested. "I know Brooke's been dying for some real Texas barbecue. What we have in Chicago is... it's okay, but it's not the same."

"Sounds good." Autumn dragged a phone out of the pocket of her wide-legged jeans and began punching the buttons. "Do you have a favorite? I normally just get a whole bunch of brisket, some sausage, potato salad and sweet tea."

"I can manage any of that," Kenneth replied.

"Done," Autumn said.

CHAPTER 13

*B*rooke slowly opened her eyes and found herself staring at a white ceiling with exposed brown beams. "What happened?"

"You passed out," Autumn informed her. "Remember?"

"Oh, yeah," Brooke replied. "That's never happened before."

"You've never been this pent up before," Autumn replied. "I bet you're hungry now."

"Ravenous," Brooke agreed.

"You also need to ground yourself. Since it's nice, let's go outside, barefoot, and eat under the tree. You'll feel better if you do. How long has it been since you had your toes in the grass?"

Brooke raised one eyebrow. "I live in an efficiency apartment in the attic of an old mansion. The nearest park is... well, I don't even know. The nearest park I know of is close to Kenneth's apartment. Walking barefoot is not wise. Dogs, you know? Plus, it's winter. I get outside, but only in the summer."

"So, years, then?"

Brooke didn't answer. She also didn't tell her sister how appealing going outside and sitting under a tree sounded.

"Am I invited?" Kenneth asked from the vicinity of her feet. "I'm still a skeptic."

"Skeptics need fresh air, grass, sunshine and food too, don't they?" Autumn challenged.

"Is everything okay?" Brooke looked upside down at her sister from the arm of the sofa. "What did you do to my boyfriend? Did you crystal him?"

"I would never," Autumn protested.

"Liar," Brooke teased. "You wave that selenite at everyone."

"He asked me to wait." At last, Autumn sounded serious. "I'll wait a while."

"I appreciate your forbearance," Kenneth said, irony dripping in his tone. "I imagine all my hang-ups are making you twitchy, aren't they?"

"You don't have *that* many," Autumn replied, eyeing him with professional scrutiny. "You seem relatively normal. Everyone could do with a cleanse now and again, but you're not in terrible shape."

"I'm glad to know that."

"Are you sure about eating outside?" Brooke asked, anxiety welling up inside her. "From there, we'd be in view of Dad's office window."

"True," Autumn agreed, "but I've never known him to be at home this time of day. It's only five. He probably won't be around for hours yet."

Brooke bit her lip.

A knock sounded at the door, and she flinched. "Who's that?" She jumped to her feet, looking for the quickest way to get out of the room.

"It's the food, sweetie," Autumn said. "My goodness, you're nervous. Are you okay?" She turned without waiting for an answer and opened the door to deal with a messenger who held two huge, fragrant paper bags.

Brooke's stomach growled at the appealing scent.

Kenneth immediately gathered Brooke into his arms. "What's going on, baby?" he asked. "Why are you so worked up? What's the worst that can happen? Your dad may be a jerk, but he has no control over you now. You're a grown-up, professional woman, thirty years old. Even if he came around, what could he do?"

Brooke leaned her forehead against his shoulder. "You don't understand. It's not just about him being controlling. I haven't followed his orders in years. He's just so mean. If I have to deal with his nasty comments, it will ruin my whole Christmas. I want to avoid him altogether."

"Okay. You know, Autumn may have a point about being in nature. Getting the sun on your shoulders would be good for you. However, I'm not saying you're wrong, either. Maybe this isn't the moment. Maybe it's best to stay inside for now. However, at my folks' house, there's a nice grassy backyard. We can walk out there barefoot. I'll make sure of it if we get even one decent afternoon of weather."

The door closed. The bags crackled, and then Autumn also laid a hand on Brooke's shoulder. "I think it would be good for you to get some fresh air," she said, "but it's totally your choice. I am a bit concerned that you're still this worried about just seeing him. Why does that scare you so much? As Kenneth says, he can't do anything to you."

Brooke looked from her sister to her boyfriend. Although her internal warning system was screaming at her to stay out of sight, she could see both of them thought she was being crazy. "Okay," she said at last. "Okay, let's go."

"Are you sure?" Kenneth demanded. "You don't have to push yourself. Not about this. You're on vacation, honey. Relax and don't feel obligated to meet anyone else's expectations."

She took a deep breath and released it through her nose, "It's okay."

Autumn scrutinized her. "I wish you lived closer. You need to continue working on keeping your chakras open and your shields closed. You're way too vulnerable."

"You can show me outside," Brooke said, gathering up a bag of food and heading for the door.

"Ooooh, the fool and the two of wands in reverse," Autumn teased, laying tarot cards in front of Kenneth. "Do you have issues with passivity, hon?"

"Maybe," he mumbled, and Brooke could see his dark skin turning even darker.

"Come on, Autumn, don't make fun of him. If you want him to buy into this arcane bullshit, you need to be nice."

"It's not me," Autumn protested. "It's the cards. They're telling him it's time to man up."

Kenneth's expression suggested to Brooke that he was chewing on the inside of his cheek.

"Don't worry about her, baby. I think you're perfect." She plunked down sideways across his lap and laid her head on his shoulder.

"Thanks, Brooke. She's not wrong though. My mom is a strong, strong woman. She has to be in order to succeed in her job—special ed is about as hard as teaching gets, and she's one of the best—but there's no doubt she struggled to deal with a musical son... a sometimes touchy, shy, passive son. I may have developed a habit of... keeping my head down and pretending to agree to keep her out of my business."

"Is she a bit of a steamroller then?" Brooke guessed.

Kenneth's face took on a number of different expressions, suggesting defensiveness, disappointment, regret, and then anxiety. He sighed. "A bit. It's easier for me to stand up to her over the phone. I can do it face to face, but... I prefer not to. It's not like she can stop me from doing my thing either way. Why discuss it with her?"

"Oh, now you're in the shit." Autumn took a sip of red wine. "A doormat and a people pleaser. She's going to stomp you both flat. Brooke, you'd better practice setting boundaries now. Repeat after me. 'I'm not comfortable discussing that.' 'Why do you need to know that?' 'I'm not talking about this with you.' 'Mind your own business.'"

"I can't say that to Kenneth's mother!" Brooke protested.

"She might respect you if you did," Kenneth suggested. "She's actually a rare creature—one who can dish it out *and* take it. She takes no prisoners, but she has respect for those who stand up to her... politely, of course. She can give a southern lady 'fuck you' like no other, but she can also hear one without holding a grudge."

"Well, I'm DOA then," Brooke said. "Kenneth, I love you, but I was scared to meet your family *before* I heard all this. Are you sure this is a good idea? What if she doesn't accept me?"

"She will one way or another," Kenneth said, "because I love you, and she loves me. It will just be easier if you push back now and again."

"She's your mother, Kenneth," Autumn pointed out. "Maybe you should set the pace. You push back on her and show Brooke that you don't expect her to lie down flat and be stomped on."

Kenneth made a face. "What else do these damned cards have to say?"

Autumn laughed and laid another card on the table. "Ten of cups. Happiness. Great!" She tossed another onto the coffee table, not laying a spread per se, just piling them up. "Also, the lovers, which is not so much about love itself, but rather making decisions together and... oh, crap." Autumn upended her wine glass into her mouth.

"What?" Brooke demanded. "The tower? Aw, man!"

"What?" Kenneth asked. He looked at the card and made a face. "That doesn't look auspicious. What does it mean? Is my whole world about to come crashing down?"

"Yes," Autumn said, "but not in a bad way. It's one of those life-altering moments in which everything you think you know is turned on its head. It's damned uncomfortable, but it paves the way for a better future. Expect to be shaken up in the next couple of days."

As though the words had summoned trouble to them, the door burst open and a short, stocky figure burst into the room.

Brooke recoiled at the sight of her father.

"Dad!" Autumn squeaked, shooting to her feet and positioning her body between herself and Brooke. "What are you doing here?"

"What do you mean?" he growled. "Last I checked, I still owned this house."

"Yes, but it's not normal for you to burst in unannounced. Remember, we talked about this? I pay rent. We have a contract. You promised to give warning."

"Unless there's an emergency." He slammed the door shut and stomped into the room. Stopping in front of Brooke, he crossed his arms aggressively over his chest and glared.

Brooke's constant anxiety flared to outright panic. She cuddled closer to Kenneth, but his usual soothing energy did nothing to help her. Her hands began to tremble. She could barely breathe over the pounding of her heart.

"I don't see an emergency here," Autumn pointed out. "No one is bleeding. We haven't called 9-1-1. We're just sitting around talking."

"With someone who shouldn't be here."

Brooke swallowed hard and spoke in a dry, rasping voice. "I didn't realize I'd been disowned."

Her father turned to her. His gaze had the impact of a punch to the belly.

She jumped to her feet and edged back around the side of the chair.

"You haven't been, of course." He edged forward. "I'm disappointed you've been so distant lately, and I'm even more disappointed you came to town without letting me know. You should be staying in your old room in the big house, and if you have someone special, I should be meeting him to give my approval. Or have you taken a page out of your sister's book and are just bringing random men around?"

"Dad!" Autumn exclaimed.

He turned to her, but instead of flinching, she stared back.

"What?" he demanded. "Have you stopped acting like a slut?"

"Shut up!" Autumn snapped. "My sex life is none of your business."

"If it's happening in *my* house, it is."

Autumn took a deep breath. "I see. Well, I guess that means I'll have to move out soon."

He laughed bitterly. "Sure. I bet." Turning on his heel, he strode past Brooke and stepped up to Kenneth, who rose slowly to his feet. Trace's eyes narrowed. "I know you. I've seen you somewhere before."

"I don't think so, sir," Kenneth said in a quiet, hesitant

voice. He seemed startled, staring at Brooke's father with wide eyes. "I've only been in Texas a couple of times, and only at the airport until today."

Trace grunted, shook his head like a wet dog and, to complete the image, barked, "Well, what do you say, mister? Do you and Brooke have a thing going, or did she just choose you for her travel buddy?"

"Yes, Brooke and I are a couple."

His glare sharpened, and he thrust his hand at Kenneth. "Trace Daniels."

"Kenneth Hill," Kenneth replied, taking the hand.

In Brooke's hyperaware state, she could see him apply a crushing pressure to match her dad's.

"What business ya in? Do you want any help with investments? I can grow wealth like no one else in the field."

"No thank you," Kenneth replied. His startled tone gave way to something flatter, an emotionless declaration of fact. "As to your question, I'm an opera singer. I just completed my doctorate."

"Great. Another hippie," Dad muttered under his breath. "So, a doctorate in *opera?*" he drawled. "That doesn't sound like it will lead to much wealth. How do you plan to make a living?"

Kenneth's eyes grew narrower with every rude word and harsh squeeze. "I'm leaving for a European tour with the opera company in the spring, and then I plan to apply for professorships in the fall."

Trace dropped Kenneth's hand. "A teacher, heaven help me. The two of you will end up on welfare," he blustered, perhaps to hide a hint of a wince.

Kenneth raised one eyebrow and stared back in silence.

"Dad," Brooke snapped. Her face felt hot and her words tried to stick in her throat, but she couldn't allow this ongoing dominance game with her beloved, "leave him alone."

"We're just making friendly conversation," Trace insisted. "There's nothing unusual about it. Besides, if you're *with* this guy, shouldn't I get to know him? Don't y'all want my blessing on your relationship?"

Brooke shook her head. "I don't care about your blessing," she said firmly. "You made it clear, long ago, that it came at a cost I'm not willing to pay."

Trace turned his aggressive stare on his daughter.

She flinched but refused to back down. From such a small distance, she could feel his attacking energy in a physical way.

"Wow. Just wow," he said sarcastically. "After all I've done for you—after feeding, clothing and housing you all those years? After paying for your education, this is how you repay me? By rejecting my advice without even hearing it? By withholding the opportunity for me to meet your partner? Have you forgotten the check I send you every month? You owe me this much."

His words ignited a white glow of rage from the molten core of her psyche. It incinerated her fear, enabling her to speak. "Have you forgotten that I've never cashed a check from you and that you stopped funding my education when I stopped studying the subjects you chose for me? I owe you nothing."

Trace shook his head and turned back to Kenneth. "Can you believe these girls? That one," he snarled and jabbed an accusatory finger at Autumn, "telling me to shut up in my own home, and this one..." He indicated Brooke. "So ungrateful after everything I've done for her? What's with these girls, eh?"

Kenneth took a deep breath. He looked at Brooke and then at Autumn before turning back to Daniel. "Well, sir," he said one eyebrow crooked in scorn, "I didn't realize kids owed their parents for providing for them. My folks have never asked for anything in exchange for feeding, clothing or housing me when

I was a kid. Also, it seems to me that respect is earned. Bursting in on an adult in the home she's renting... I wouldn't tolerate that from a landlord, and she's right to be angry. If you showed some respect, maybe you'd receive some."

Brooke's jaw dropped. She'd never heard such a cold, severe tone from Kenneth, nor seen him so confrontational.

"She's cast a spell on you!" Trace exclaimed, "if you can't see something so obvious. I thought the other one was the witch."

"That's enough," Brooke said. She dug her phone out of her pocket and pushed a few buttons. The phone began to ring.

"Metro Taxi," an accented voice said.

"I need a cab at 1723 Central Hills Road."

"Going where?"

Brooke paused. "Um... airport hotel. I'll specify which one when the driver arrives."

"Sounds good. How many riders?"

"Two."

"It's pretty far out. We'll be at least 30 minutes."

Shit. "Okay." She hung up. "I'm sorry, Autumn. I can't stay here tonight after all."

"I completely understand," Autumn replied. "I'm sorry."

"It's okay. You didn't know this would happen. I believe you didn't mean to ambush me."

"I sure didn't," Autumn agreed.

"What the hell!" Trace bellowed.

"Never mind, Dad," Brooke drawled. "If you can't stand me in *your* house without me prostrating myself and kissing your ring, I'll just take myself out of here." She turned to Kenneth. "Let's get our stuff, honey, and wait outside. The atmosphere in here is getting obnoxious."

"Where do you think you're going?" Trace shouted.

Brooke ignored him. She made her way up the stairs to

claim her pack from the bedroom, before hurrying to the bathroom to collect Kenneth's toothbrush.

"Did you get my shampoo too?" he asked, meeting her in the hallway.

She nodded, extended the bottle and the brush, and made her way back down the stairs, only to stop dead halfway down. Her dad stood at the base of the stairs, blocking the way.

Kenneth bumped into her back, thankfully not with enough force to unbalance her.

"Why run off?" Trace asked. Underneath his perpetual expression of anger, she could see his confusion.

"Because you're being rude," Brooke stated flatly, "just like you always are. You burst into a visit you weren't invited to, made insulting remarks to everyone and now you're being physically aggressive. You *know* people don't like these things. You have clients. They respect you. Why do they deserve your respect and we, your own flesh and blood, don't? Does a paycheck really mean more to you than family? If so, there's nothing more for us to say to each other. Now get out of my way or I'll call the police."

He blinked twice. A third time. Then he stepped aside.

Brooke shoved past him, her fingers laced through Kenneth's.

"Brooke, wait!" Trace shouted, but she had stopped answering.

Brooke led Kenneth through the living room, out the door and shoved it shut behind her.

Just before it clicked into its frame, she heard Autumn say, "Look what you did now. If you ever want Brooke to give you the time of day again, stop humiliating her."

Trace's reply got lost in the slamming of the door, but his sarcastic 'I'm never wrong' tone rang loud and clear in Brooke's ears.

"What a charming man," Kenneth commented. Once out of sight of the house, they slowed their pace to a comfortable walk and made their way to the end of the drive. "I understand things better now."

"Like why I'm such a basket case?" Brooke demanded bitterly, stopping her headlong rush toward the road. "Why changing *any* plan freaks me out? Why men and relationships scare the shit out of me?"

Kenneth turned to face her for a long moment. Then he engulfed her in a massive, cuddly hug, laying his lips on hers.

Brooke tried to melt. She could feel—finally—the tempting warmth of Kenneth's presence, but it was no use. Being on her father's property left her too exposed and vulnerable.

"Are you okay, baby?" he asked, tucking her against his chest.

"No, not really," Brooke replied honestly. "The last thing I wanted was to expose you to my dad and his stupid ideas. We should get out of this driveway. The taxi will be here soon."

She began walking again, and this time, the shadow of the big house felt even more menacing than before. It was as though it had the power to trap her in this mire of bad intentions and habits that had been plaguing her for so many years.

It's a choice, she realized. *Every time I choose to let Dad's stupid beliefs about human worth trickle into my decisions. Every time I let myself get anxious because he wouldn't approve of what I'm doing. Every time I choose to pass up an opportunity to live, to experience, because I should be saving every penny to buy a house, which is the only sign of wealth I'll ever be able to afford, he's taking me over again.*

She thought of how close she'd come to losing—no, to intentionally giving up—her relationship with Kenneth based solely on this sort of warped reasoning, and a deep shudder rolled up her back. Her hands began to tremble.

The long, dark shadow gave way to weak, evening sunshine at last, and a few more feet of gravel brought them to the gate. She stepped through onto a typical Texas highway lined with large family homes and small farms.

"That's the gate to my soul's prison," she commented, not exactly to Kenneth. "I escaped once. I should never have come back."

He engulfed her again, resting his chin on the top of her head. "He only has power over you if you let him," Kenneth pointed out. "He's not God or a king or president. He's a tiny tyrant, yes, but his empire only exists inside that gate. Now that you know, you can start rounding up all the things he gave you to send them back where they belong."

"He didn't give me anything," Brooke protested. "I wouldn't have it."

"Ideas, baby," he replied. "Thoughts that don't serve you. Attitudes that hurt your life and keep you small, that make you think your happiness ought not be your priority. You can see, can't you, that what he was saying made no sense? That even *he* didn't believe it?"

"What do you mean?" Brooke turned and looked up into Kenneth's face, shocked to see a hint of amusement in his expression. "This isn't funny."

"It could be," he argued, "if you think about it. He just said that musicians are hippies and teachers are homeless. Does that even make sense to you?"

She blinked.

"Not that there's anything wrong with being a hippie," he added thoughtfully. "Several of my professors have that look about them. Know what else they have? Homes. Cars. Retirement plans. They go on vacations in Europe, South

American and anywhere else that takes their fancy. Some of their kids go to private schools. They're not rich per se, but they earn enough to live a comfortable life and to buy peasant skirts if they want them. Does that really sound like the epithet he tried to make it?"

Brooke shook her head.

"And he also implied that teachers are homeless. Honestly, your apartment kinda sucked, it's true, but why did you live there? Was it really the only place you could afford?"

"It's the only place I could afford on my savings plan," Brooke muttered.

Kenneth nodded. "You lived there so you could save up and buy something better. Teachers earn a living wage at any public school. My family did just fine on two teacher salaries. He's dumb."

"He is," Brooke agreed. "He swallowed the whole 'teachers aren't professionals' bullshit so many people seem to think is true. He glories in it."

"That's because he's an asshole. A rude, ignorant one," Kenneth reminded her. "I think you can safely ignore any of his life advice. Look how much better you did when you didn't let him push you around."

Brooke nodded. "I know that, but it's hard. His voice is always in my head."

"Well, then you'll have to banish him. Does your sister know a spell for that?"

"Probably," Brooke replied, "but it'll have to be over the phone. I'm never coming back to this place."

A rattle of tires on gravel drew her attention to a yellow cab just pulling up beside them. The window slid down. "Two riders to an airport hotel?"

"That's us," Kenneth agreed.

"Which one?"

"I'll make some phone calls and tell you for sure once we get closer," Brooke promised. "Aren't we like an hour from there?"

"About that," the driver agreed, stroking a wild, wooly beard. Get in."

They jumped into the back seat and Brooke dragged her phone out of her pocket. A quick search and a brief phone call later, they had settled their destination. Brooke leaned her head back against the seat and closed her eyes, fighting to keep her mind blank.

Kenneth's hand crept into hers, lacing their fingers together. He held her gently, her hand on his knee, his hand on top of hers. "Be easy, honey," he murmured. "You were right about him. He's hopeless. Who greets long-lost family and total strangers in such a way?"

"I don't think he was expecting you," Brooke replied. "He thought he would just steamroll me and guilt me back into his net, but when you were there, and he'd already begun his tantrum, he just had to go with it."

"That seems possible, though unlikely to be the whole reason."

Brooke winced and admitted the painful truth. "And then you challenged him. He's not one to take a challenge from anyone he views as... inferior. You were supposed to accept his 'sage wisdom,'" She made finger quotes in the air and rolled her eyes, "and agree with everything he said. You didn't back him, so..."

"So he took aim?"

She nodded.

"Inferior?" he raised an eyebrow. "Because I'm also a teacher and musician?"

She shook her head. "No, not only. I mean, you might rise in his estimation if you had tons and tons of money, but..."

Kenneth twisted his lips to the side and half-closed one eye. "Charming. Well, that may explain his terrible behavior, but it doesn't really help, does it?"

She shook her head. "Another reason I didn't want him to meet you. I know what he's like, which is why I didn't want to see him or expose you to him. But, damn it, why does it hurt? Is it so wrong to want a father who does... fatherly things? I mean, would it be too much to ask for a vote of confidence, an acknowledgment that I'm doing okay? A friendly greeting from him to the man I love?"

"It's not too much, no," Kenneth reminded her gently, "but it's not going to happen for you. Not with him. You weren't blessed with a supportive father, and that isn't going to change. You're probably better off to toss this one back. He's a bad fish."

"I agree," Brooke said. She tried to think of something to say, but her breath sucked painfully, and her lip quivered, so she remained silent.

A moment later, they pulled up in front of an inexpensive airport motel, and a few minutes after that, they made their way up to a plain, simple room.

Brooke stripped off her clothes and hurled them against the wall as though they were poisonous. Then she tossed the covers away and flopped onto the bed in her underwear, her face buried in one arm.

Kenneth sat beside her, big hands covering her back.

"Everything I've ever based my life on is a lie fabricated by a man who doesn't love me. He arranged for another man not to love me, blamed me for it, and did his damnedest to prevent me from loving myself. It's not fair." She punched the pillow with one balled-up fist.

"It's not," Kenneth agreed. "It's not fair and it's not right. You deserve better, baby. But know this. You're not alone. I'm here, I love you and I'm not going anywhere. Your issues don't scare me, and now that you're fighting free of his influence, you're going to feel so much better. Your sister loves you, too. Did you see how upset she was when he showed up?"

Brooke didn't answer. A lifetime of acute, suppressed misery radiated out from the dark, tangled corners of her heart. Her eyes burned and her breath caught in her throat, but she couldn't cry. Her tears felt stuck. "Do you think I need therapy?"

"I think," Kenneth said, "that it would be wise for you to use some of your savings to process and release the old goat, even if you end up delaying your ability to buy a house for a couple of years."

"What are you saying?" she demanded, rolling over and sitting up.

"I'm not sure," he said, eyes narrowed as though looking at something far away. "I just have a feeling... but you shouldn't worry. It will be worth it."

"You sound like Autumn," Brooke pointed out.

He shrugged. "Maybe she's right. Who knows? Maybe there's a lot of mystery out there, and we can only see it if we believe. All I know is, when something feels right, I have to embrace it. And if it feels wrong..."

"You walk away?"

He nodded.

"I wish I'd walked away a long time ago."

"There's no time like the present," he pointed out.

"Kenneth?" Brooke asked.

"Yes, baby?"

"Will you hold me?"

"Gladly. Lie back."

Brooke flopped back on the bed, and Kenneth snuggled up against her. "I love you," he reminded her. "Try to be okay, honey. Try to let it go."

"I can't," she choked.

"No, I know. Not now. For now, you need to feel this, not stuff it down, isn't that right?"

"It hurts."

"I know, baby. I know. Life hurts so bad sometimes."

Brooke gave up trying to communicate and just let herself feel, really feel the pain of her father's lifelong criticism and rejection. The pain of her mother's death, so early she only had the faintest fuzzy recollection of a warm lap and a soft singing voice. Her disappointment when her beloved sister went astray. The anxiety she lived with every day, that in the end, she would not be enough. It cut deep into her, making her heart pound and tightening her guts until she wanted to retch. Her shoulders and jaw ached.

Kenneth cuddled her close, but even his presence couldn't help her.

Nothing can help me. I'm broken. So broken even my own father rejected me. So broken that I don't deserve my job, my man... "Why does he hate me?" she whispered. "What did I do that was so terrible?"

"Nothing, baby," Kenneth breathed. "Nothing at all. It's his fault if he won't acknowledge your worth."

Brooke didn't believe him. She'd been trained her whole life to accept less, to expect less. Even to be less. Less than a full person. Less than worthy of love, attention or autonomy. To accept control with thanks and insults with gratitude. Her early training urged her to call her father and apologize for anything —nothing.

No, she told herself. *I didn't do anything wrong. It's right to protect myself from unprovoked attacks. It's right to distance myself from someone so cruel. Would I accept this from a total stranger?*

Sadly, probably, she would.

Somehow, a slow peace started creeping into her awareness. It touched all her sore places with soothing energy. It strengthened and supported her. Not to heal her—that would be her own work to do—but to provide a framework on which her new spirit could hang.

I'm not unlovable, she reminded herself. *Autumn loves me enough to cut away my emotional ties to dad and try to 'cleanse' me in the best way she knew how. Having me in the line of fire would take the pressure off her and provide her with a sense of superiority, yet she didn't want it. She wanted my happiness more than she wanted his brokenness.*

And Kenneth. She opened burning, aching eyes and looked into his warm, brown gaze. *Beautiful man. The epitome of tall, dark and handsome. He loves me. He loved me when I pulled back. He loved me when I ran. He welcomed me back again. He has remained constant and true, no matter what nonsense I came up with to push him away. Somehow, he found something worthy in me and has stuck around for it.*

Another dark realization dawned. *I let myself be drawn away from my own happiness because I couldn't stop chasing my father's approval.* "This stops now."

"I beg your pardon?"

"Kenneth, I need to rework my entire worldview, and I don't know who or what I will even be when I'm done. I've been a phony my whole life, and I just can't live that way anymore."

"You're not a phony," he replied. "You're coming to terms with a difficult childhood and the coping methods that came with it. That takes time, especially if you're completely isolated, which you were. You took five whole years to come out of the fog, and now, you're ready to move on. Yes, it's going to be hard, but you're strong. You can do this."

"Will you still be there for me?"

"Oh, yes. Brooke. All I want is for us to be happy and fulfilled together. You're actually so close. If you could believe it, you'd be there."

Brooke drew Kenneth's face close to hers for a kiss. His lips compressed hers with wanton sweetness, a tender touch that activated all the shattered pieces of her. Connections illuminated, linked, locked.

Suddenly desperate for human connection, she slid her hands under Kenneth's tee shirt and caressed his chest and belly.

"Hmmm, that feels nice," he mumbled against her lips.

"Take it off," Brooke ordered.

"Oho!" Kenneth whistled through his teeth. He tugged his shirt over his head.

Brooke reached behind her back and unhooked her bra, spilling her breasts free.

"I love these," he rumbled. "Full and soft." He cupped one generous globe in each hand. A wide thumb stroked over each nipple.

She let out a little whine.

"Good?" He stroked again, and then adjusted his hands so he could grasp her nipples between his thumbs and forefingers, gently rolling them to increase her pleasure.

"Oh, yes." She reached around Kenneth, stroking his back.

He released her breasts and crushed her close in his arms, claiming her lips in a hot, wild kiss. The banked passion that always lingered between them flared easily to life.

"Kenneth," she breathed against his mouth.

He kissed her again. Their tongues tangled together in a mutual exercise of unbridled desire.

Brooke's sex moistened and tingled. She arched her back, wanting the closest possible connection to her lover, and she could feel the firm thickness of his erection against her pubic bone. "Hmmmm," she hummed.

Kenneth cupped her mound through her panties, sexy and slow.

She bit her lip and met his eyes with flirty shyness.

"Too much?" he asked.

She shook her head.

He slid his hands inside her underwear and cupped her mound again, sliding one finger along the opening of her body and feeling the moisture. "Oh, baby. You're so ready, aren't you?"

"Ready to get busy with my man? Hell yes," she replied, dropping the timid demeanor.

He curved his finger and the tip of it penetrated her ever so slightly. His palm compressed her clitoris.

She hissed.

"Shall we get these off you?" he suggested.

Brooke didn't even answer. She just grabbed her waistband and started tugging. Her panties surrendered easily to the pressure, pooling around her ankles. She pushed them away with one foot.

Kenneth rose briefly and returned to the bed, naked. His long, brown form contrasted with the white sheets.

"You're so gorgeous," she whispered, running one hand down his body until she could grasp the tempting fullness of his sex. When he dropped a condom packet on the bed beside her, she smiled. The tingling wetness between her thighs increased.

Kenneth, it seemed, was just as ready. A drop of moisture beaded at the tip of his penis.

Brooke caught it on her thumb and smoothed it over the head. He groaned, low and deep. Brooke set out to pleasure her man, wrapping her hand around him and moving his foreskin gently up and down.

"That's so good," he moaned. "Yeah, baby."

Kenneth tolerated her touches only for a moment before he took hold of her shoulders and tumbled her back on the bed. Crouching over her, he grasped her thighs in his hands and opened them, exposing her to his gaze. He settled between her legs, laying them on his shoulders, and dipped down.

"Ooooh," she breathed as he kissed her sex.

Then he stroked along the seam, feeling the neatly trimmed curls. Parting them, he kissed her again, directly on the clitoris this time. He manipulated it with exquisite skill. As Kenneth began to lay wild, luscious pleasure on Brooke's most sensitive spot, she fisted the sheets with both hands.

She panted and moaned as he gently urged her toward orgasm.

Two thick fingers invaded her, touching secret places inside her. "Come, baby," he encouraged. "Come on. I want to see how good you can feel."

The vibration of his voice and the tickling against her g-spot ignited her, and she rocketed past the stars to a place where only love existed. There, Kenneth cocooned her in tender passion, and all her fears and insecurities faded away.

This is joy. This is rightness. I need nothing more. I have nothing to prove. My existence is proof enough that I am not a mistake. I am. I matter. I love and am loved.

Pleasure faded to a slow hum, and Brooke returned to her body long enough to retrieve the condom from beside her. She tore open the package as her legs slid down Kenneth's arms.

He released her onto the bed, so she could reach low.

With practiced ease, she sheathed him. Then she squeaked in surprise as he rolled, tugging her on top of him.

"Let's take you for a little ride, baby," he suggested. "What do you say?"

No words emerged to respond to his request, but she didn't

need them. Taking hold of his thick shaft, she angled it upward and let gravity do the rest. He slid into her depths, fully penetrating.

Her head fell back. Little whimpering sounds escaped with each breath.

Kenneth wrapped his hands around her hips and guided her upward. He let her sink back down before he lifted her and allowed her to lower back down again.

Oh, yes, she thought, adding her own motion to the thrusts, so they surged together, again and again, seeking the perfect fulfillment of their mutual climax.

They found it.

Between one enthusiastic thrust and the next, the fuse lit, burned and burst. It left them both frozen and shuddering, trapped at the apex of pleasure. Again, as always, that sensation of perfect oneness drew Brooke out of her busy mind and into her body, allowing Kenneth's soul to caress hers with irresistible sweetness.

Nothing is more important than this—than us. We have each other, and for now, that's enough. She sank slowly down so her head rested on his chest.

He laid both hands on her back and they drifted in an afterglow that merged relaxation with delicious fatigue.

Soon, I'll sleep, but first, a long cuddle to enjoy this connection with the heart of my heart, with my soulmate.

Long moments passed. Kenneth's erection began to wane, and he reached down to grasp the condom as he eased out of Brooke, but always he kept one hand on her back.

A soft chirp invaded their drowsy cuddle. It grew louder and more insistent.

Brooke ignored it, determined to hang onto the moment. When it finally stopped, she relaxed. At least, until it started again.

"Damn it," she muttered. "What now?" She hoisted herself from the bed, groaning at the pleasant ache in her muscles.

The ringing stopped as she made her way toward her purse, abandoned near the door of the hotel room, but started again immediately.

"Jeez! What?" she groused, dragging the bag up by its strap and rummaging in its depths. Retrieving her cell, she registered Autumn's number and frowned, pressing the button and lifting the phone to her ear. "What's up?"

"I need your help," Autumn wailed.

"What?"

"It's Dad..."

"I don't want to hear about Dad," Brooke said. "I'm done with him."

"He's at the hospital."

Brooke froze, her angry tirade silenced. "Ugh. What? Why?"

"He had a heart attack." Autumn sobbed. "He was in my living room, yelling and stomping around, the way he always does when you don't give him what he wants, and he suddenly grabbed his chest and..."

"And?" Brooke demanded, her mouth still barely connecting with her brain.

"And he fell down. I called the ambulance. He's at UT Southwestern. It's only a few minutes from where you are. Can you please go to him?"

"Autumn, I... I don't know. I don't want to see him."

"Brooke, he's having a *heart attack*."

"I don't want to be mean, but he probably brought it on himself. Stomping around like a toddler over something that's none of his business..."

"Brooke!"

"I'm not sure," Brooke told her sister. "I just don't know. He still likes you. Can't you go?"

"I can't!" Autumn wailed. "River's dad just called me to say he's dropping him off early. River's got a cold, and Braden won't deal with a sick kid. I can't bring germs around Dad. He's already in a weakened state... and River... he's already sick. I don't want to take him to the emergency room where he might come in contact with who knows what! Please, Brooke. You have to do this!"

"Autumn, your ex is an ass."

"I know," she snapped. "That's why he's an ex, but it doesn't matter. One time, I wasn't home when he decided his custody time was over, and he left River in the big house, assuming the cleaning lady would watch him. He likes messing with me, and there's nothing I can really do about it. But Braden being an ass is neither here nor there."

"It is, actually," Brooke said. "You have two asses to contend with, and you're trying to push one off on me."

"Don't start with me," Autumn snapped. "Do you want Dad left alone to face all the crazy stuff they might do to him?"

"Well, in an objective, human way, no," Brooke said, trying to be reasonable. "No one should go through a heart attack alone, but I didn't like facing what he did to me either. Might this not be Karma for him? He's been a jerk to everyone, so no one wants to support him in his hour of need?"

"I mean, I'm not saying that's without some validity," Autumn agreed, "especially for you, but at the same time, do you want to be the person who let her dad have a heart attack alone when she was literally a ten-minute drive away?"

Brooke bit her lip. "I'm so done with him."

"I understand. Can you be so done with him, like, tomorrow?"

Brooke took a deep breath. "I have a flight out tomorrow

morning that I will not miss. Certainly not for Dad, but if it means that much to you, I'll stop in, see how he's doing and give you an update. I'll make any further decisions based on what I see."

"Thank you, Brooke! Thank you."

"And, Autumn?"

"Yes?"

"You need to get away from Dad. Letting him spoil you and River might be nice in some ways, but it only encourages him to meddle in your life, and then he makes insulting remarks to you. He's still abusive to you, just in a different way."

"I think you might be right," Autumn acknowledged. "At this point, my whole life is so enmeshed with his, I'm not sure if I can get myself free and still have a pot to pee in, but today's experience has definitely been eye-opening."

"I agree," Brooke said. "My eyes are open for sure. Maybe we can help each other by staying accountable to each other in the future."

"Maybe so," Autumn agreed. "Okay, text me when you find out what's happening."

"I will. Bye, Sis."

"Bye."

Brooke hung up the phone and dropped it back into her purse.

"Surely, you don't mean to go?" Kenneth exclaimed, leaning up on one elbow and regarding her, his languid, passion-heavy eyes opening wide.

"I suppose I must," she replied. "What if he dies? A heart attack is no small thing. I need to see him, for the sake of my own conscience if nothing else."

"I think you'll only succeed in making yourself feel worse," he muttered. "Brooke, I wish you would reconsider. I don't see what good it will do for you to subject yourself to his rudeness again. You don't deserve it."

"I know that," she replied quickly.

"Do you? Do you honestly know, in the deepest places of your heart, that his choices are his own and have nothing to do with you, that you don't deserve the treatment you have received? That you don't deserve to be treated like shit while your sister is pampered like a princess?" Kenneth paused, seeming to consider his last words. "Honestly, he even abuses her, too. Did you notice?"

"I noticed," Brooke said darkly, "but if my father dies... What would people say if they found out I abandoned him in his final hour?"

"What people? Who would know? People only need to know what you choose to share with them. If he passes, just say your father passed away and leave the details out."

"Because I have something to hide?" she challenged him. "Because I'm ashamed of my behavior and need to keep secrets? I'm going, Kenneth." She turned away from him, hunting for her clothes and purse.

"Wait, Brooke, hold on," he urged, tugging on his underwear.

"Wait for what?" she demanded, pulling fresh panties from her pack and stepping into them.

"How will you get there? You don't want to blow more money on a cab, do you?"

"I'll take the DART," she replied. "There's a stop a couple of blocks from here."

"What the hell is a DART?" he asked.

"The DART is Dallas's metro line," she explained. "It's cheaper than a cab and more convenient than a bus."

"Well, if you're going, I'm coming with you," he insisted. "I won't have anything happening to you, and that's a fact."

"Come if you'd like," she replied. "I wouldn't mind the company, but if you feel the need to say I told you so, skip it."

"Understood," he acknowledged. "Though I still think this is a bad decision, it's your decision to make, so have at it. Just understand that I will be hanging around to keep you safe."

Brooke pulled her shirt over her head, added a light jacket and went hunting for her shoes.

CHAPTER 14

"Well, here we are," Kenneth said, looking around the emergency department's lobby. "Now what?"

Brooke approached the check-in window.

A young woman who had frosted her hair silver and wore it in a long, messy ponytail opened a plastic sliding cover. "Can I help you?"

"I was told my father came in by ambulance a while ago. Trace Daniels. Do you know where I can find him?"

"Daniels?" The young woman clicked a few buttons on the computer. "He's been admitted, but he's stable at the moment. Would you like someone to show you the way?" She glanced at Kenneth. "Due to his fragile condition, we don't want to excite him. One visitor only."

"No worries," Kenneth replied. "I'll just wait here. He's your dad, and frankly, he didn't seem like someone I want to support. Text me to let me know what's going on, okay?"

"Sounds like a plan." Brooke stepped closer. "I know you're mad," she muttered, "but I'm scared. Please hold me?"

"I'm not mad," he said. "I'm annoyed that you're doing this to yourself, but it has to be your choice." He enfolded her in one of his soul-soothing hugs. "I'm here for you, Brooke. Nothing will change that. I'm not going to reject you just because we disagreed, okay?"

A deep shudder ran through her as a weight she hadn't realized she was carrying released itself. "Thank you."

He kissed her forehead.

"Ma'am?" An orderly called to Brooke. "If you'll follow me."

Reluctantly, she pulled herself from Kenneth's arms. Bereft of his warmth, a chill sank into her, leaving her trembling. She followed the young man through the twisting maze of hallways. When he indicated a room, Brooke paused, took a deep breath and steeled herself before stalking into it. Her heart pounded, but a strange calm had fallen over her.

The tormenter of her childhood lay on an adjustable bed. A hospital gown was barely visible under a thin, white blanket. His small, frail appearance left her feeling confused. Trace's personality had always taken up more than its fair share of the oxygen, but not anymore.

For the first time in her life, Brooke stood over her father looking down.

His face, relaxed from its habitual molar-clenching scowl, looked haggard and gray. The skin around his eyes crinkled heavily. Black, bruised-looking bags stood out in sharp relief against his ashen skin. His unshaven jaw appeared messy instead of rakish and sweat slicked his graying hair.

He looks like bitterness brought to life, she thought. *No wonder he's so unpleasant. He's been carrying his unhappiness for years. He can't part with it.*

He opened his eyes, and despite his obvious fatigue and strain, she could still see the vivacious snap.

"Didn't expect to see you here," he commented.

"I didn't expect to *be* here," she replied, her voice cool and flat.

"So why are you then?" he asked. "Go on. Run back to your lover. Let him coddle you. Leave me to my fate."

Brooke raised one eyebrow. "I might," she replied. "It would be no more than you deserve, and after everything you've done, I would feel no guilt about it."

He opened his mouth, and she recognized his expression of impish delight.

"Dad," she interrupted, "you are about one insult away from never seeing me again. Then you really will face whatever's ahead of you alone, because Autumn can't make it until morning."

He shut his mouth and considered her with narrowed eyes. His thick eyebrows made an angry line across his forehead.

"What did the doctor say?" Brooke asked.

He glowered another minute, but when she didn't break down gibbering or grow defensive, he sighed, relaxed his shoulders and answered like a human. "They're sure it's a heart attack. I've had some heavy-duty meds to break up the clot, but I need a catheterization procedure to assess the damage. From there, they'll decide whether to go forward with balloons or whether I need bypass surgery."

"Oh," Brooke replied. She had no idea what to say. "None of that sounds pleasant."

"It's been awful so far."

She sighed and sank into a nearby chair. "Any idea when the procedure will begin?"

He rolled his eyes. "Nobody tells me anything. I wonder if it won't be until morning. Guess I'm lucky, though."

He had that baiting look on his face again, but for some reason, Brooke wanted to know. "Why is that, Dad?"

"Because you're here."

This is a setup. I can feel it. She waited for the other shoe to drop without a flash of dawning hope.

"I mean, if you had a *real* job, you'd be working right now, so..."

Anger flared, and for once, she didn't try to tamp it down. "Right now? At eleven at night? I don't think so, and if you did, that would explain why you're here."

"I beg your pardon?" he drew back against the bed, offended "The reason I'm here, missy, is your disgraceful behavior—"

"Dad!"

Trace cut off his tirade mid-word and looked at her.

"Shut up." Strangely, he did, so Brooke continued. "It's your own fault you're here. Between your horrible diet, stress, overwork and your obsession with controlling things that are none of your business, you made yourself sick."

"Well!" he huffed. "Well, that just goes to show... I mean..." Trace spluttered to a halt.

"Good. Now, you've been warned to be polite, and I mean it. Teaching is a real job, and by pretending it isn't, you're insulting everyone who took the time to teach *you*." She crossed her arms over her chest. "If you can't be proud of my numerous accomplishments, I'll thank you to keep it to yourself."

"I don't understand why you never would take even the tiniest morsel of friendly advice," he groused, but the combination of his poor physical condition and her unexpected defiance seemed to have taken the wind out of his sails.

"Because it's not friendly advice. One, I never asked for any and two, it's just meant to be controlling. Most parents help their kids figure out how to pursue *their* dreams, not their parents'. You had your chance to create your career path. Let me do the same. I'm content with where I'm at, and I wouldn't change a thing."

"Well, I wouldn't expect you to admit it at this point..."

She started to rise.

"Wait, wait. I'll stop."

Brooke remained standing.

"Won't you please stay?"

She shrugged. "There doesn't seem to be a reason. All this controlling bullshit isn't good for your heart. I should leave and let your blood pressure settle."

He sighed. "Please, don't go."

"Then quit picking on me. It isn't funny. I'm tired, and I have a big day tomorrow. You're damned lucky I came at all."

"You do? What are you doing tomorrow?" he demanded.

"Well, contrary to what you might think, Dad," Brooke drawled, "I do have plans. We only meant to spend one night at Autumn's on a long layover. I'm on my way to Atlanta to meet Kenneth's family."

"Wow. Serious, eh?"

"I suppose we'll get married someday," she informed him blandly. "Time will tell."

"*That* serious, hmmm? Are you sure it's a good idea to marry another musician? You know what they say..."

"No, Dad. I don't know, but the last time I checked, a teacher and a professor equaled a decent, middle-class life, which sounds absolutely perfect to me."

"I mean, if that's the best you can do..."

"Okay, that's it," Brooke snapped. "You have no self-control at all, do you? Listen here. It's not the 'best I can do.' It's what I want. What *I* want, Dad, for *my* life, which you don't get to live for me, dictate to me or judge. You've used up your chances. I'm leaving. Enjoy your recovery, and you might consider getting therapy for your personality disorder while you're at it."

She turned on her heel and stomped out of the room. *Coming today might have been a mistake, but at least now I can cut him off without guilt. Even as sick as this, he still has no self-control, no manners, no kindness. I don't need a dad like that.*

Brooke found Kenneth in the lobby, sitting on a low armchair. "Back so soon?" he asked.

"You were right," Brooke replied with a sigh. "He's stable enough to be an ass and persistent enough to try it. I'm done with him. Let's go back and get some sleep before our flight in the morning."

"Best suggestion I have heard in..." he glanced at his watch. "hours."

Brooke giggled, though she felt far from calm. "Let's go, okay?"

Kenneth rose to his feet and scrutinized her face. "Yes." He held out one hand and she took it. His warmth tempered her righteous anger to a manageable simmer.

Brooke felt strangely numb as she sat on the DART. Clutching Kenneth's hand, she stared out the window at the artificial light of Dallas in silence. Her chattering mind finally went still, her pounding heart slowed to a steady throb.

They walked the two blocks from the stop to the hotel in the quiet, humid night. The temperature had dropped, not to Chicago cold, but she didn't feel comfortable in her thin jacket. She ignored it, even when shivering set in.

"Come on," Kenneth urged. "Hurry." He increased his stride, his long legs eating up the distance while Brooke trotted to keep up.

The quick pace warmed her body, but it did nothing to return her to full awareness. Not when they entered the hotel, not when Kenneth swiped the room key and ushered them inside, not when he handed her the toothbrush and toothpaste, and not when he urged her into bed.

Brooke kicked off her shoes and stripped off her jeans. Turning on her side, she lay cradled in Kenneth's arms, staring into the darkness with sightless eyes.

"Baby," Kenneth murmured in his husky rumble, "are you okay? You seem a bit like you're in shock."

"In a real sense, my father—the father I always wished I could have—just died. I expect to rage, but at the moment, I feel... numb."

"I'm sorry," he whispered, his lips touching her ear. "I'm sorry you didn't get the father you deserved. I'm sorry you didn't have a mother to help you find your way. I'm sorry you're hurting. Is there anything I can do?"

His love at this tense moment touched her in a deep, sensitive place. A cold place. He warmed her there, deep in the frozen part of her soul, and it melted in a flood of tears that clawed their way into her chest. She tried to swallow them down, but they overwhelmed her. She turned her face into the pillow and sobbed.

Kenneth rubbed circles on Brooke's back as she cried out a lifetime of being the designated family screw-up. The scapegoat of a toxic man who didn't know how to love, only to manipulate. Pain and injustice poured from the festering wound in her heart.

"It's not fair," she gasped, punching the pillow. "It's not fair. I don't deserve that. I never did anything wrong. I didn't deserve it."

"I know, baby. I know. It's so wrong."

Though Kenneth's breathing eventually evened out and his body relaxed, Brooke remained awake through the night, crushed under a weight of grief. She closed her eyes moments before the room phone rang their wake-up call, accompanied by alarms ringing on both their phones.

"Well," Kenneth said, "time to go. Planes don't wait. You ready?"

"Ready as I'll ever be," Brooke replied. *Just what I didn't want... to meet Kenneth's family when I'm so tired I can hardly move. I hope they'll like zombie Brooke.*

CHAPTER 15

*T*he cab pulled up in front of a string of cute townhouses. The one Kenneth indicated as his family's home was clad in white, with a prominent dormer on the front and a sharply peaked roof. The ones on either side were red brick.

Brooke looked up at the house nervously as Kenneth hopped from the taxi, circled around the back and opened the door for her.

"Come on," he urged.

Drawing in a deep breath, she said, "Okay." Then, she accepted his hand and allowed him to escort her out.

They moved along the sidewalk toward the front door when a mob of people poured out. Three male youths with matching flat-topped haircuts—obviously Kenneth's younger brothers—streaked down onto the sidewalk. Three adults approached behind them.

"Mama, Dad, Granny, I'd like you to meet my girlfriend, Brooke Daniels. Brooke, this is my family."

Brooke examined the faces before her. Kenneth most

closely resembled his dad, Walker. Both had blunt, broad features tightly curled dark hair cut close to the head, and wide, charming smiles.

Walker extended a hand, and Brooke shook it before he turned to hug his son.

His mother, Shayla, clearly had a more mixed heritage. Her smaller features and wavy rather than curly hair rendered her ethnicity ambiguous. Her stature, on the other hand, fit her profession.

Tall and stout, Shayla's arms and shoulders bulged with muscles, visible through the thin sweater she wore over her sundress. Her calves, bare beneath the hem of her dress, also showed the muscular development indicative of someone who did heavy lifting on a regular basis. However, her shrewd, intelligent face showed she was no mere sturdy back.

This is a woman who uses her brain and body hard, every day. She intimidated Brooke more than a little, a reaction that did not ease when she simply regarded Brooke with a raised eyebrow before turning to engulf Kenneth in an embrace.

Then, an older woman stepped forward, hands extended, and grasped Brooke. "Welcome, honey. So glad you're here. I'm Della." Her accent was black and southern, warm as cinnamon and sweet as cane syrup. Each of the wrinkles covering her medium-brown face contained a smile.

Brooke couldn't help but smile back. "Pleased to meet you, ma'am," she said, trying to sound confident, but her throat tightened with nerves and fatigue, and emerged as a tiny, squeaky whisper.

"Now, don't you be nervous, not one little bit. You're here with our Kenny, and I've never seen him look so happy." Della beamed.

"Thank you," Brooke murmured.

"You know, he could be happy because he just finished his doctoral degree," Shayla pointed out.

"Don't start, Mama," Kenneth warned his mother.

"Oh, are you *not* happy with your degree?" his mother asked, blinking. "You certainly put a lot of time and effort into it."

"Cool it," he said mildly. "That's a loaded question, and you know it. Of course I'm happy to have finished my degree, but I'm even happier to have met someone special. Now, I warned you not to go there, and I meant it."

Kenneth's mother pursed her lips and crossed her arms over her chest. Her eyes narrowed.

"Shayla, this is no way to welcome a guest," Della scolded her daughter. "Kenny is a big boy with a good heart, and he's wise. He brought this woman home because she's part of the family now. You can see it plain as day if you look at them."

"But..." Shayla sighed, shoulders sagging.

Wonderful, Brooke thought, echoing the sigh. *Just what I needed. What past life sin did I commit to deserve this?*

Then, Shayla steeled her spine. "Won't you come in?" she invited stiffly.

"Thank you," Brooke replied.

Kenneth pressed gently on Brooke's back and escorted her up to the front door.

"Did you have a good flight?" Kenneth's father asked, drawing close to them.

"Not bad," Kenneth replied. "It was bumpy from Chicago to Dallas, but from Dallas to here was smooth as glass."

"That's good," he replied.

They entered a narrow hallway that led to a spacious living room with white walls dressed in richly warm artwork, leather furniture and an antique piano in the corner. They passed through into a large dining room with a huge polished wood table and ten matching chairs. This opened into another hallway lined with two bedrooms, a den and a powder room. It ended with two staircases; one going up, the other down.

"Mama, Dad and Aniyah sleep on this level," he explained, "and the boys share the entire upstairs. They didn't stick around to introduce themselves, but Jackson is seventeen and a senior in high school, Jamal is nineteen and working for a year while he considers his options and Paul is twenty-two and finishing up his bachelor's at the University of Atlanta. He's studying engineering. He's only home for the break, which is good because it can be a bit tight up there with all three of them grown so big. It's not a bedroom exactly, but more like an efficiency apartment with three beds and a sitting area."

"Keeps them out from under my feet," Shayla quipped with a tight smile.

Brooke smiled back, more out of courtesy than humor.

"And I have a suite downstairs," Della added. "Kenny's room is down there too."

"Ah," Brooke said. "Sounds like a nice setup."

"It's worked well for us," Shayla informed her. "With so many people in so few square feet, we had to be creative."

"Looks like you succeeded," Brooke said. "This home is wonderfully cozy."

"Thank you," she replied, though her tone still sounded less than welcoming.

"Mama, we're going to spend some time downstairs resting. It's been a long day of travel and a long few days overall."

"Okay, Kenny," Shayla acknowledged easily. "We'll have dinner in about two hours. Christmas Eve dinner, of course, and will you two be going to the service tonight?"

"I would love to," Brooke said eagerly, though formal religion had never been part of her life.

"Sure, why not?" Kenneth agreed.

"Now, that's just lovely," Della responded with a wide smile.

"Thanks, Granny," Kenneth said.

"It was wonderful to meet you all," Brooke said. "Kenneth has told me a lot about you, and I'm so glad to be here."

"Nice to meet you too, Brooke," Walker said kindly.

Shayla grunted.

Kenneth wrapped his arm around Brooke's waist and escorted her downstairs.

"Can I get you anything?"

Brooke jumped to see Shayla standing beside her. "No thank you, Ma'am. Kenneth decided to take a nap but... I couldn't seem to settle, so I decided to read for a while...." Realizing she was babbling, she stepped away from the bookshelf she was perusing and trailed off.

Shayla sank to a seat on the basement family room sofa; a cute, squishy piece of furniture with a pattern of big yellow daisies.

Uh oh. I wonder if this is how the inquest begins. "Um, I appreciate your hospitality, welcoming me into your home," she stammered. "Sorry if I've been a bit... quiet. I didn't sleep well last night."

"Sorry to hear that," Shayla replied. The curt tone she'd used earlier had softened to one of curious scrutiny. "Come have a seat." She indicated the armchair beside her. "I want to talk to you."

Brooke obeyed the command, though her heart pounded with anxiety. "What did you want to talk about, Ma'am?" she asked, though she felt she knew.

"I'm sure you can guess. You and Kenny. Have you dated a black man before?"

Brooke shook her head. "I haven't. I..." she trailed off, not knowing what to say.

"I hope you're aware of what you're up against if you move forward with this."

"Ma'am?" Brooke eyed Shayla curiously, saw the solid set to her jaw, her strong hands fisted, not tightly clenched but definitely not calm and relaxed.

"Come on, Brooke. Don't be obtuse. You know what I mean."

Shayla's blunt, confrontational manner ratcheted Brooke's anxiety to even higher levels. After her devastating confrontation with her father and her sleepless night, she struggled to produce words that expressed anything useful. She swallowed, willing her busy mind to settle on something, anything that would help. Nothing coalesced.

Shayla pursed her lips. "What even made you want to be with him? His handsome face? His gentle soul?"

"Those things, yes," Brooke agreed, "and his musical talent, of course. I've had quite a crush on him for a long time. When he... asked me out, I couldn't say no. He's... he's very special to me."

"Yes, he's special, all right," Shayla agreed. "Have you considered, though, that the gentle soul you and I love lives a hair's breadth away from violence every day of his life? All he has to do is dress wrong, go into the wrong neighborhood or *look at* someone in a way they don't like, and it could cost him his life? What if one of your white friends decided he was a threat and called the police?"

Brooke licked her lip. "I wouldn't be friends with someone like that," she blurted.

Shayla frowned.

"Okay, okay." Brooke sucked in a deep breath. "I'm sorry. I'm not expressing myself well. I... Like I said, I had a rough night. Give me a moment, please." She paused, bit her lip. "Yes, I know these things can happen. I hate it. If I lost a connection because they couldn't see the man, only the stereotype, I would consider it the trash taking itself out. Um, I've taken courses in diversity and while I have more to learn, I am aware of privilege including my own, and I try to use it every day to help *all* my students find a better place in the world."

Shayla nodded. "It's different though when it's a student. There's distance in those connections. You do your job and you go home. Now, you're moving towards making a family with a man many will never take the trouble to get to know. They'll either fetishize him or dismiss him... or fear and blame him."

"All I can do," Brooke said softly, "is keep fighting it. And keep loving Kenneth."

"I like the sound of that."

Both women looked up to see the subject of their conversation striding into the room, his long legs eating up the distance. He sank to a seat next to his mother and reached beside him to take Brooke's hand. His warmth crept up her arm, strengthening and settling her the way it always did.

"Hello, Kenny," Shayla said coolly. "I was just having a little chat with your lady."

Kenneth screwed his lips to the side. "Sounds more like an interrogation. Did you find out what you wanted to know?"

"Not really," Shayla replied. "If you two plan to make a go of this, you can't skip the hard realities. You can't just be infatuated and forget that there's a whole world out there filled with hate that will fall on you, Brooke, in a way you've never experienced before."

"Let them come," she said, at last finding something strong to say. "I won't falter."

Shayla closed her eyes and pursed her lips. "Easy to say, but do you really understand what you're talking about. Kenny, have you told her just how many times you've been pulled over for absolutely nothing?"

Brooke turned to look at Kenneth.

"It has happened," he admitted.

"It happens *often,*" Shayla corrected. "Almost monthly."

Brooke felt herself frowning.

"And every time it happens, it comes with a threat of death. See, you, Miss Daniels, can get pulled over, reach into your glove box, pull out your license and registration, smile at the cop and drive away unscathed. It's only by the grace of God that Kenny hasn't been harmed in these unnecessary harassments. And what about when you rented your apartment?"

Brooke's mind set to whirling. "What happened?"

Kenneth heaved a sigh. "The management said that my credit score was too low, and I couldn't get in."

A sneering echo of her father's voice reverberated through her mind.

That's also something we've never discussed. Does he have good credit now? Has he fixed it?

"His score was actually fine," Shayla interjected, "but Kenny had to pull it up himself and show them. They didn't look. They were just trying to keep him out. He had to do the same for the electric *and* the cable company."

"Wow. That's... that's rotten," Brooke stammered.

"See, this is what I'm afraid of," Shayla continued. "You two haven't dealt with reality at all. You say strong things about fighting discrimination, but you're not even aware of all the ways it plays out. You have a long way to go before you're ready."

"It's a path we'll take together, Mama," Kenneth said.

"Yes," Brooke agreed, trying not to show how shaken she felt, not only about the conversation but about how woefully unaware she had been. "Yes, I... I... um..." Words failed again. "I'm sorry that happened to you, honey," she told him, not sure what else to say. "And to you too, Ma'am. It does, doesn't it?"

"Somewhat," Shayla agreed. "Black women face a different kind of discrimination than black men do, and of course, these problems only the tip of the iceberg. You could go on forever studying all the ways large and small that *your* people protect themselves and their advantages at our expense."

That stung. One part of Brooke wanted to protest, to list out all the ways she worked hard to help her students of all colors rise, but she forced it down. *Remember to listen to her experiences, not argue with them. It's the system, not you personally.* "I'm so sorry it is this way," she said softly. "It's not right."

Shayla acknowledged her response with a nod that wasn't as curt as it could have been, but still, she pushed on. "So I have to ask again, Brooke. Are you ready to face what's ahead of you? Are you ready to find out the hard way who will suddenly turn against you when you step outside your race? Who will suddenly reveal themselves as racist? If you to stay together, marry, there *will* be someone you care about who has some kind of feeling about it, and if you have kids..."

"Ahem," Kenneth cleared his throat.

"What, Kenny? So far it seems like you two are just floating along. Can't keep that up forever. Are the two of you ready to be the parents of a biracial youth? I can tell you, that's even *more* complicated. All the risks and prejudice black people face, but they also might struggle to find their place in *any* community or group of students. Ask me how I know."

"Mama, believe me," Kenneth said, and his voice had firmed from its usual tinglingly-sexy friendliness to something powerful, "when we decide *if* we want children, we will consider all the possibilities, good and bad."

"Um... I'm glad you brought this up, Ma'am," Brooke rushed in nervously. "I'll certainly take the time to continue to educate myself in any case. You're right that I'm overdue to face these realities. But I will reiterate that anyone who has some kind of issue with Kenneth—or people of color at all—is no friend of mine and no one I want to keep in my life."

"And on that note, let's bring the confrontation to an end," Kenneth said firmly, giving Brook's hand a gentle squeeze. "Mama, that's enough. You've said your piece and we're not going to harp on it. It's Christmas. We're supposed to be enjoying the holiday."

Shayla opened her mouth to speak, closed it again and gave the couple a long, considering look. Then she nodded, rose and walked away.

Brooke sagged. "Why didn't we ever talk about this?" she asked him under her breath. "It *is* something we should have discussed long since."

"You weren't ready," he replied. "I didn't want to overwhelm you."

"Kenneth," Brooke said firmly, "I am *not* too fragile to hear about what you have to *live* with. It's part of who you are. Don't you think I need to know?"

"Well, now you do," he said. "It's not my whole life, but it does matter."

"It does." Brooke rose from the chair and sank onto the sofa beside him. She slid her arms around his torso. "It matters a lot. You don't deserve it." Her forehead came to rest on his shoulder.

"No one does," he agreed. "Baby, we've only been on this roller coaster since October. No need to discuss a lifetime's worth of complications in the first second. Let's not forget—the world is stupid, but this relationship is not."

"Definitely not. It's amazing. Eye-opening and life-changing. But like all relationships, there's a reality we have to face. For us, it's how race affects us as individuals and a couple, which is a conversation we needed—*I* needed—to have. It's a step in my journey as well. Ignoring the truth also won't help our relationship grow. We have a chance to take things deeper." She lifted her head and met his eyes. "It may hurt, but it's worth it."

He grinned, though she could see the strain around his eyes. "I agree. Okay, baby. Let's incorporate harsh reality into our idyll."

Brooke bit her lip.

"You okay?"

She nodded.

"I'm gonna get a glass of water. Want one?"

"Please," she agreed.

Kenneth kissed her forehead. "I'll be right back."

Lost as she was in dark, complicated thoughts, the moments it took Kenneth to complete the task passed without her knowledge. She passed the time blindly through her messages until something caught her attention.

"Oh, my God," Brooke said, eyeing her cell phone. "Ha, that's too funny."

"What's happening?" Kenneth asked, plunking onto the downstairs family room's sofa beside her and handing her a glass of cool water.

"An email from my dad. He offered me a bribe to forgive him. Look." She extended her phone as she accepted the drink and took a sip.

"What's this? Why is my picture on this page?"

"Remember Dad said he'd seen you before? It was in a

magazine. Apparently, those two dweebs I chased away the night we first met wrote their article after all. Heaven only knows how they managed it, particularly without your consent, but they submitted it to *Top Ten Percent,* and there you are... in my dad's favorite magazine. It's his way of giving the approval I never asked him for."

"What's *Top Ten Percent?*" Kenneth asked.

"Just some magazine about the movers and shakers in various fields. Business, the arts, science, education. I have no idea what criteria they use to determine who is more 'top' than anyone else, but it's kind of a big deal. I suppose you'll be getting job offers from all over now." She winced internally as she voiced the words. *He agreed, remember?* she reminded herself, forcing down again the thought that limiting his options in this way wasn't really fair. *Autumn said I could get a job anywhere. She's not wrong, but...*

"That depends," Kenneth replied, interrupting her runaway thoughts, though a maelstrom of feelings raged through her. "Their interview was pretty... fucked up. What does the article say?"

She scanned it while he sipped his drink. "Not what they were asking you, that's for sure. It just talks about how you're bringing a new face of diversity and talent to the Chicago music scene. It's actually really nice."

"Huh. Okay then. So, uh, what about your dad?"

She shrugged, setting her water glass onto a coaster that rested on the side table. "It's not an apology or a plan about how he's going to do better. It's just another manipulation. I'm going to ignore it. I have better things to think about." Though she tried to sound brave, her voice wavered again.

Kenneth set his cup aside and enfolded her in his arms, dragging her onto his lap. She leaned her head back on his shoulder. "It's okay not to be over it yet," he murmured.

"I'm ruining Christmas," she whispered, the confrontation with Shayla, her sleepless night and the painful reality of cutting off her father crashing over her at the same time. A wave of anxious despair rolled over her.

"No, you're being so brave. Here you are, after everything you just went through, being so strong and friendly."

"I shouldn't have come," she whispered. "I should have just stayed up north. There, things make sense."

"It's okay," Kenneth murmured, running his fingers through her hair. "It's okay, honey. You're okay."

"No, I'm not. Why do I bother? My father hates me. Your mother hates me. I shouldn't even be here."

"No one hates you, honey," he reminded her. "Your dad is a sick man. Mama... well, give her some time. I know she'll come around eventually."

Brooke turned, buried her face in Kenneth's shirt and dragged in huge lungfuls of air scented with his essence. They soothed her but didn't entirely banish her misery.

"On this, the day in which we celebrate your birth, Lord, bless this meal, we pray, and the hands that prepared it. Amen," Della said.

"Amen," the other family members echoed, and then the boys, starving in the way only young men can be, pounced on the massive quantities of food that crowded the table.

"This smells lovely," Brooke said as the platter of honey ham headed her direction. She accepted a slice and passed it on. Next, she piled up greens, potato salad and cornbread on her plate.

"What does your family normally eat at Christmas?" Della asked.

"Nothing special," she replied, not sure how to begin the conversation, or that she even wanted to.

"Why do you ask, Granny?" Kenneth asked.

"Well, if Brooke is going to be family, we should incorporate some of her traditions as well," Della explained.

Brooke choked and took a sip of water. "That's sweet. Um, I really don't have any traditions." She tucked a bite of ham into her mouth. "Mmmm. This is so good."

"No traditions? My lands, what does that mean?" Shayla demanded. "What kind of family doesn't have *any* traditions?"

"Uh, well... my father... he usually worked. My sister and I... well, we were just kids. We didn't have a chance to make any of our own."

"He worked on *Christmas Day? At supper time?* Why didn't your mother put a stop to that kind of nonsense?" Shayla asked, looking at Brooke, dismay lowering her elegantly-arched eyebrows.

"I don't have a mother," Brooke replied. "She died when I was five. I barely remember her. It's just been me, Autumn and Dad... and now Autumn's son River."

"I'm sorry to hear that," Della cut in, sending her daughter a quelling glance. "I grew up in an orphanage. We didn't have much in the way of anything to pass down either. A few churches would send charity baskets around the holidays, but that was about it. When I left there, I decided I was going to celebrate the *hell* out of anything and everything that took my fancy. Life is too short to be an object of pity, don't you think?"

"Definitely," Brooke agreed. *I may not have had quite the same experience, since the person who thought I was so pitiful was part of my family, but still. She has a point. Why be pathetic when you can choose to celebrate* anything *that pleases you? I need to think about that.*

"When I met Kenny—not you, Sugar." She reached out and

squeezed Kenneth's arm. Then she turned back to Brooke. "My late husband was also Kenneth. It's a family name."

"I have an Uncle Kenny too," Kenneth pointed out. "He lives in Baton Rouge now. I prefer to go by my full name, just to keep things straight, but of course, parents and grandparents get a pass." He winked at Brooke and she smiled, thankful for the brief explanation.

"Anyway," Della continued on with her story, "When I met and married my Kenny, we had a long talk about how we wanted to celebrate various events. It was so exciting to realize that our rituals and traditions would become our children's memories... and ours." Her eyes glowed as she related the tale. "Now, those memories are all that remains of him, but I'm not sorry. We had a good life together, even if it was shorter than I would have liked."

"Yes," Shayla added, "family is very important, and you live so far from yours... did I hear they're all in Texas?"

The warm nostalgia of Della's story faded as Shayla resumed her sharp-edged questioning. *Here we go again.* "Yes, that's right. This is the first time I've been back in five years."

"Long time to be away from family."

"I talk to my sister often," Brooke said.

"Well, that's good. And your dad?"

This is the last thing I want to talk about. "Um, my dad is... difficult. We don't get along." *There. No need to say anything more. My dad's taken up enough of my headspace already.* "What kind of greens are these? I've never tasted anything like them."

Shayla gave her a disapproving look, but Della launched into a lengthy description of the recipe and preparation of good Southern collard greens, and Brooke sagged with relief.

Kenneth's hand slipped into her lap, squeezing her fingers, and she turned to him with a smile.

"Anyone want dessert?" Della asked, indicating a massive red velvet cake displayed in the place of honor on the sideboard, under a glass dome.

"Oh, I couldn't!" Brooke laid a hand on her belly. "I'm so stuffed. The food was delicious."

"Maybe in an hour or so," Kenneth suggested. "We'll have had a chance to let our food settle a bit."

"Good idea," Walker agreed.

The younger brothers groaned with disappointment, but then Jackson, the youngest, suggested, "Let's shoot some hoops while we wait."

Though the pastime seemed more fitting to Jackson's exuberant seventeen than Paul's somber twenty-two, they all ran for the door.

The phone in Brooke's pocket chimed. "Excuse me," she said. Gathering up her dishes, she made her way to the kitchen, loaded them in the dishwasher and took a seat in the formal living room, checking the text message.

"What's that?" Aniya, Kenneth's sister, asked, sprawling across the sofa across from Brooke. Her long braids hung over the arm and trailed on the floor. She held a phone in front of her face as she talked to Brooke.

"My sister sent me a text."

"About what?"

"This and that," Brooke said, not wanting to discuss it.

"What's it like having a sister?" Aniyah asked.

"Mostly nice," Brooke replied. "My sister, Autumn, is a great listener. Sometimes she's bossy, but I know she always has my best interest at heart."

"Oh." Aniyah looked deflated. "Sounds like a brother."

"I suppose so," Brooke replied, "but without the farts and smelly feet."

"And *sweat!*" Aniyah added.

"And that. Plus, she doesn't inhale every mouthful of food in the entire house." Brooke cast a sly glance at Kenneth's sister. "Don't tell anyone I said this, but Kenneth still does that."

"Do I hear someone taking my name in vain?" Kenneth meandered into the room and plunked down on the arm of the chair Brooke was sitting in.

"Of course not," Brooke lied, giggling.

"She totally was," Aniyah tattled.

"Traitor." Brooke rolled her eyes.

"What did your message say?" Kenneth asked, looking over Brooke's shoulder.

"Nosy much?" she teased. "She let me know that Dad is doing okay. He had the catheterization and they decided he won't need bypass surgery. The balloon angioplasty will suffice. He's likely going to make a full recovery."

"What are you going to do?" he asked.

Brooke shrugged. "Probably nothing. I've wallowed in that pig trough long enough. It's about time I block him."

"Block who?" The rest of the family came trooping into the room, but it was Shayla, of course, who addressed Brooke.

Great. Now, what do I say? That's not something I want to talk about with her. I mean, it's really not her business. What did Autumn tell me I should say? In the moment, her brain froze. "Uh, my dad," she stammered. "I mentioned we don't get along."

"Hm," Shayla grunted. "Move your feet, Aniyah." She shoved at her daughter, urging her upright and perching beside her, "and put that damned phone away. It's not polite."

"Brooke has her phone out," Aniyah pointed out.

Brooke quickly tucked her phone into her pocket. "Sorry. I don't mean to be rude. It's just... my dad's in the hospital and my sister is giving me an update."

"Your dad's in the *hospital*?" Shayla leaned forward.

Shit. This is not getting better. "Yeah. He's going to be okay."

"But if that was ever in question, why are you here and not there? I mean, I was under the impression that y'all didn't celebrate Christmas, so you being away from them didn't matter, but he's *sick?* I'm not comfortable with that."

Brooke sighed. "Remember I said we're not close? I visited him. It was good enough."

"I'm sorry, but I just don't agree. I would hate to think that any of my children would act in such a way." She crossed her arms over her chest.

First time we meet, and things are already falling apart. Plus, she has no fucking clue what she's talking about. Shayla's bossiness finally succeeded in getting on Brooke's overwrought nerves. *This is* not *the same as our previous conversation, which really was important. This is just meddling.*

She suddenly recalled Kenneth telling her his mother respected women who stood up to her. *Well, she's already looking for reasons not to like me. Might as well give her one. Can't exactly make things worse.* "Ma'am, with all due respect, you don't know what you're talking about. My father is a nasty person."

"He's abusive, Mama," Kenneth added. "A real bully with some suspicious attitudes about race and gender. I met him for all of ten minutes, and I saw it. I've never met such a rude, unpleasant man. Brooke is right to cut him off, and I've encouraged her to stick with it."

"Thank you, Kenneth," Brooke said primly. "He is everything you've said and worse, and thus, has no place in my life. But I don't want to get into all that. Remember I said I didn't want him ruining Christmas? Well, I aim to keep that goal."

She turned back to Shayla. "So, since you've barely met me,

and you have no idea what my father is like, it would be better if you didn't make assumptions."

A gasp sounded from Aniyah as her three huge brothers raced into the room, flopping onto the furniture. Their movement drew Brooke's attention and inspired her next words.

"If your children acted this way, it would say something about you, not them. Clearly, that's not the case, because here are your loved ones, all around you." Brooke gestured at the various members of the Hill family. "My dad is not like that, and I'm not going to talk about him anymore. Please drop it now."

Shayla opened her mouth and then closed it again with a snap. Her features scrunched down until she looked like a storm cloud.

"Cool it, Shayla," Della said sternly, bustling into the room. "Don't pick on her. Brooke, honey, it's not sitting right with me that you don't have any holiday traditions. Does it bother you?"

"Sometimes," Brooke admitted, her heart still pounding.

"Well, here's an easy one. Should be right up your alley. Let's sing carols. Kenny, come over here, Sugar."

Brooke looked at Shayla and found the woman regarding her with an unreadable expression. Mentally shrugging her shoulders, Brooke let Kenneth take her hand and lead her to the piano.

"Do you know 'Go Tell It on the Mountain?'" Della asked.

"I've heard it a couple of times, but I don't know the words," Brooke replied. "Do you have any sheet music?"

"Songbooks on the bookshelf," she said, indicating a sizable collection to the left of the piano.

Brooke grabbed a book and leafed through the pages. *Thank you, Della, for saving me from that conversation.*

Della struck up the opening chords and Kenneth chimed in

on the chorus. Brooke followed along for a verse or two, enjoying the liquid velvet of her lover's voice. Then she joined him, selecting an alto line so she could harmonize with him. Kenneth reined in his massive voice, jumping up an octave to the highest point of his comfortable range so they could blend.

We've never sung together just the two of us like this, Brooke realized, remembering how she'd once wished to do so. *It's so fun!*

On the next verse, Della joined in, singing a tenor line in her low, sweet but warbling timbre that allowed Kenneth to drop back down.

By the time they'd finished the song, most of the family had gathered around the piano to join in.

This really is *a Christmas tradition,* Brooke realized, *and they've included me in it.* Though still not sure where she stood with Kenneth's mother, Brooke felt cautiously hopeful about the rest of the family.

Shayla hung back from the singing, studying the woman her son had brought home. Brooke's firm rebuff stung, but in all fairness, Shayla had to admit she'd pushed her luck. *Pushed and got pushed right back. In that, at least, I can't complain. Yes, her family is her business, and yes, cutting off a parent is a huge deal few would make for no reason. Can't fault her for making decisions about her own family, and she's right. I don't know her well enough to have an opinion on it.*

Brooke's voice rose in joy, high and sweet with a hint of the depth the years would eventually bring her.

She's good at that. It's surely one thing they have in common, but is it enough? Has her casual examination of privilege allowed her enough insight to make this relationship work? Will she ultimately choose Kenny over her friends and family if they fail to examine their own? Will she put Kenny in danger?

"Take the lead," Della urged, and Brooke picked up the melody.

Shyly, Aniyah joined her. A moment later the two synced up.

Brooke grinned, encouraging the young woman with a wink.

Aniyah picked up strength, matching her and together they created a vortex of feminine strength that rang through the house.

Aniyah's grin grew as Brooke decreased her volume, allowing the young woman to rise to the forefront. She belted out the carol, bold as a music show contestant, a feat neither Della nor Shayla herself had ever managed.

So, Brooke has a heart for the young folks, like she said, and a way with them. Even caught my prickly baby girl in her snare. Brook does seem sweet and all, but... Shayla sighed again as a lifetime of oppression rose like a dark cloud in her soul. *How can a white woman come into our family? What does that even mean for us?*

Kenneth's glorious bass twined with Brooke's delicate soprano, incongruous as a flute with a trombone, and yet they possessed an unexpected harmony.

Brooke slipped her hand into his and squeezed gently

He stroked her thumb.

Shayla sighed as understanding clicked into place. *They shouldn't fit together, but they do. It's not a crush. Not a rebellion, though I've always seen a hint of that stubbornness underneath Kenny's oh-so-polite 'yes ma'am.' He didn't argue with me. He just did what he wanted... and now he's doing it again.*

Kenneth wrapped his arm around Brooke's waist, drawing

her closer to himself. In defiance of his mother's concerns, he stood strong as stone. This was his choice and he would tolerate no interference. Kenneth was, as always, very much his own man.

"He's wise," her mother's voice rang in her ears.

He is that, Shayla admitted to herself. *Strong too. Stubborn, I could say. He could have stayed home and followed in our footsteps, but instead, he chased his dreams to the other side of the country and found wild success. Now, he's about to launch a new adventure... and this is the woman he's chosen to take that journey with him.*

Back straight, shoulders relaxed, Brooke looked like a queen. Her blue eyes sparkled.

She has steel in her, too. Stronger than she looks. Maybe even stronger than she knows. Time will tell what will come of this relationship, but they both intend to try. What more can I say? The decision was never mine to make. All I can do is embrace it... or not.

Brooke dropped back to the alto line, letting Aniyah take the melody. The boys joined the music, contributing melody and harmony, as their skills allowed. Della took the tenor, Walker doubling the bass line with his son, and the family began to weave a little bit of Hill family Christmas magic—a longstanding family tradition—with Brooke fitting in perfectly in the midst.

Well, all right then.

Rising from the sofa, Shayla picked up the descant and joined the song.

~

"Brooke, wait!" Shayla called.

Brooke turned away from the taxi that would carry her and Kenneth back to the airport. "Ma'am?"

"I wanted to give you something."

"Oh?"

"Here." She extended a regular college-ruled notebook, of the sort a person could find at any discount or grocery store.

Brooke accepted it and regarded the cover, and then looked up at Shayla, a question in her eyes.

"It's a collection of recipes... family recipes... for all of Kenny's favorites."

I wonder what I'm supposed to take from this. Is she implying I can't cook? I'm not the best but... "Thank you?" She couldn't quite banish the question from her voice.

"Sorry it's so late. I didn't have time to put it all together before Christmas."

"Oh, that's okay," Brooke told her. "I don't mind."

"They're *family* recipes," Shayla reiterated. "The ones Mama has developed over the years and passed down to me... and to Aniyah." She watched closely for Brooke's reaction. Then, seeing she still hadn't made her point, added, "Only to family members."

Understanding dawned. "Thank you, ma'am." Her voice cracked, but she pressed on. "This means a lot to me."

Just to drive the point home, Shayla added, "If you're Kenneth's choice, then that's just fine with me."

This time, Brooke's voice cut off altogether. She answered the much-coveted comment with a watery smile.

Maybe things will be okay after all.

CHAPTER 16

a week later, back in their apartment, Brooke and Kenneth lay in bed together, cuddled up and relaxed, passion spent.

"My mom called today," Kenneth mentioned, "while you were at school. Were you really filing sheet music all that time?"

"You'd be shocked how long it takes. What did your mother say?" Brooke asked, knowing she cared entirely too much about the answer.

"She said she was glad to meet you, and you laid a lot of concerns to rest."

"I'm surprised," Brooke replied.

"Oh? Why's that?"

"I mean, I essentially told her to mind her own business, remember?"

"Oh, yeah," Kenneth said, grinning at the memory. "She told me you were strong. I guess that's what she meant. I did tell you she would respect your boundaries, right?"

"Yes, you did," Brooke agreed, "and you were right. I

thought I was going to have my own heart attack when she started pushing, and I had to tell her my dad and I would most likely never reconcile, and he was and not a topic of conversation, ever."

"That must have been difficult, but you know, I've seen you stand up before. I knew you had it in you."

She snuggled up against his chest, basking in the afterglow and the warmth of his compliment. "Kenneth?"

"Yes?"

"I love you."

"I love you too, baby," he assured her, laying a big, warm hand on her back. "Um, Brooke?"

"Yes?"

"I have a question... a request for you."

"What's that, honey?" She laid her forearm on his chest and met his eyes. Even in the dark, they glowed with warmth and life... and nerves.

"I'm gonna miss you like hell when I'm in Europe."

"Oh, I know," Brooke agreed. "I wish you didn't have to go, but it wouldn't be good to pass up such an amazing opportunity."

"Right. Um, I know you'll be working, of course, but... I saw your school calendar in the kitchen. When you're on spring break, I'll be in Prague..."

"Oh, how cool!" Brooke exclaimed. "I've always wanted to travel. There's this amazing 15th-century clock in Prague that I heard of in high school, and I would *die* to see it."

"Well, you could," he pointed out. "I mean, think about it. The ticket is pricey, but you could stay in my room with me..."

"Oh, honey, I would love to, but I can't."

"Why not?" he asked. "It's not the money is it?"

"No," she told him quickly. "Not the money. It's just... the school hosts a choir camp every year during spring break. It meets each day, and we invite singers from all over the city and surrounding areas to come for clinics, sectionals, and big rehearsals. They practice for the state choir competition. I help every year. It's important to me."

"I see," he replied, his eyelids drooping, and his tense lips going slack. "Sounds lucrative."

"It's not, actually. I don't receive any additional pay for this project. It's all volunteer, so we can keep the tuition low and the kids can afford it."

He lowered his eyebrows. "You know, your dad's not the only person who doesn't treat you right."

Kenneth's non-sequitur puzzled Brooke. "What do you mean?"

"I mean, your job doesn't pay that well. Decently, but it's just a public school. A living wage but nothing extravagant, am I right?"

"Well, yeah," she agreed, "but it's an honor to work there."

"I agree. However, how many things do you do outside of contract hours for which you receive no compensation? How many after-school rehearsals? How many choirs. How many camps? Are there summer camps too?"

"There are," she admitted, "but, Kenneth, that's just part of the game. When you get a job, you'll see. There's a lot more to teaching music than just showing up during contract hours. The long days are normal."

"I realize that, Brooke," he replied, "but remember that you have to keep things in balance. You need to tell them no sometimes so you can have a life."

"What are you specifically asking me, Kenneth?" she demanded, though she thought she knew.

"Tell them no to volunteering this year," he told her bluntly. "Come meet me in Prague instead. Otherwise, you do realize I'm leaving mid-January, and I won't be back until the end of April? Does that sit right with you?"

"Of course not!" She rained kisses over his chest. "I'll die of missing you, but we knew this was coming, honey. It sucks, but your career and mine don't always align. You need to go, and I need to stay. If only it was a year or so from now. Once I have that promotion in hand, I'll be a lot freer to pass off some of these projects, but until then, I need to look like the one they can't live without. Does that make sense?"

"It does, but I think you're overthinking it. How many years in a row have you done this camp?"

"Four," Brooke replied. "Since I started."

"And summer camp?"

"Same."

"I think you've made your case with them long since. I want you to think about this. Think hard, Brooke. It's really, really important to me that you come."

She took a deep breath, her desire for Kenneth and his happiness warring with her eternal need to prove herself at work. "I'll see what I can do," she said at last.

He frowned. "I know what that means. Is it too much to ask, baby?"

"I don't know," she replied. "I have to have time to think. Can I take that time, Kenneth, without you being angry with me?"

"I suppose," he said, dejection heavy in his voice. "Though I had hoped for a more enthusiastic response. Do what you gotta do, Brooke, but understand how much this means to me. I hope that figures in."

"It does, Kenneth. I promise it does."

"Okay, baby. Go to sleep. Think on it. Let me know when you're ready."

He turned around with his back to her and made deep, sleeping noises.

Well, shoot. How am I supposed to sleep now?

"Oh, man," Brooke groaned.

"What's wrong?" Nancy called from the next office over.

"Faculty meeting at three," Brooke replied. Then, a petulant whine escaped her. "I don't want to go to a meeting. I want to go home. I'm tired."

"I noticed," Nancy called back. "You've certainly not been your usual energetic self lately. Is it Kenneth, hon?"

"Yeah, probably," Brooke answered. "I've been bummed since he left. I bet I won't be back to normal until he gets home. I miss him."

"Of course you do," Nancy said soothingly. "How long has it been?"

"Eight weeks," Brooke replied with a sigh. "Eight weeks, and we still have six weeks to go. I don't know how I'm going to hold out that long."

"I guess, just keep busy," Nancy suggested. "But since it's already 2:45 p.m., shall we walk over together?"

"Okay." Brooke sighed, stood up from her desk and grabbed her keys. She pulled the office shut behind her and joined Nancy in the main choir room.

Nancy smoothed her steel-gray curls away from her face. "You know, Brooke, you should get a bit more sunlight. You look almost gray."

"I feel gray," Brooke replied. "I'm a creature of the southern sun. This winter crap is weighing me down. I need some fresh air, but it's too darn cold."

"It's not that bad, once you get used to it," Nancy soothed.

"How long does that take?" Brooke demanded. "I've been here five years."

"Well, now I surely don't know," Nancy replied, leading her out of the choir room and locking the door behind them.

They headed off down a long hallway with a shiny tile floor and the smell of teenagers lingering in the air.

"I'm from here, so I hardly notice anymore—that is to say, I hardly notice the cold. The snow really bothers me. I guess some people adjust and some don't. Maybe you could cultivate an interest in winter sports?"

"I could try that, I suppose," Brooke replied listlessly, her momentary passion falling back into lethargy. "I suppose I could."

The warren of hallways leading from the choir room to the cafeteria had been the bane of freshmen since the school opened. Brooke herself had taken a couple of months to figure it out. Now, she could find her way in the dark, blindfolded. Thus, her busy mind took the opportunity to ruminate again on her misery. Her dark mood deepened until it matched the gray sky outside the high, rectangular windows.

In the cafeteria, a scent of macaroni hung heavy in the air, and a slick of mop water glistened on the floor. The cinder block walls echoed with idle conversation. Nancy joined several of her friends, while Brooke found a seat near the back and sank into it. She rested her head on her folded arms on the table.

"You okay, Brooke?"

She looked up at the assistant band director. "I'm okay, Mike. This grayness is getting me down is all. How are you?"

"I'm hanging in there," he replied, running his hands through his thinning, sandy hair. "You'd think I'd have gotten used to it by now."

"Maybe we never do," she murmured. "Maybe we just

endure—burning up our strength to keep going—and then sleep our vacations away."

"Sounds about right," he said, plunking down in a chair near her.

"Good afternoon, everyone," the principal called, stepping up to a small, portable podium with an embedded microphone. A loud buzz of feedback threatened to blow out their eardrums. "Sorry. Sorry. Let's get started. I'd like to get home before supper time."

The mumbling died down and a rustling hush fell over the room. Someone drummed a pencil on a table in a complicated rhythm. A shoe tapped. Heel, toe. Heel toe. Someone breathed through their mouth. Huff. Huff. The disjointed sounds jangled Brooke's nerves. Exhausted and jittery, she longed to escape. *I feel... unsafe*, she realized, *like something is looming over me.*

Tugging her phone out of her pocket onto her lap, she texted her sister. **My intuition is driving me bonkers. Something is coming. What can it be?**

A moment later, the silenced phone buzzed in her hands. **I pulled the tower again. Something IS coming. It's going to shake you up. Try not to freak out. It will be for the best**.

Gee, thanks, Brooke typed back.

"All right, all right now, where did I leave my notes?" Principal Jones patted his pockets: inside his blazer, his shirt, both pants. "There it is. First of all, detentions are down 10%, so our security team would like us to remember that our new discipline initiative is working, and we must continue to be diligent and consistent. Kids who are learning aren't kids who are getting into trouble."

Some teachers nodded while others looked mutinous.

There's always someone willing to protest any change, no matter how positive.

"Maintenance will begin painting classrooms next week. If you received an email stating your room was due to be painted, remember to remove any posters, signs or other objects from the walls."

Muttering greeted the announcement, not all of it friendly.

"A student group has requested to begin a Rachel's Challenge. They're looking for a teacher to be their sponsor. This appears to be a temporary group, but who knows whether it might take off and linger. Volunteers should email my secretary before Friday."

Silence. Everyone's faces took on a matching fixed expression.

"Next, ummm... Oh, yes, we've qualified for state again, in all choirs: freshmen boys, freshman girls, mixed, men's chorus and women's. Let's give our esteemed directors a round of applause."

The other teachers clapped. Nancy rose to her feet. Brooke waved.

"That leads me to my final point. Our beloved head director, Ms. Nancy Schumacher, has submitted her retirement, effective at the end of the school year. We will miss you very much, Nancy, and appreciate all your hard work. We will have a retirement party for her April 1st in the music hall teacher's lounge. Be sure you sign the card. It's with my secretary."

He waited for a round of murmurs to subside before he continued. "We've hired a replacement, who is called Miss Lizbeth Gomez. She will be arriving in July and assisting with summer camps. If you'd like to know more about Miss Gomez, her bio will be in the weekly newsletter. That is all. Have a good evening."

He stalked away. The teachers resumed murmuring as they rose and sauntered toward the parking lot, their classrooms and who knew where else. All but Brooke. She remained at the table because for a long moment, she wasn't sure she remembered how to breathe.

"Nancy," she croaked, snagging her colleague's arm as the woman shuffled past. "What's happening? Who is Lizbeth Gomez? Why didn't I hear about this until now?"

"I don't know, hon," Nancy said gently. "They didn't tell me anything about the process, and really, why would they? I'm leaving. Who they bring in doesn't concern me, so I haven't been kept in the loop. Maybe you should talk to Principal Jones."

"Oh, I aim to," Brooke replied. She finally managed to draw a full breath into her lungs and rose on legs that felt far from steady.

She swept down convoluted hallways, barely noticing bulletin boards filled with posters, walls crammed with student paintings, sketches and watercolors, some with ribbons. Display cases clustered with trophies and sculptures.

This really is a special group of kids to work with, she thought, momentarily distracting her mind from her distress. It sank back in almost immediately.

The principal's office stood in a brightly-lit corner. Floor to ceiling windows, both within and without, invited in the most sunlight in the entire building. Brooke grabbed the handle and swung the door open, stalking in.

Tanya, the principal's secretary, had hair that looked like iced tea and a face that looked like a walnut. Deep fissures surrounded tiny, squinting eyes, and a barely-visible nose. Her mouth disappeared among the wrinkles. She looked up at Brooke and her creases formed themselves into a stressed and irritable expression. "Can I help you?"

"I need to talk to Principal Jones right now," Brooke said. Her distress warred with her desire to sound professional, leaving her tone flat. *I sound like a damned robot.*

"I'll see if he's in," she said, reaching for her phone.

"Miss Daniels?"

Brooke looked up to see Principal Jones standing in the doorway of his office.

"I have a minute. Come on back."

Brooke began shaking with nerves and rage, so badly that she had to place each step carefully to ensure she neither tripped nor ran into anything. Despite her care, she scraped her shoulder on the doorway. *I must look drunk. I feel drunk. My ears are ringing.*

"Take a seat," he said, indicating the chair on the non-business side of his desk. He sank down across from her. "What can I do for you?"

Could he really be that *oblivious?* "I was surprised to hear you'd hired someone for the head choir director position."

"Why would that surprise you?" he asked. "You probably knew Mrs. Schumacher was retiring before we did."

"Of course," Brooke replied. "What I want to know is, why didn't I hear anything else about the process?"

"You didn't need to," he replied.

"But *I* applied for that job," Brooke stated.

"Yes, I saw that application," Mr. Jones informed her. "Damned nuisance. You were supposed to be on the committee, but as an applicant, you couldn't be."

"What do you mean, 'on the committee'? Why would I do that? I wanted this job. In fact, after working here so successfully for so many years, I expected to get it."

"No, we really didn't consider you for the position," he told her bluntly.

The words hit Brooke like another heavy blow to the gut.

She doubled over, her arm against her belly, struggling to breathe. "Why not?" She dragged a shaking breath into her lungs. "Why didn't all my years of service, the awards my students have won, my frequent accolades, even your own acknowledgment that the choir has been better than ever since I started... why didn't that matter? I *earned* this promotion."

"Calm down, Brooke," he told her. "You're getting emotional. You have done very good work for us, yes. We all felt that it was in the school's best interest for you to keep doing what you're doing."

"But that's not how it works," Brooke cried, her tone shrill. "People want and expect to advance in their careers, not remain stagnant. Does this Ms. Gomez have tons of experience or some kind of amazing degree or something?"

"She has a master's degree, and I believe five years of experience, come the end of this school year. She is currently at a Catholic school in Texas."

"Five years?" Brooke gulped. "Five? I have five years *here*, at this school!"

"Yes, we were all aware of that. Miss Daniels, you really need to settle down. The decision has been made, and this expression of your... emotions is becoming distasteful."

Brooke's nostrils flared. "You denied me a promotion I've earned MANY TIMES OVER with someone who has the same amount of experience as me, and now you don't want to hear my untidy FEELINGS about it? Sorry, Bill. It doesn't work that way. I'm *furious* that you've denied me the career advancement I have earned by giving *my job* to someone who isn't even a stronger candidate than me."

She took a deep breath and continued her tirade. "How could you even consider doing such a thing? Do you have any idea how many extra hours I've put in, without compensation or complaint, to show you all I could handle leading the program, that I was ready for the next level? Do you know how much I have invested? What I've risked in my personal life for this promotion? You need to reconsider this decision. Ms. Gomez can come as MY assistant. That's the right thing to do."

Mr. Jones raised one eyebrow, clearly unimpressed. "The director position was never yours to have. Assuming was not a wise idea, Miss Daniels. Look at how you've disappointed yourself. Nothing will change. The entire committee, as well as the board of directors, all agree that you are doing what we most need you to do by remaining with the freshmen. There are so few teachers who are as excellent as you are with beginners. It's a gift of yours we have honored by keeping you where you do us the most good. Once the beginners have learned what you teach them, anyone can carry them on to success. You're doing your best work where you are."

"But that's not how a career works!" Brooke exclaimed, her tone rising again. "I have a right to advance in my career."

"Your career is not our concern," he informed her coldly. "Only our program. You will remain in the assistant position for the time being. In the future, if the lead position opens up again, you're welcome to apply..."

"No," Brooke responded flatly. Her distress had at last awakened her backbone, which would not tolerate her succumbing to such rank injustice. "No, I won't. I refuse. There's no telling how long it would be before *Ms. Gomez* moves on. It could be decades, and I refuse to beg again for a promotion I earned long since."

Her heart began to pound as the only solution to the problem dawned on her. *Oh, shit. Could I really?* But there was no alternative. "I ask you one last time. Reconsider whether it's right for you to do such a thing to an employee as loyal as I've always been."

"There's no way I will reconsider," he told her. "You will continue to work with the freshmen. Period."

"Actually, I won't," Brooke said. She gulped. "I will *not* allow this to happen. I will not give my heart, soul and all my time to a job that doesn't respect me. If you do not give me this promotion, I will leave. Find a school that appreciates what I can do and rewards me with appropriate promotions when the time is right."

"What?" Mr. Jones rocketed to his feet, his face like a thundercloud. "You'd rather start over as nothing?"

"No," Brooke snapped back, rage flaring hot and bright inside her. "I'll never start anywhere as nothing. My choirs' accolades come with me. My success comes with me. My experience comes with me. Unlike here, where I'm expected to stagnate in the same position, I can take my accomplishments with me and find a job that respects me instead of taking advantage. Since you all took me for granted, you will *not* get my work with beginners anymore. Consider this my official resignation. I'll turn in the paperwork to HR before I leave today. I'm done here, effective the end of this school year."

Rising to her full height, she sailed out of the office, leaving her boss spluttering behind her. As she made her way back down the hall to the choir room, her pounding heart threatened to shatter her ribs. Her breath caught in her throat, leaving her gasping.

Oh, God. What have I done? Quit my job? The job I sacrificed everything for? The job I almost lost Kenneth for? The job I gave up five years of my life, day and night for? What do I do now?

"Anything you want," a little voice whispered in her ear. "Find another job. It should be easy. Get out of this cold place. Like Autumn said, the country is full of jobs that will appreciate you, where you can establish better boundaries and live in balance. Places with better weather and a better cost of living. Think about what else you can do..."

"Ooooh," she whispered as she staggered into the choir room.

"Are you okay, Brooke?" Nancy asked. She turned from the bank of filing cabinets that lined the wall of the room.

"I'm not sure," Brooke said. Unlike before, her voice sounded thin. She felt fragile, like a well-placed shove might crush her into a thousand pieces. "Um, you should know I won't be volunteering for spring break camp this year."

"Oh?" Nancy raised her eyebrows. "Why not?"

"I'm going out of town," Brooke told her firmly.

CHAPTER 17

*K*enneth stared up at the ceiling of his Prague hotel room. *Spring break has started, and yet, here I am... alone. She's not coming.*

At some time in the past, a pipe had leaked. The brown stains on the ceiling followed a clear, straight line to the corner, where a spider worked hard to build a web the maid would wipe away at her next cleaning.

I know how that spider feels, he thought. *I've worked so hard to build something with Brooke, only to have her job come in and sweep it away every time. I love her, but I feel like I'm beating my head against the wall trying to make a life with her. I practically had to bribe her to move in with me, and the rest has been one step forward, two steps back.*

Kenneth let loose of a rumbling, closed-lipped groan. *I had so hoped, after her confrontation with her father, that she would stop following in his footsteps, but it seems overwork is a habit she's not ready to give up. Am I okay with that? It's pretty clear it will never change.* He sighed, rolling onto his side.

In the street—barely visible outside the window—cars honked, and gravel crunched as the traffic streamed past.

People heading off to work, to join friends for breakfast. In a few hours, I'll leave to attend my daily opera rehearsal, though we don't need it. This is our third night in Prague, and we already have the stage, the orchestra and everything else figured out. It's fun, but... I want to go home.

"Where is home?" a voice in his head demanded. "Where is the place you belong? Chicago, where you've agreed to stay despite not liking the place all that much? Atlanta, where your family lives, but you don't? Somewhere else? A mythical place where you can build my future... but only if you go alone because Brooke will never leave her job?"

Kenneth shook his head. "Am I really thinking about breaking up with her?" he asked himself aloud. "I'm not sure, but being in second place in her life, tolerable as a partner so long as I don't interfere with her single-minded dedication to her job... Well, that's an unflattering position to be in."

It hurt, and now, without Brooke's compelling presence to wrap him around her little finger, he finally let himself feel it. "She doesn't care as much about me as I do about her," he admitted aloud. "She likes me, likes talking and singing with me. She likes sex. But nowhere in that does she commit herself to me. Not if it conflicts with her job. Am I prepared to spend my life as a mistress to her work?"

He sighed, not sure what the answer was, but quite sure the question cut him deeper than he'd ever been cut before.

His cell phone chimed like bells; Brooke's special ringtone. He reached out a lethargic hand and dragged it over to him, looking at the screen without much interest.

How's Prague?

It's okay, he sent back. **Cool architecture.**

What have you seen so far? Have you gone to the astronomical clock?

Not yet. I had thought about going today, before rehearsal.

Send me pics?

Kenneth sighed. He started typing **You could have taken pics yourself if you had decided to come see me**, but then he deleted it. *What's the point?* **Ok. I'll go in an hour or so. Keep your phone handy.**

I will. Thank you. I love you.

"Do you though?" he asked the phone aloud. "Do you really love me? I wonder sometimes." He set the phone aside and headed to the shower.

Before he could turn on the water, his phone rang. Hoping it might be Brooke, he grabbed it and answered before the caller ID could appear on the screen.

"Son?"

His shoulders sagged. "Hi, Mama."

"Did I get the timing okay? What time is it there?"

"It's 9 a.m. You're fine."

"Oh, good. How are you doing? Where are you now?"

"I'm in the Czech Republic, and I'm doing fine." He flopped back on the bed and stared up at the ceiling again.

"You don't sound fine. What's wrong, Kenny?"

"Nothing," he replied, but a heavy sigh belied his claim.

"Humph. If you say so. Listen, I got word from your uncle that Louisiana State University in Baton Rouge is looking for an assistant professor of music... I did a little research, and they have an opera company as well..."

"Thanks, Mama, but I'm planning to stay in Chicago," he replied. *But why though? Why stay when Brooke isn't even going to be around most of the time? She works until seven or*

SIMONE BEAUDELAIRE

later almost every night. Weekends. Summers. Even spring break. Whenever there's something to be done, she's there.

"Are there any jobs there?" his mother demanded.

"Not many," he replied. "I've got an application in at a high school in the suburbs, but that's the only thing I've found so far."

"Since when did you get a doctorate to teach high school?" his mother demanded. "Aren't you overqualified? Will they even hire you?"

"Unlikely," he admitted, "but I'll keep trying."

"But why?" Shayla demanded, her incredulity loud and clear despite the thousands of miles between them.

"I promised Brooke," he explained. "She's building her career there in Chicago. I promised not to let my job search interfere with that."

"Oh."

What do you mean by that, Mama? Oh? "So, I guess I'm stuck at the moment."

"You might consider whether it's worthwhile to redo that conversation with her. Your career is not of less importance than hers. It may be that you two could find a place where both of you could advance. Perhaps a place closer to home..."

"I would love that," he admitted, "but Brooke is adamant. She'd never go for it."

"Have you asked?"

He sighed. In the corner, the spider connected the threads of its web into a messy tangle. *Messy, like my love life.* "It's the basis of our whole relationship. She was so afraid this would happen—that my career and hers would drag us apart—that she almost refused to date me."

Kenneth realized he was oversharing something with his mother—who had never been fully on board with the relationship—that was none of her business. *Here's your*

270

chance, Mama. Talk me out of it all. Give me permission. Give
me a reason to question everything I've done so far.

"Well, honey, that's rough for sure," Shayla said,
measuring her words carefully, "but hasn't a lot changed
since then? You all have been a couple for a while. You've
met each other's families. You live together. It's worthwhile to
revisit the conversation, given that your relationship has
matured."

"I can't do that," he said flatly. "I made a promise." Kenneth
sighed again. "Maybe she was right. Maybe, if we cared about
each other so much, we shouldn't have gotten in each other's
way like that."

"Kenny, listen," his mother said, "I may not have been
completely comfortable with Brooke at first, but the more I
think about it... you and she have a good thing going. If you
don't at least discuss your reality with her, you're going to
resent her. Resentment kills a relationship much more than a
difficult conversation."

Shayla paused, though not nearly long enough for
Kenneth's swirling thoughts to gel. "Tough discussions are part
of everyone's relationship, especially if y'all marry eventually.
No one gets an award for suffering in silence. Don't do that to
yourself... or to her. Lay it on the line and brainstorm a solution
together."

"I don't think she'll entertain it," he began.

"You don't know that, and you won't unless you try. Maybe
what she was saying made sense at the time, but now,
everything's different. Don't you *dare* assume she's too weak to
handle a tough discussion. She's so much stronger than you
think. Remember how she weathered a confrontation on little
sleep when she'd just cut off her father, without becoming
defensive? Remember how she put me in my place?" Shayla
chuckled at the memory. "You're treating her like a fragile

flower who will wilt if she has to do anything difficult. I don't think that's the case."

"I don't know," Kenneth said. "I still don't think it will work. If I break my promise, she'll probably dump me."

"Then she does," his mother said bluntly, "but at least you'll know instead of assuming. Just think about it. Promise me?"

"Okay, Mama. I'll think about it. I have to go now. I need to take a shower and head out. Love you."

"I love you, Kenny. Talk to your lady. You both deserve honesty between you."

The line went dead, and Kenneth headed to the shower, more confused than ever.

An hour later, he found himself staring at an ancient building with a single towering turret. On the side, two dials—one with a second dial inside it, the other ringed inside with concentric yellow circles—ticked off the time by tracking the heavens. He regarded it with a certain detached interest.

"If only you were here," he whispered. "This would mean a lot more if you were seeing it with me."

Looking at the landmark Brooke had wanted to see so badly, Kenneth could almost feel her presence. It felt like she was standing behind him. *Don't be stupid and turn around. She's in Chicago. You're in Prague. There's no one back there but tourists.*

The hour sounded. A skeleton sculpture at the corner of the upper dial came to life, ringing a bell. The coverings of two windows above the dial opened and a procession of hyper-realistic apostles passed, each one pausing to 'look' out the windows at the street below.

The sense of a familiar presence grew until it was all he could do to fix his eyes on the clock. *Take the picture,* he urged himself. *Send it to her and be done. She's chosen her priorities. The only thing you can do is honor them.* What that would mean for their relationship, he felt sure he knew, and the pain of it cut into his belly like a knife.

The chiming stopped and the windows slammed shut again. *It's like our relationship. It was cool for a moment, but the time is passing, and I fear it will soon be gone.* Dejected, he studied his shoes.

The sense of presence increased again, bringing a warmth he could feel on his skin. The hairs on the back of his neck rose seconds before his vision went black as two hands covered his eyes. "Guess who?"

He whirled around. "Brooke?! What are you doing here?"

She grinned, showing her teeth. "I wanted to surprise you. Surprise!"

Surprised? Astonished is more like it. "What about camp?" he demanded.

"I opted out," she explained. "It really was voluntary, you know. I told you that, right?"

"You did," he agreed, "but you also said you would probably do it anyway." *And yet, here you are. What does it mean, Brooke? What are you telling me by being here?* The impossible contrast between where his mind had been moments ago, and her unexpected appearance left him confused and numb.

"I changed my mind," she told him. "Besides, I missed you, and I decided that it was more important to spend spring break with the man I love than to spend it at work again. Haven't you always said I need better balance? I wanted to see you. Besides, it occurred to me that I wasn't doing a good job of putting you first. There's no denying you're my life partner, and it's about time I acted like it."

Brooke realized it? On her own? Good Lord. She was coming around all along. Mama was right. I shouldn't have assumed. A ribbon of joy unfurled in Kenneth's heart, calming the uncomfortable pounding. "I'm glad," he murmured. "I was... concerned. At some point, Brooke, the balance will have to shift. Our relationship needs to come before work, and we *both* need the opportunity to pursue our goals." *There. I broached the subject.*

"Oh, I agree," she said, and he could see by the openness in her expression that the defensiveness that had always clouded her features had vanished. "Kenneth, I need to tell you something."

"What's that?" he asked. *What will she come up with next to shock me?*

"I... um..." her eyes darted to the side, and then she took a deep breath, raising and releasing her shoulders. "I quit my job."

"What?" Kenneth's jaw dropped, and his eyes felt like they were bugging out of his head.

"Yeah. Remember that I was so sure I would be promoted to head choir director?"

He nodded.

"They never even considered me for the position. In fact, they hired someone with the same amount of experience as me and gave her the job I wanted. They thought I would be happy to go on being the assistant forever."

"Wow. That's messed up," he told her.

"I agree," she replied, reaching up and laying a hand on the back of his neck. "I wouldn't tolerate being treated that way, so I put in my resignation, effective at the end of the school year, and I have no intention of going above and beyond for a single thing between now and then. They've hogged my life—with my unfortunate consent—for too long. I'm going to reclaim it."

"So, what does that mean then, for us?" he asked. "Where do we go from here?"

"I guess, you pursue your dream. It's your turn. Apply everywhere. I'll follow you wherever the wind blows."

This is so huge I almost can't take it in. Did she really, finally put her job into its proper perspective? Wow! "No, that doesn't work for me," Kenneth told her solemnly. With one finger, he smoothed a strand of hair away from her face.

"What do you mean?"

"I mean, Brooke, that we need to go where they can support us both. Where both of us can pursue our dreams... side by side. No one sacrificing. No one left out."

"That sounds great," she said. "Um, Kenneth?"

"Yes, love?"

"Can we focus our search somewhere... warmer? To be honest, I don't want to do winter anymore. I'm not suited for it."

"Oh, sure," he agreed. "There are great musical opportunities in the south. My mama mentioned Baton Rouge, for starters."

"I would love that," she agreed.

"Then we should be just fine. Brooke?"

"Yes?"

"I love you." He drew her close, and the warmth of their undeniable connection sank into the hurt, healing his heart, healing their bond and leaving them ready to face a future neither of them could foresee.

It's okay, Kenneth realized. *As long as we're together, going where the wind blows will be just fine.*

AUTHOR'S NOTES

I'm not a choir director, and I don't play one on television, but I've been in choirs—church, community, school and university choirs—for as long as I can remember. Some of my fondest memories are singing with the Valley Symphony Chorale, which is the basis for the chorale Brooke and Kenneth sing in. For me, with a high-tension job, singing is like therapy. Choir directors, whether paid or volunteer, provide a needed outlet for so many people. They work when others are on vacation, work extra at holidays, work nights and weekends, all so the music can keep flowing. They're unsung heroes... pun intended.

ABOUT THE AUTHOR

In the world of the written word, Simone Beaudelaire strives for technical excellence while advancing a worldview in which the sacred and the sensual blend into stories of people whose relationships are founded in faith but are no less passionate for it. Unapologetically explicit, yet undeniably classy, Beaudelaire's 20+ novels aim to make readers think, cry, pray... and get a little hot and bothered.

In real life, the author's alter-ego teaches composition at a community college in a small western Kansas town, where she lives with her four children, three cats, and husband—fellow author Edwin Stark.

As both romance writer and academic, Beaudelaire devotes herself to promoting the rhetorical value of the romance in hopes of overcoming the stigma associated with literature's biggest female-centered genre.

THANK YOU

Thank you for taking the time to read *Where the Wind Blows*. If you enjoyed this book, please consider telling your friends and posting a short review. There is nothing more valuable to an author than the praise of their readers. Your time and support are greatly appreciated!

BOOKS BY SIMONE BEAUDELAIRE

Si tu m'Aimes (If you Love me)

Where The Wind Blows
ISBN: 978-4-86745-659-0

Published by
Next Chapter
2-5-6 SANNO
SANNO BRIDGE
143-0023 Ota-Ku, Tokyo
+818035793528

31st May 2022

Lightning Source UK Ltd.
Milton Keynes UK
UKHW010649270123
416064UK00004B/406